P9-DGF-011

FALL
BACK
DOWN
WHEN I
DIE

ALSO BY JOE WILKINS

MEMOIR

The Mountain and the Fathers: Growing Up on the Big Dry

POETRY

When We Were Birds
Notes from the Journey Westward
Killing the Murnion Dogs

FALL BACK DOWN WHEN I DIE

A Novel

JOE WILKINS

Little, Brown and Company
New York Boston London

Though many of the places named in the novel are real, the author has invented a number of place names and has shifted the nature of others (e.g., history, location, population, businesses, schools, etc.). He has as well taken some liberties with the geography of eastern Montana; for instance, while it was often rumored that wolves had made it as far north and east from Yellowstone as the Bull Mountains, it was never verified and, considering the distance, is unlikely. Here, the author has ignored the distance and confirmed the rumors. Finally, though the author has used for many of the characters variations of names he knew and heard growing up, the characters herein are fictional; any resemblances to actual persons are entirely coincidental.

Little, Brown and Company
Hachette Book Group
1290 Avenue of the Americas, New York, NY 10104
littlebrown.com

First Edition: March 2019

Little, Brown and Company is a division of Hachette Book Group, Inc. The Little, Brown name and logo are trademarks of Hachette Book Group, Inc.

The publisher is not responsible for websites (or their content) that are not owned by the publisher.

The Hachette Speakers Bureau provides a wide range of authors for speaking events. To find out more, go to hachettespeakersbureau.com or call (866) 376-6591.

ISBN 978-0-316-47535-8
LCCN 2018956883

10 9 8 7 6 5 4 3 2 1

LSC-C

Printed in the United States of America

For Alexis and Mike
and for all those
trying to find better ways
in the far places

If I am native to anything,
I am native to this.

—Wallace Stegner, *Wolf Willow*

FALL
BACK
DOWN
WHEN I
DIE

VERL

Day Two

Not out in all this country. Not even with your ATVs and radios and such as that. Not even. What I'm saying. You won't find me. Not out in all this country. I can run and hide and run and even if it would be only a moment at six hundred yards and you would have to put a bullet in my back these mountains here are mine you fuckers you fuckers and you cowards I am telling you for fuck all and ever these Bull Mountains are mine.

WENDELL

As the neighbor girl's SUV disappeared down the road, Wendell watched the tire-kicked dust bloom and sift through shades of gold, ocher, and high in the evening sky a pearling blue. Harvest light, late-August light—thin, slanted, granular. At his back the mountains already bruised and dark.

Wendell stepped back into the trailer and the screen door banged shut behind him. He considered the boy, sitting on the front-room floor, scribbling in a spiral notebook, pencil marks so dark and hard as to sheen to silver. Of a sudden the boy closed his notebook, jammed his pencil into the whorled spine. He looked right at Wendell, the dark of his eyes the biggest thing about him.

—Bet you're hungry, Wendell said. Let's get us something to eat.

The last weeks of harvest hadn't seen him home much, and though he preferred beef stew or chili all he found in the cupboard were cans of chicken noodle. Wendell realized he'd have to do more regular shopping now, with the boy around.

—Looks like it's chicken or chicken, bud.

Wendell pulled a can off the shelf and sliced into it with the opener, then spooned the clotted mess into bowls and set the bowls in the microwave and punched the buttons. The light was broken, but he could hear it whir, knew it was heating. The boy stood and waited, itching the

5

side of his face, then sat at the small round table in the trailer's kitchen and kicked his thin legs. Seven years old, maybe fifty pounds soaking wet.

The social worker from Billings, a frumpy, jowled woman, had brought the boy out yesterday. Said they'd had him at the hospital for a few days, just to make sure, and had thought to take him to a group home but then found out there was an uncle south of Delphia. Took them a while to track him down, but, well, here they were, she said, stepping to the side, motioning toward the boy. Here was his nephew, this scrawny kid with a plastic grocery sack of clothes and a spiral notebook. Wendell was just back from hours on the combine. He held up his hands, explained he wasn't an uncle to the boy but a cousin. Lacy, the boy's mother, had come to live with Wendell and his mom, Maureen, because Lacy's father had left to work a fishing boat in Alaska and her mother, Maureen's sister, had died in a car accident years before that. When her father's letters quit coming, Lacy had simply hung a curtain across the room that she and Wendell shared and stayed with them through most of high school. Yes, Lacy had been like an older sister to him—they were a year apart—but she was really only a cousin. He wanted to make sure that was clear.

The woman considered this, regarded the Keystone Light cans scattered across the countertop, then asked about his mother. He could tell she was hoping she wouldn't have to leave the boy in a trailer way out in the Bull Mountains with a man not much more than a boy himself. But Wendell shook his head, told the social worker his mother had died about a year ago. The woman stared at his work boots, his sleeveless T-shirt covered in grease stains and chaff, the burnt umber of his sun-blasted arms and neck and face, the stark white line on his forehead where he pulled his ball cap low. It seemed to Wendell she studied him for hours, days, a reckoning thorough and strict and piling up like all the rest. He didn't need a boy to look after, that was for sure, but Wendell still wanted this woman up from Billings to see him and think something good, think he might be able to do whatever it was that needed to be done. And so he felt strangely relieved when she finally sighed and said she was sorry to hear about his mother, then went ahead and pulled a file folder out of her satchel and told him about the boy, how he was "developmentally delayed," "variously involved," and, the kicker, how he hadn't said so much as a word since they'd found him. As far as they could figure, the boy had been locked in that apartment on the south side of Billings all alone for more than a week.

The microwave whirred. The boy brought both hands to his face, began tapping his fingers across the stretched skin of his cheeks, making a hollow drumming sound. He was somehow cockeyed, this boy, his shoulders kinked to the right, his neck skinny and long and stretched to the left, ears delicate and wide as monarch wings.

The boy drummed at his cheeks, stared at the table, shivered. Kept drumming.

—Me too, bud. I'm hungry too.

At the ding Wendell popped open the microwave door, grabbed the bowls, and burned his fingers. He cursed, glanced at the boy—still tapping away—and apologized. Then crumpled up a couple of paper towels and ferried the bowls to the table that way.

Wendell got two spoons and filled two glasses of water and stepped back, surveyed the table.

—This sure don't look like much.

He rooted through his cupboards again, found a package of saltines and paired it with a stick of margarine from the fridge. Then sat down and scooted his chair up. Smiled at himself for his quick thinking.

—Butter crackers, bud. Butter crackers'll stick to your ribs.

The boy stared at him, then at the crackers. Wendell took a cracker, put a thick pat of cold margarine on it, and handed it to the boy.

Until his mother had gone on that health kick, they used to get butter crackers with about every meal. There'd be meat, butter crackers, potatoes of some sort, a plate of pickles, and, for dessert, peaches or pears in heavy syrup. That was the sad, good time when it was just the two of them—after his old man had vanished, before Lacy.

The boy shoved the cracker into his mouth, worked it around in there a moment, then reached for another. Wendell grinned at him.

They ate for a time. The scrape of spoons, the soft shatter of crackers. After he finished, the boy just sat there, staring at his bowl. Wendell opened another can and poured half into the boy's bowl and nuked it and set the bowl in front of him. The boy ate that one, too, along with another plateful of butter crackers. Then he leaned back in his chair, eyes not quite so wide, his shoulders and jaw seeming to relax.

The boy was sleepy, Wendell thought. Or full. Or, hell, he didn't know. He didn't know what he was doing.

Before she left, Jackie, the neighbor girl who'd sat with the boy all day, had said she couldn't come by tomorrow. Said she had to drive into town, to the library at the school, where there was internet, so she could register for fall classes. She was starting at the private college over in Billings the next week. Wendell hadn't realized. He still thought of Jackie Maxwell as the new kid, the one whose parents had moved from Colorado and bought the Shellhammer place after Art Jr. lost it to the bank and had begun raising goats, of all things—a line of organic goat meat that took off when a chain of fancy grocery stores in California started buying it all up months in advance. There was a year, before he saved up and bought his Chevy LUV, that he and Jackie had ridden the same bus, the south bus. South-bus kids, north-bus kids, east-bus kids, west-bus kids. And town kids were a different bunch altogether. Jackie was a skinny kid with round glasses and two long braids, but one day she had worn her hair down instead, and on a dare Wendell had waited until the bus driver wasn't looking and then flicked a wad of bubble gum from way in the back and hit Jackie square in the head. Her brown hair had gotten all mushed up in the pink gum, and the whole bus had just laughed and laughed. Now here she was, grown up and nice-looking and telling him she was registering for college classes while he was living in his mother's trailer, bringing in someone else's wheat. He hoped Jackie didn't remember that about the gum. He didn't know who he'd get to sit with the boy tomorrow.

—How about some TV, bud?

He flipped it on for the boy and set himself to cleaning up the kitchen. Wiping down the table, Wendell thought he heard the boy hum or maybe laugh, but when he looked up, the boy, who hadn't been sitting there more than five minutes, had fallen asleep on the floor. Jesus. He finished with the dishes and pulled a can of Keystone Light from the fridge and took a drink. The light of the television played across the boy's small body. Wendell's heart knocked about in his chest.

Two shows later, Wendell knelt on the floor and picked the boy up in his arms. Just a bundle of skin and sticks, he thought as he laid the boy in his mother's bed, with its cream comforter and lace pillows. He hadn't been in her room much since she'd died and had sort of forgotten about her dresser, which had a big lead-glass mirror atop it. When he was a boy that mirror had scared him something awful, the stretched angle he saw himself at after he slipped into bed between his sleeping parents early in the morning. He rooted in the closet and found a sheet and draped it over the mirror.

The boy clenched and the whole of him went hard and rigid, his skinny arms thrown above his head, his eyes snapping open—but then, just as quickly, he relaxed and his eyes fluttered closed again. The social worker had mentioned fits, had shown Wendell what to do. Sound asleep like this, though, it didn't seem possible. Sound asleep and small and so out of place here in this woman's room. Wendell thought maybe he should get some sheets with cars on them or basketballs or something, hang a few posters on the wall. He wasn't sure. He opened a window against the heat, and the room filled with night sounds: crickets, mosquitoes, wind in the dry grass and pines, the far yips and calls of coyotes. He looked at the boy once more, his head turned to the left, knees pulled nearly up to his chin now. He's the smallest thing around, Wendell thought. The tiniest little thing for miles.

Wendell went for another beer, sat at the kitchen table, and drank it down. The boy was asleep, which was as it should be, and the night was all about, and he was tired from the day's work, the long muscles in his shoulders sizzling, shifting against the bones. He rubbed at his eyes with his thumb and forefinger, reds and purples swirling behind his lids, and took stock of his situation: He was twenty-four years old. He owned the trailer and the pickup outright but owed back taxes on what land was left—the old farmhouses, the shop, most of a section to the west—and had overdue payments on two of his mother's last surgeries, surgeries that hadn't done any good anyway. Glen Hougen, his boss, had let him fill his truck up the other day, so he had most of a tank of gas. Maybe a bit less than a hundred dollars in the bank, a few bills in his wallet. Considering he didn't know what he'd do with the boy tomorrow, didn't know whether he could afford to hire a permanent babysitter, this was about as much as he could make sense of, this and the night.

It was just him now, he thought, the beer can insubstantial in his hand. Him and his girl cousin's bastard kid. They were the last Newmans left in these mountains.

The next day he brought the boy with him to the field, asked Glen if, considering the circumstances, there not being but the one seat in the combine, he could drive the grain truck for the day, so the boy could ride along.

Glen spit, wiped his mouth with the back of his hand.

—Christ, Wendell. I know you've had a rough shake lately. But this ain't ideal.

—I know.

—Tell you what, you give Lanter a quick-and-dirty on how to run the combine. Take him around the field one time while I watch the little shooter. If Lanter can get his mind around it, you can drive the truck.

—I appreciate it.

—You goddamn better. I ain't got but one full-time hand, Wendell, and I need you doing the jobs that matter most. Even if Lanter gets it, he'll be slow. Won't get near as much done today.

Wendell helped the boy out of the LUV, and the kid stood there in the stubble at the field's edge, blinking in the blue-yonder light.

Glen came right up to him and leaned down.

—You ain't a bad-looking little fella. Got yourself some nice black hair.

At this, Glen pulled off his ball cap and rubbed his own slick, bald head.

—I'm downright jealous. What say we shake?

The boy pulled away, and when Glen reached out and took hold of his hand, he began to tremble and a breathy wail rose from his throat.

Embarrassed, Wendell set his hand on the boy's shoulder.

—Hey, it's okay, bud.

But the boy broke into a saw-blade scream that rose and broke again. Wendell knelt and tried to shush the boy, took him by his arms. But the boy only got louder. He jerked, kicked, shrieked in Wendell's face.

Now Glen took Wendell by the shoulder.

—Hey, loosen up that grip. That's right, okay, go get him a drink out of your canteen or something.

Dust in Wendell's eyes, the building heat of the day at his throat. He did as he was told and hefted the boy, who flailed and yowled, banging the back of his head into Wendell's shoulder and chest, and hurried across the field toward the grain truck. The boy's wails ripped through him. The cut stalks snapped beneath his boots. Wendell stumbled and righted himself and whispered to the boy that he was his good uncle and would do his honest best to take care of him, his honest best. And by the time they got to the truck the boy had quieted some, though he continued to shiver and jerk.

With the boy in one arm, Wendell hauled open the heavy, creaking door of the grain truck and set the boy up on the high bench seat, got him his notebook and pencil, the canteen. The boy's breath began to smooth and slow, and he put his fingers to his face and played the sides of his cheeks. Wendell leaned into the truck and showed him the old AM radio, how you could turn the silver knob and swing the dial up and back through the numbers. The boy watched a moment, his hands still at his face. Then reached out to take the knob.

Wendell fumbled his can of Copenhagen from his back pocket and pinched off a chew, spit, wiped at his forehead. Walked back across the field.

Glen shook his head.

—Goddamn. You don't even know what you're in for, son. Who'd you say the boy's daddy was?

—Lacy never did let on. His last name is Burns, though.

—And you never knew Lacy to run with a Burns?

—There's a lot I don't know, I guess.

Glen shook his head again and sucked at his teeth.

—That girl was buck wild from day one. No disrespect. But there was nothing your mama could've done. You start messing around with that methamphetamine—well, you're up shit creek. That boy ain't quite right, is he. Poor kid's gonna have it all kinds of rough. What's his first name?

—Rowdy.

—Rowdy Burns?

—Yeah.

—Goddamn.

His junior year was the year Delphia was finally going to make State again. Everyone said so. Wendell could shoot the lights out, Daniel McCleary was quick and smart with the ball, and the Korenko boy, despite his general lunkheadedness—he'd been held back two grades and was twenty years old—was six and a half feet tall.

The championship game at the divisional tournament saw two of the three news stations in Billings send reporters. Wendell scored thirty-three points and with just over a second left had a chance to tie the game, send it into overtime, with a one-and-one from the free-throw line. He made the front end, then clanked the second. That night, after the oblivion of the ride home on the team bus and the many dark turnings of the gravel road back to the trailer, Lacy came into his room and crawled into bed with him. Spooned herself up against him. Small as she was, she took him in her arms and held him. The summer before, he and Lacy had played a thousand dusty, furious games of one-on-one at the hoop nailed to the barn wall. She was quick and sharp-elbowed. She'd pushed him hard and could be downright mean about it. All that long ride home, he'd thought of her, of what she might say. But she hadn't said a thing. Just held him. He cried, really cried, and then like a tumbling stone in a river fell into a black, thrashing sleep.

He dreamed, as he often did, of wolves, their great forepaws soft and sure on the earth, and later woke to find Lacy standing over him, a rifle in her hands.

—Let's go.

—Where?

She turned toward the door.

—Just get the fuck up, she said.

Wendell followed her into the mountains. Black, high-running clouds, the light of the late-winter moon watery and blue. Grass and sticks and the night's freeze sharp beneath their bootfalls, scratch of pine bark, grit of rocks. The chatter of coyotes. A great horned owl's *whoo, whoo, whoo-whoo*. Then all was still, silent. And as the howl rang and rose around them, Lacy stopped, took her bearings, and followed that fading bell of sound. The slim, shifting, indomitable bit of darkness that she was disappeared into the fuller darkness. And he followed.

They walked all night. Dawn found them near Hawk Creek, where before hiking back they slept a cold hour huddled beneath a pine.

They never saw the wolf.

Stopping for Rowdy to piss, running back to the trailer because he'd forgotten to pack butter crackers, slowing to comfort the boy when something set him off—it all had Wendell back to the field slow, the combines full and waiting and Glen shaking his big bald head, spitting in the dust.

13

Otherwise it was a good day. Wendell liked how the boy's presence gave him an excuse to talk or gripe or act goofy. And for the most part Rowdy seemed to do fine. He liked to spin the radio knob. He liked the ups and downs of the dirt roads, the bumps and turns and washboards. Wendell gunned the engine now and again just to see his eyes go wide.

Once, midafternoon, the boy got some chaff or something stuck in his throat and couldn't seem to stop coughing. He got redder and redder, and Wendell pulled over and clapped him on the back and tried to get him to drink some water, and Rowdy finally did get a little water down and was okay then, though in the dusty, angled light Wendell felt wrung out.

Late in the evening, the sun bleeding through the pines, the broken land about going shadowed and blue, Wendell turned to find the boy sitting ramrod straight on the bench seat, like he'd been most of the day, scrawny shoulders cockeyed, eyes wide as skipping rocks. Wendell figured Glen would most likely work them until midnight to try to catch up, and remembering the tall bedtime tales his old man used to spin for him, he thought he might tell a story to help the boy relax, maybe even curl up and close his eyes.

—What say I tell a story? What would you say to that?

The boy turned and blinked, waited.

—All right, then. Let me get a dip here first.

Wendell reached for the can of Copenhagen he'd left on the dash, thumped it once, and set it on his thigh. Left hand on the wheel, he carefully worked the lid off with his right and set it too on his thigh and pinched up a chew. Just as he got the tobacco situated in his lip, the boy reached over for the tin and the lid and clicked the two together and handed the can back to Wendell. Wendell smiled, winked at the boy.

—I don't care what anyone says, Rowdy Burns, you're a gentleman.

Wendell told the boy about the long days of tilling and leveling and planting in the spring, the hope of rain hooked to the inside of you like a weight on your heart, and how when the rain comes, hope pulls the other way, lifting the heart like the rain does the green shoots, which poke up and lengthen and before you know it dry to gold and deeper gold. He told the boy about the tremendous red machine of the combine, the spinning forks that feed the wheat to the cutter bar, the triangle blades that snip the wheat, the thresher that does the sorting—sending chaff spinning out behind the combine onto the stubbled field and collecting hard red durum in the hopper—until the combine makes for the edge of the field, the auger bar straightens out, and the wheat spills into the empty bed of the grain truck.

—And here we are, bud, driving these dirt roads back and forth, carrying the wheat to the silos, where we auger it up into the silos, and then it waits in the silos to be sold, and then it's sold. And then, well, it's sold.

Wendell glanced at the boy, who was listening hard, watching him like a pilgrim watches the sky for a sign. Before them the road unspooled and narrowed off into the far reaches of the gathering night, starlight sliding down through road dust. In the silence Rowdy blinked and shivered, leaned into the bench seat, relaxing his shoulders ever so slightly. Wendell went on. He told about what came next and easiest to him, which was high-school basketball, how everyone in a fifty-mile radius showed up for home games, with more than half that traveling to away games and tournaments. He told about how goddamn much he missed playing basketball, coming hard and sharp off Toby Korenko's pick—the squeak of his sneakers, the slick of sweat as shoulder bumped shoulder—and catching the pass from Daniel McCleary and squaring and rising and at the apex of his leap levering the ball up and out and watching, as he dropped back to the hardwood, the ball snap through the net. How the crowd rose up then and hooted and hollered and stomped on the old wood and steel bleachers, and how the gym, a tight cinder-block square with the out-of-bounds lines right against the walls, fairly shook with that unbridled sound.

Basketball had set things right for him, he told the boy. With his father gone and most of their land sold or leased, he'd been the odd one out on the playground. Here, in this far place, a frontier that was all men and territory, he was the one without, lacking both, and the rules concerning such things were hard and fixed and applied with full and violent force to everyone—but Wendell couldn't find the words to explain this except to say again that basketball had saved him. He closed his eyes for a moment, felt the gravel and the ruts and the old cracked tires and the wheezing metal frame, the secret worries of the stars. He opened his eyes. After they won the district tournament his junior year, he told Rowdy, Glen had bought the whole team dinner at Jake's, the best steak house in Billings. Wendell had scored twenty-six points and grabbed eleven rebounds, and Glen had come right up to him special and said he couldn't order anything but prime rib, the most expensive thing on the menu. That steak, Wendell told the boy, was as big as the plate.

The sweet, bracing burn of tobacco was in his throat. The boy had curled himself into the passenger-side door, eyelids drifting, falling shut. The two of them were close enough to touch but they were not touching. They were alone in the old rattletrap grain truck, traveling through the dark, one small, true, utterly unseen thing in a universe of such things.

Now Wendell told this sleeping, shirttail relative of his something he'd never told anyone, that even though he didn't take much but basketball seriously in high school, he loved nothing more than when Mrs. Jorgeson, the English teacher, ancient, stern, an angry-looking mole on the side of her nose, would assign a new book. *A Tree Grows in Brooklyn, The Outsiders, Cannery Row*—he would come home and say barely two words to his mother or Lacy before disappearing into his room and from there into the strange, particular worlds of those pages, places and times where the rules were sometimes the same and sometimes different, and the place he knew so well, Musselshell County, with its residents numbering fewer than five thousand, was suddenly, frighteningly one of many. It confused and thrilled him—that the world was mutable, variegated. He told the sleeping boy that even though you were supposed to turn the books back in after the quiz and the report, he started keeping them. Mrs. Jorgeson must have known, but she never told him to stay after so she could ask him about it, and even if he didn't much have the time to read anymore, those books were still stacked on his bed stand. Lacy had teased him about getting his nose stuck in those books some, and his mother had thinned her eyes at him not turning the books back in to the school, but they'd been good enough to mostly let it pass. They were like that for a while, he thought, a family of sorts, each with a room of the trailer to clean on Sunday, each carrying wounds and sadnesses.

The moon came up whistle-thin. A tooth, a claw, the leanest blade. And a low wind skulked among the twisted knots of sage and greasewood and drifted down the hills, its breath cool and dry where it touched him on the inside of his arm, the hollow of his neck. Because he wanted to, because he'd realized in the telling there was so much to tell, he told Rowdy about the countless days he'd spent tromping through the woods, trapping and hunting in the Bulls. He told about the sheer sides of canyons, the faded markings that Indians and homesteaders had carved into the sandrocks. He told about the elk herds growing year after year, surprising everyone, and the beetle-sick pine trees, whole ridges gone orange with chewed, dead trees. He told about the time he and his old man were checking their trapline when they came on a lynx, the first and last he'd ever seen, just as it was about to gnaw through its own front left knee. His father, calm as could be, raised up his .22 and put a clean hole in the cat's head. They skinned it out that day and cured the hide, and even now that banded, dun, three-legged lynx hide hung across the back of the easy chair in the trailer.

The memory of his father quieted him. There was a sheaf of coyote pelts in one closet or another and any number of fox and raccoon and rabbit skins tucked here and there. He'd get a couple out for the boy, he thought. Hang one in his room, maybe. Put one on the floor by his bed for when he got up in the night. He and Glen had gone into town a couple of weeks ago and stopped for coffee at the drugstore, and all the talk was of the upcoming wolf hunt, the first fair-chase wolf hunt in the history of the state of Montana. "You ever run your hand across a wolf hide?" one of the old-timers, milky-eyed Kreele Poole, had asked him before remembering who it was he was asking. Wendell thought again of his father, how in one motion full of grace he could lift the rifle, firm the butt, and fire.

Wendell came up a low hill, and the headlights of the truck slid from dark sky and star-scatter to cheatgrass and gravel road. He still had a few rifles, and he still had his father's old traps, though for how busy Glen kept him he hadn't buffed the rust from the teeth or boiled them in dye for a long, long time.

The boy shifted in his sleep and stretched his thin legs out until one of his socked feet just touched Wendell's leg.

Wendell showed up with Rowdy again the next day, and Carol, Glen's wife, met them at the field. She was hot at Glen for not letting her know the day before. Just what was he thinking, allowing a poor, troubled child of God to ride in that nasty old grain truck all the long day? And she was hot at Wendell for not calling her to sit with the boy, as he knew very well she was a Christian woman and would surely look after one of God's innocents if Wendell had only had the good common sense to ask, which Maureen had had in spades and he ought to think on his mother more. Why, he surely ought to have known, Carol continued, stamping her foot, that with her own grandboy living nearly over in Billings now, she was lonesome to look after somebody and here was this little boy right close by needing taking care of and no one had thought to even tell her.

She shook her head at the both of them, then came over to Rowdy as sweet as you please, pulled out a packet of gummy worms, and fussed over him. As Rowdy gnashed the gummy worms like they might get away, she straightened up, her hands on the boy's shoulders, and told Wendell he could pick him up after work. She'd make sure that by then Rowdy would have had his supper and said his prayers and be ready for bed.

Wendell worked the toe of his boot against the dry earth, the cut stalks.

He'd already had it in mind that Glen would let him drive the grain truck another couple of days or so, and Rowdy would ride with him. He'd packed butter crackers and two gallon jugs of water and had been thinking of stories to tell, even stories about the boy's mother, Lacy, about her time with them, how beautiful, fierce, and fun she was. But Rowdy's mouth rolled with bright bits of gummy worm, and Carol held him close.

Wendell knelt in the stubble and touched the boy's chest.

—You gonna be all right?

Rowdy rooted around in the plastic package, extracted an orange gummy worm, studied it, and shoved it in his mouth.

Wendell stood and thanked Carol.

—I imagine he'll be fine, he told her.

And a couple of weeks later, he was. He'd even played some with Tyler, Glen and Carol's grandson, when he visited over the weekend, though Glen told Wendell one morning, grinning, that Carol was more than a little distraught that Rowdy still hadn't opened his mouth, not even to say his prayers.

VERL

Day Three

Goddamn but I have been running. I hear engines and the squawk of
your radios and once like revelation a glassy helicopter lifted itself over
the ridge and flattened the grass and cracked three sick trees. My heart I
thought would charge out of me. But even then you missed. I hunkered
down. Then ran. When I had to do what I had to do. I did. I shot the
wolf clean. I did not miss. Each time you have missed me.

GILLIAN

THE FARMSTEAD, AS IT CAME INTO VIEW DOWN THE WEEDY ROAD, LOOKED like most farmsteads this far north of the Yellowstone, this far into the Bull Mountains—a break in the cottonwoods or jack pines sheltering an outbuilding of corrugated tin, some falling-down corrals, the hulks of old pickups and tractors, a two-story farmhouse in some late stage of collapse, and off to the side of the house a double-wide with cinder-block steps surrounded by a yard of cheatgrass and dust. And here, at this particular Bull Mountain outpost, beneath a lightning-split pine by the barn, a pack of dogs—brown, mottled, rib-skinny—bellied down in the dirt, chewing on what looked to be a fresh deer hide.

Gillian slowed her Prius and parked near the trailer, then breathed a prayer, a habit from her Catholic girlhood that she'd never kicked. She clicked open the glove box and reached for her pepper spray, slid the cold cylinder into her purse. She eased out and shut the door gingerly. The dogs—three, four, maybe five—ripped at the hide and growled at one another. She quickstepped across the dirt yard and checked for rattlers before hurrying up the cinder blocks. She knocked. The trailer door swung open beneath her fist. The smells of grease and cigarettes and closed spaces washed over her.

—Hello? she called. Ms. Wilson? Hello?

A door opening, closing. Footsteps. A small woman, large-eyed, maybe thirty, emerged from the back hallway. She wore charcoal pajama pants studded with little pink hearts, and a faded pink hoodie.

Gillian introduced herself as the assistant principal and counselor at Colter Schools. She mentioned the phone message she'd left the day before.

—You just barge on in, huh?

—I'm sorry. Your door swung open when I knocked.

—Oh yeah, it does that. The latch is busted.

Gillian held her hand out, and Tricia Wilson hesitated but took it, her own hand small and cold, the purple on her fingernails chipped.

—I can heat some coffee up in the microwave if you want.

—That'd be lovely, Gillian said.

She followed Tricia into the trailer—*Kiss This* scrawled in bubbly, pink cursive across the rear end of her pajama pants—and waited in the living room, where a shampoo commercial twisted across the screen of the muted television. On the wall hung three framed paintings featuring sharp lines, shadowed figures, a girl's naked back—everything black, electric blue, or silver, punctuated with a few bursts of hot pink or blood red. Suicide art, Gillian had dubbed it. The sort that led not to an art scholarship but to a stint as a tattoo artist. She'd seen it again and again during her nineteen years in the Montana school system.

The microwave whirred. On the television, Dr. Oz threw his arms wide and the camera cut to the studio audience, all clapping fanatically. Standing in the kitchen, Gillian toed a small burn mark at the edge of the dark green shag, took note of a blue satin Delphia Broncs jacket lying on the wraparound couch. Delphia was north of the Bull Mountains, along the Musselshell River, and Colter was south, along the Yellowstone. Only fifty crow-fly miles separated the two small towns and their schoolhouses, but it was fifty miles of canyons and cutbanks, of jack pines and cactus, of wild mountain country. Still, it happened most every year: A kid would get kicked out of one school and enroll in the other. Then get in trouble there. Come back to the first school for a time. Maybe fail a few classes and leave again. A dance over and across the mountains that most often ended in the kid dropping out—or going to juvenile or jail or simply disappearing. Gillian had done the dance in her own way, starting as a science teacher at Delphia in 1990, then taking the assistant-principal position at Colter in '98, more than a decade ago now. Though that was for different reasons altogether.

The microwave dinged. Tricia clicked open the plastic door and handed Gillian a boiling cup of mud-colored coffee, then poured herself a cup as well and stuck it in the microwave. Gillian thanked Tricia and sipped at hers. Jesus, it was terrible.

Gillian ran her hand over the polished wood of one of the kitchen chairs, the fine grain of the wood, the sure, sloping lines of the lathe work. The table and chairs, far too big for the trailer's kitchen space, were a beautiful set. They were built with great skill and care and had belonged to Tricia's grandmother, it turned out, though all Tricia could say was what a bitch they'd been to move. The table was covered now in junk—plates crusted with ketchup, binoculars and fencing pliers, a slung hunting jacket.

The microwave sounded again and Tricia began to transfer the detritus to the kitchen counter, which was itself covered in dirty dishes and half a dozen pink plastic Mary Kay starter kits. She grabbed at the hunting jacket, and as she balled it up to toss it down the hallway, Gillian couldn't help noticing that the sleeves from just below the elbow, as well as the entire bottom half, were stained a dark, rusty color, as if the wearer had waded up to mid-torso into a pool of motor oil or blood. Gillian's vision thinned. She took an awkward step. Coffee lapped over the edge of the mug and slapped the linoleum.

Tricia stared a moment, as if trying to decide whether to be angry, then crumpled a few paper towels and tossed them to the ground.

Gillian braced herself against the nearest chair.

—I'm sorry, she said. I should sit.

Tricia dumped the wadded towels in a plastic garbage can and leaned against the counter.

—What did you say your name was?

Gillian breathed and crossed her legs, collecting herself.

—Gillian Houlton. I'm the assistant principal over at Colter. I called about Tavin, your son.

—Right, yeah. Well, what's he done?

Tavin had been missing a lot of school, Gillian explained. It was only the middle of September, and he'd already missed six days, and ten was the state limit for the whole year. After that, if his teachers were of a mind, they could fail him and he'd have to repeat the eighth grade, which might be especially tough since he was already big for his age.

Tricia flipped her bangs off her forehead.

—Christ, she said. I can't make him go. He's so big, like you say. And he just worships Brian right now. Brian doesn't think much of government education.

Tricia paused, poked her left thumbnail in her mouth, and chewed at it until little bits of purple polish winked from the corners of her lips.

—He was a little boy for so long, you know. And now he's not.

—I know what you mean, Gillian said. Mine is a senior this year, and I can't figure out how it happened.

She paused and sipped at her coffee.

—If Tavin really idolizes his father, maybe I should talk with him?

Tricia stared at her for a time, as if she couldn't quite decide. Then grabbed a pack of menthols off the shelf over the sink, cranked one of the stove coils to a red-orange glow, and lit the cigarette off it. She spoke in a rush of smoke.

—Brian isn't Tavin's dad. I had him by Jimmy Stensvad.

—I see. Does Tavin still have a relationship with Jimmy?

—Jimmy's dead. Fell out of a truck bed.

Tricia took another drag and sat down. She wiped at her eyes.

—They were all out drinking and driving around and raising hell, spotlighting coons or something. Stupid son of a bitch. He was so good and so stupid. It wasn't but a couple of weeks after graduation. I was pretty far along but still wasn't showing. We were planning the wedding, a honeymoon in Rapid City. Everything.

How much to reveal? Gillian wondered. Enough to make a connection but no more.

—I'm so sorry, she said. It won't help, but I know how you feel. I lost my husband too. Years ago now, but I don't know that I'll ever really be over it.

Tricia coughed and stood and spit into the sink. She wiped her nose on a paper towel and dried her eyes with the sleeves of her sweatshirt. It was a strategy that had worked for her in the past, Gillian could tell, using her sorrow this way. But she wasn't in control of it. Not really. She loved that boy. Maybe he loved her too.

—Tricia, I'd like to talk to Tavin, if it's all right. I'm not the cops, I'm not here to get him in trouble. I just want to talk. He's done well up until now, and I'd hate to see him throw it away. Eighth grade is a pivotal year. Any chance he's around?

Tricia dropped her cigarette into her coffee mug, where it hissed against the dregs.

—He's out with Brian. Probably miles out into the mountains now.

—Hunting season doesn't start for another month, Gillian said.

She'd tried to stop herself before she spoke, but couldn't. All these years later she could still hear his voice.

Tricia tensed, her pack of menthols scrunched in her hand.

—I thought you said you weren't the cops.

Gillian took a big swallow of rancid coffee, punishment for her stupidity.

—Christ, I'm sorry. My husband used to be with Fish and Game. Guess I'm still in the habit. It's none of my business.

Tricia shook another cigarette out of the pack and slipped it between her lips.

—No, she said, it isn't. And I think we've talked this out. Leave the cup over by the sink. Make sure the door latches behind you.

Gillian cursed herself as she slammed the car door, cursed herself as she twisted the wheel and gunned the engine, the dogs finally noticing, barking and chasing and biting at her tires before falling away. She cursed herself as the Prius fishtailed up the draw and spun through the loose gravel and dust. Cursed her own stupidity as she turned onto the county road and drove south through the dry coulees and over the windburned ridges of the Bulls, drove as fast as she could back toward the Yellowstone Valley and what passed for civilization.

She wouldn't see Tavin for the rest of the year now. Not after that. Tricia would say something to Brian, and Brian would go apeshit, and Tavin would get sent to Delphia, or they'd say they were homeschooling. Kent Leslie, the principal, would fuss and fume in response, worried as he always was about their state funding, which was directly tied to the number of students, and when you had only seventy-odd students in the entire district, even one mattered. And the boy himself, Tavin, would end up just about like his stepdad—running a few cattle, poaching, drinking, doing terrible things to this girl and that girl and having a kid or three, voting Republican even as he lived off the usual rural welfare: government grazing leases and Conservation Reserve Program payments. God, the cycle of rural poverty. Rural stupidity. It was enough to make her insane.

As she dropped out of the Bulls and into the valley, Gillian thought for a moment about turning west, breezing along the interstate back to her house in Billings, forty miles distant, showering, getting dinner ready, having a glass of chardonnay as she waited for Maddy to finish her after-school shift at Starbucks—but it wasn't yet four thirty, which was when Kent officially let the staff go, and beyond her own fuckup, she couldn't think of a good enough excuse. Like she'd known she would, she turned east and a few minutes later got off the interstate at the lone exit for Colter.

Though Colter looked encouraging near the freeway, at least by small-town Montana standards, with Edna's, the one surviving diner, and a new Chevron boasting an A&W Restaurant both within sight of the exit ramp, its promise soon played out. The frontage road cut through a scrubby patchwork of ditches and overgrazed fields littered with rusted farm equipment, and then, slumped along old Highway 1, came the city proper: a four-by-five grid of gravel and dust featuring an impressive collection of crumbling brick false-fronts, one or two of which, depending on the year and the severity of the most recent drought, housed saloons with names like the Grand, the Branding Iron, and the Ace. Just off Main, as if in counterpoint, lay the old mission Catholic church and the steeply roofed Lutheran church, both sanctuaries shaded by massive, ancient cottonwoods, and on the edge of town, near the rodeo grounds, stretched the brand-new, shedlike evangelical church, the Church of the Plains, whose oiled parking lot baked in any kind of sun. Along the grid of gravel roads in between, scattered here and there, lay a motley collection of maybe three dozen farmhouses, double-wides, and camper trailers, half of which were empty and the other half of which sheltered all the souls of Colter. And of course, at the top of the hill, sat the school—grades K through 12, all in the same low-slung brick building.

In her office Gillian made some notes on her visit and was about to slide Tavin's file into the drawer for old cases but caught herself and opened the upper drawer, which was for current students, and put the file in there. Oh, Tavin. Round-faced, beady-eyed, his hair cut so short his scalp was pink with sunburn most of the time. It was possible that Tricia might try to do right by the boy. But what about the stepdad? That's where the trouble usually was, with the fathers and grandfathers and uncles. What about that Brian? She should have gotten his last name. Another fuckup.

Gillian leaned back in her chair and eyed the clock—4:17 p.m. Despite days like this, she loved her job, she did, but she'd been at it a long time now and the list of wins in the past couple of decades was short—she put the number of students who'd managed to make even a few solid choices about their lives at maybe a dozen, maybe a few more. It wasn't for lack of trying on her part. Gillian had planned late into the night, every night, her first years of teaching and still attended conferences every summer. Even before she became assistant principal, she was the one other teachers came to when they needed help, when they needed someone to observe a troublesome class or design an intervention for a particular student. The only reason she'd driven out into the Bulls today was that Mr. Paysinger, the English teacher, had come to her pursing his thin lips and worrying his scraggly chin beard, telling her that Tavin Wilson was already failing eighth-grade language arts, tapping his attendance log to show her how many days the boy had missed. And even as Gillian had known right away what she had to do, she'd also known that it likely wouldn't be enough, that for most of these kids it would never be enough—a knowledge that was only confirmed when she saw the shivering rib slats of those dogs, the pearlescent underbelly of that deer hide, the hunting jacket dipped in blood. The way Tricia lit her cigarette on the stove coil, her face so close to all that bright, hard heat.

The first time Kevin Kincheloe ever spoke to her was to ask her to the Foresters' Ball. That was the fall of 1980 and Gillian was a senior at the University of Montana, working the midnight shift at the library reference desk. She'd seen him around, a skinny, long-legged kid whose sandy hair hung down to the collar of the snap shirt he tucked into dark blue jeans. Often, he would be at a study table in the middle of a jostling group of boys who periodically broke into snorts of laughter that rippled through the silence of the second floor, where Gillian restacked books, her favorites the slim volumes of poetry, which almost disappeared as you shelved them.

She was taking her last few classes that semester, waiting for her student-teaching placement in the spring. Her father, a thirty-five-year veteran of Kaiser Aluminum in Spokane, a broad man whose back clacked now like dominoes in a wooden box as he reached for his coffee at the breakfast table, had insisted on the double major in education and biology. She didn't mind. She liked school. As a young girl, she'd almost always finished her seat work long before her classmates, which afforded her plenty of time to daydream herself into the role of teacher. She was sure she'd be both more fun and more firm than her own instructors had been—middle-aged men and women who snuck out for cigarette breaks during reading time and let the boys who made the most trouble put their heads down on their desks and sleep.

She loved ecology and knew she'd make a good science teacher. Last week for her advanced ecology class, they'd all tromped down to the Clark Fork and pulled caddisflies from the shallows. She'd held one in her hand, watched as the larva slowly hauled its thin legs back into its gravel casing, a fragile assemblage of sticky silk and tiny river stones. What she was less sure about was Montana. When she was applying to college, she'd picked Missoula mostly for the way the town was nestled in a river valley and ringed by green mountains, a nice contrast for a girl from industrial Spokane. But she was discovering that small towns came with their own grim realities. Even the college boys in Missoula, many in from ranches and outpost towns, were somehow louder and harder, their hands thicker than those of the boys she knew back home, who, while they could be coarse, were still city boys, complete with bell-bottom corduroys and hifis that spun the Rolling Stones, boys who wore Jimmy Carter lapel pins given to them by their factory-working fathers, union to the core. Until she could apply for licensure in another state, she hoped she might land a teaching position in Missoula, at least, where the university provided a little culture and leavened the politics. After Missoula, she didn't know where she'd go. Spokane didn't much feel like home anymore. Her mother had died, of pancreatic cancer, almost a decade ago now, when Gillian was in sixth grade, and after she left for college, her father remarried. He'd even recently built an addition onto the house for his four young stepchildren. She thought she'd travel, thought she'd like to live near a river, someplace thick with birds and trees and trails to the water.

In the library the fluorescent lights fluttered off, then on, and she continued tracing the life cycle of a caddisfly. Though it didn't matter for her grade, she was trying in her illustration to get the gravel casing she'd seen on the Clark Fork right, to shade it just so, that bumpy, bright, perfect little house of mottled river rocks.

—That's pretty. What you're working on there.

She startled, looked up to find the boy from the second floor. Tall, wide-faced, smiling. She asked him if he needed to check out some books and when he said he didn't she returned to her drawing. But he didn't move. Just stood there.

—You ever seen a hatch? he said. A caddisfly hatch?

She swung her head back up, studied him, as if she might find in the slope of his cheekbone whatever it was that had just set her heart to thumping.

The hatch was really something, he said, and told her about driving a hundred miles up the Musselshell River just to see it—it was like fog coming off the water. Then, as if this was what naturally came after such an anecdote, he said he was in the forestry school and asked her if she'd like to go to the Foresters' Ball with him.

She hadn't been on a date in over a year. On the last one, although she didn't smoke, she'd tucked a lit cigarette in her mouth all night to keep the stupid galoot from trying to kiss her. But there beneath the fluorescent light in the library she said yes even before she got the boy's name.

After dinner Maddy claimed an Oh-my-God buttload of homework and shut herself in her room. Gillian cleared the dishes and wiped down the counters and the table and loaded the dishwasher, then poured a second glass of wine. She puttered in the backyard for a time—filled the birdbath, splashed water on the tomatoes and herbs—and then sat on the patio in the shade of the ash trees as *All Things Considered* leaked from the outside speakers, a piece about the developing health-care bill. Last year, Gillian and Maddy had watched the election results come in with all their fellow Obama volunteers at the new brewery downtown. The celebration started early and continued right through the results in Montana, where Obama had cut the distance to just over two percentage points. There'd been lots of talk that night about this being the beginning, about Montana soon turning blue. Gillian sipped at her wine and smiled at the memory. The station cut to local news and her heart stilled a moment, then crashed against the bones of her chest—three quick interviews, all with men who had put in for the wolf lottery and were hoping to draw hunting tags. She could almost smell the tobacco on their breath, see the devil in their eyes. The sunset brightened and twisted in the haze of the city, and Gillian lifted her wineglass to her lips, only to find it empty. She went back inside.

Maddy's muffled humming and singing drifted down the hall. Gillian set her glass on the counter and gave in to temptation. She started toward her office but paused by her daughter's door, straining to hear the words: *Sometimes it did get lonely but it—*

Silence for half a beat.

—Mom? Is that you?

—Oh, sorry, honey. Can I come in?

—Mom, don't be creepy. Just knock.

Gillian gave a slight knock and opened the door, found her daughter sitting on the floor, knees pulled up to her chest, her long, raven-colored hair swept over her head. She had a textbook lolled wide on the floor in front of her and her phone firmly in hand, earbuds dangling around her neck.

—You have such a nice voice, Gillian said. I miss it.

Maddy rolled her eyes and turned back to her phone's glowing screen, balled herself up all the more tightly.

—You were singing Lightfoot, weren't you. You know your dad had all his records. After work he used to sit in the basement—remember that old swamp cooler we had in the house along the river?—and he'd listen—

—You've told me this story at least a thousand times.

Gillian studied her daughter, how long and lean she was—that was all

Kevin. And her smile, slight dimples even now. That was Kevin too. God, the man could just smile. She tried to hold back, but the years collapsed, and she felt her eyes go watery.

—Oh, Mom, don't cry.

Maddy rose and in two graceful steps was there, her arms around her mother. Though taller than Gillian by a couple of inches, out of habit she nestled her head into the crook of her mother's neck. Gillian hugged her back tightly.

—Thanks, honey. You know you just remind me so much of him. More and more all the time. You were so young. Sometimes I worry you'll forget him.

Maddy pulled away.

—Why don't we ever visit? Delphia, I mean. It'd be a way for me to know him, right? To see where he grew up? Where the three of us lived?

Gillian let go a long breath. Though Maddy hadn't asked in years, she used to, often, and Gillian had had to plan, practice, and revise her responses. Kevin's mother, Elner, was in Delphia, and it had been hard convincing a little girl it wasn't a good idea to go to Grandma's house. But Gillian had done it. She had to—she knew she wasn't strong enough to face them. Not there, anyway. Not in those mountains. Before Elner got so sick with Parkinson's, she had visited Gillian and Maddy in Billings a couple of times. She'd been funny and irreverent, as she always was, but Gillian could no longer write off Elner's ignorance as the harmless quirks of an old country woman. No, these ideas had real consequences, and Gillian seethed whenever Elner mentioned another farm foreclosure and blamed it on what "they" were doing to rural America. Gillian couldn't stand the camo-and-pink outfits Elner bought for Maddy or the GLOBAL WARMING: ANOTHER LIBERAL TAX SCAM bumper sticker on the back of Elner's truck. She dealt as best she could with the visits in Billings, but whenever Maddy asked after her aunts or for a visit to the ranch, Gillian explained to her daughter that sometimes a family just couldn't spend time together, that it was sad but true, and that after what had happened to him, her father wouldn't want them to know that place or those people—not anymore. Gillian repeated that mantra now with little variation from when Maddy had been a newly fatherless six-year-old.

—We're what mattered to him. You and me. Not that place. I promise you, he's here with us more than he is anywhere else.

Gillian touched her own chest, then her daughter's.

—He's right here, honey.

—I know, Maddy said. In our hearts.

It was a familiar recitation. *He's right here, in our hearts.* Mother and daughter could have chanted it together, if they'd wanted, with the same attendant intonations and pacing, yet even for their familiarity, the words still touched all the old delights and wounds. Now Maddy's eyes slicked with tears, and she stood there a moment longer, letting Gillian look at her, take her in, then wiped at her eyes and slipped away, settled back onto the floor. She winged her arms behind her, twisted up her hair, and pinned it with a pencil. Plugged in her earbuds once more.

She moved like a ribbon, Gillian thought. A spill of ribbon. She shook her head. That long, thick raven hair wasn't Kevin's. That was hers. When Maddy was twelve, thirteen, fourteen, Gillian remembered wishing she'd end up as straight-hipped and slim as Kevin. But though Maddy had Kevin's height, her chest and hips, her every curving, were Gillian's. The girl would be downright gorgeous in a year or two when she figured out how to put it all together. Gillian hoped, anyway, that it would take a year or two, so that when it happened Maddy would be off at college meeting people as smart and as interesting as she was. Gillian watched her daughter's lips move, in silence at first, then with a throaty whisper. Though she would have liked to stay and listen, she closed her daughter's door and made her way back down the hall.

In the kitchen Gillian rooted in her purse and found her phone. She poured another glass of chardonnay, then called Dave Coles. The phone rang, and rang, and beeped:

—*You've got Dave Coles, publisher, editor, lead reporter, and errand boy at the* Colter Courier, *eastern Montana's best newspaper! Leave a detailed message, and I'll get right back to you. That's my newspaperman's promise!*

—Hi, Dave. Gillian. Haven't seen you over at the Boiler Room lately. Want to grab a drink this Friday? And, if you would, check around for anything you have on a Tricia Wilson. And a guy she's associated with named Brian. Maybe a husband, maybe just shacked up. I'm not sure. But probably a Delphia graduate. Or not necessarily a graduate but, you know, a Delphia kid. Anyway, it's about Tricia's boy, Tavin. Hoping we can keep him in school. Thanks. See you Friday.

Gillian took her wineglass to the couch and clicked a lamp on. Dave Coles's great-grandfather had published the first edition of the *Courier* in 1908, and alongside churning out the weekly, Dave now curated a dusty, slipshod museum of sorts out of the newspaper offices. Two years ago, when Gillian was filling in for a social studies teacher who'd quit midyear, she and her students spent a good chunk of the semester at the old brick *Courier* building on Main, researching and putting together a town-history pamphlet. Dave was kind and peculiar and full of stories, and though his goofiness always made her shake her head, he truly cared about his community. He'd helped her out before, when it meant getting a bond passed or not letting the school-board members fire a good teacher because of their problems with her politics or just keeping a kid out of trouble. And though he was Colter through and through, Dave liked to dip his toe into the city. He enjoyed the rib eye over at Jake's and often held court at the Boiler Room.

Gillian took a swallow of wine, and another, and soon set the empty glass on the coffee table. The streetlights came on. An evening breeze drifted through the ash trees, knocked against the sliding glass door. She tried to read her novel but couldn't concentrate for the wine behind her eyes, for hearing her daughter's voice, indistinct but rising now and again into a pure, sure note.

VERL

Day Six of the New Dispensation

You see now I have given this here a fine new title. I have said no to your laws that would not let a man shoot a vicious animal on his own land. That would neuter a man on his own land. You are the ones that put the wolves back in this country that was just fine without them. And I have said no and am here in this country that has borne me and held me and that I have loved.

I am living this new way. This is a new dispensation.

Also you best understand this isn't for me. This isn't some kind of diary book my boy's mother would keep. I've no need to write this down. Don't mistake it. I could live out here on the land without another soul around the rest of my born days and be goddamn happy as a buck goat.

Later

I have been thinking. All this day I have been walking. I have not done such walking as I've done here lately in a goddamn time and even over the banging of my fat heart I have been thinking and have stopped and read over what I wrote (for I have nothing to read but this with my Louis L'Amours back at the trailer) and had another thought. What I mean is

I ~~wander~~ wonder at myself for writing this. Why tell the cowards and the fuckers? Won't do a lick of good. Sick in the head as they are. They would never see the truth of any of this. I guess this ought to be for those it could do some good.

Well this is for my boy then.

For you boy. I speak to you now. Listen. It takes training to be a free man. Your television and your schoolteachers will feed you all kinds of rot. I want you to know rot for rot. Even years on I want you to know what kind of a man your old dad was. A free man. A man of hands and plans. A man of mountains. These Bull Mountains. You hear me?

Listen so as you'll know. Carry my voice in your head.

What is most important is I have my .270 and a thirty box of shells. I have my lace-up steel-toe boots a pair of wool socks heavy Carhartts a tee shirt flannel shirt duck jacket scotch cap. I have a wolf's tooth and two wolf's claws on a length of fishing wire strung around my neck. I have thirty-two dollars (not that I will ever need such funny money again might as well roll it up and smoke it for the good it will do me) a two-liter stainless steel canteen and a jackknife. My coat pockets stuffed to busting with candy bars and copenhagen and antelope jerky and it is no shame to raid the odd henhouse. A hen's head yanks right off and if you roast them in their feathers under a pile of rocks there is not much smoke. I'll suck an egg too. Like an old dog. I'll not think twice for an egg is full of vitamins and fat and good especially for a man's body sucked right out of a little tapped hole in the narrow end of the shell.

I saw that once about vitamins on a morning show your mother watches. That's how I know.

It is late now boy. Dark but for the stars. The air sharp and cold. Writing to you this way I think of you. And your mother.

WENDELL

Aᴌᴛʜᴏᴜɢʜ ᴡᴇᴇᴋs ʟᴀᴛᴇʀ ᴛʜᴇ ʙᴏʏ sᴛɪʟʟ ʜᴀᴅɴ'ᴛ sᴀɪᴅ ᴀ ᴡᴏʀᴅ, ʜᴇ listened well enough. When Wendell told him to pick up the pace, Rowdy lifted his knees and fairly hustled through the dry grass and duff.

Mid-September, early morning, cool, the sky the blue of birds' eggs—they'd finished harvest yesterday. Since Glen had worked them through the past two weekends, he'd given Wendell this Thursday and Friday off. And here they were, then, he and the boy, their first full day together since they'd rode in the grain truck, and the soap smell of sage was sharp in the air, meadowlarks letting loose their liquid, six-note songs.

Wendell unlatched the wooden door of the shop, which slumped some fifty yards back of the trailer, and they went in together, the musk of grease and rust and still, dark spaces enveloping them. Wendell readied the workbench and then told Rowdy to bring him the number threes and fours out of the tangle of traps hanging by that spool of twine. Rowdy didn't hesitate. He sorted through and hefted the traps by their dark, clanking chains—bending his small body against the awkward weight of them, jaws and springs knocking against his belly—and hauled them over to Wendell. He strained to get them up onto the oil-stained bench.

—That's right, set those right up there. We'll work the dirt off with this brush and get the worst of the rust off with steel wool. You want the brush or the wool? Okay, the brush. That means you take first crack. There you go. When you finish, slide them my way.

They scrubbed the traps side by side, the boy's bony shoulder every once in a while bumping Wendell's waist. Once they finished, Wendell handed the number threes to the boy and took up the fours himself. They came out into the light, blinking and shying a moment for the dark of the shop, then crossed the dirt yard and hung the traps from sixty-penny nails Wendell's father had long ago pounded in a spiral around the trunk of a sizable pine.

Wendell set up the propane burner, and the boy watched wide-eyed as he lit it with a long-handled lighter and the flames leaped up orange and gold and settled into a ring of shimmering blue knives. Wendell had the boy turn on the garden hose and fill the big, smoke-black pot. Then Wendell heaved it up onto the burner.

—Pine needles, bud. We need some pine needles.

The boy looked up at Wendell, then took off running into the woods.

Wendell grinned, pulled a can of Copenhagen from his back pocket. Another meadowlark called. The wind turned in the trees. As far back as he could reach, he found in memory the oily dark of the shop, the feather blue of the sky, and the bubbling pot of trap dye. There was his father, sharp-eyed and black-whiskered, hands rangy and sure, and his mother, slender, her hair undone, stepping out the back door, shivering in her nightdress as she waved them in for a breakfast of eggs and deer sausage, with black coffee already on the table. Hadn't they had a good number of years like that? Sometimes he wasn't sure, as he couldn't ever call to mind those good years without thinking about what came after.

The boy came pounding down the hillside, his arms full of pine branches.

—That's the ticket. Drop those right here and let's shuck the needles into the pot.

The smell of the boiling pine needles was green and heady, and Wendell gathered the traps and dropped them one by one into the pot, where they clattered and shook.

—Some trappers dye and wax. But my old man only ever dyed. I figure that ought to be good enough for the likes of us. What d'you say?

The boy stared at the pot, his fingers at his cheeks, though he seemed to have forgotten to drum them. From somewhere off in the trees came the *hack-hack-hack* of a magpie.

—We'll let these boil for a half hour or so and then bury them out back of the shed. Then when we dig them up, maybe a couple of days, we'll be ready to run us a trapline. Sound good?

The boy looked from the pot to the shed and back to Wendell, then reached both hands out and took hold of one of Wendell's hands and stared up at him.

With the traps buried they gathered Wendell's guns, at least the few he hadn't sold to pay down the medical bills he discovered after his mom died: a .243 with an adjustable nine-power scope for deer and antelope; a 30.06 with a six-power scope for anything bigger; and his grandfather's old bolt-action .22 for varmints and plinking.

They hiked back of the trailer, skirting the collapsing farmhouses that were once Wendell's great-grandfather's and great-great-uncle's, and turned south down the draw, moving through sagebrush and bunchgrass for a time, before rising into jack pines and cedars. To their right a sand-rock ridge jutted up. The junk coulee widened and fell to their left.

Wendell hadn't taken the boy up this way yet, and when he glanced back, Rowdy was standing stock-still at the lip of the junk coulee, study-ing the mess as if reading runes or auguries. Wendell swung the rifles off his shoulder and took a look himself, the first good, long look he'd had in years. Here was the scrap and evidence of not quite a century of New-man settlement. First, the recent castoffs: maimed toys and cardboard boxes and piles of mice-infested clothes; a ridiculously large projection TV; a toaster shaped like a Trans Am; at least three microwaves, one nearly the size of an easy chair; two actual easy chairs, pea green and sun-washed blue; a set of frayed and faded lawn furniture; and smashed pallets, mangled irrigation siphons, old wooden fence posts, and countless car batteries and tires. Next, deeper in: a slope-sided Ford truck, an agitator and matching wringer, a refrigerator with a long silver handle, and the moldering but intricately carved and inlaid boards of what might once have been a traveling trunk of the sort you see being unloaded from trains in old Western movies. Last, at the very limits of vision, deep in the crevasse: a steam tractor, a seeder, a subsurface packer, and some half dozen other ancient, alien-looking farming implements, their architecture bewildering, their names and uses long forgotten, though a splash of paint on a row of tines remained as red as a wound.

They stood there at the edge of time and distance, scions, inheritors—and the wind flung dust at them, the grit of it gathering at the corners of their eyes. On the ridge above, a flat ten-inch whorl of sandrock, balanced just so for millennia, slipped and came rolling down the cliff and over the trail, where it landed with a crunch in the face of a microwave.

The boy startled and fell onto his backside, his breath whistling, thin. He sat in the dirt and drummed his cheeks.

—Hey, bud, you're all right. Just a rock. Wait, tell you what you do at the junk coulee.

Wendell turned and unzipped his pants. He pulled himself free and out over the edge of the crevasse loosed a great stream that spattered below, among the molder and rust. Rowdy stared a moment, then scrambled to his feet and unzipped and dug in his jeans and pissed all over a cracked tire.

They'd lost their BLM land, three good sections with plenty of grass and an artesian spring, in '95. Then, for lack of rangeland, they had to sell off what was left of the cattle. His old man cursed how far they'd fallen.

—I guess we're sheepmen now, he said. Fucking wool farmers.

Yet for months they ate steaks from the last few steers they'd butchered, and even though Wendell intuited, from his parents' evening arguments and morning silences, that they'd lost the section because of something his father had failed to do, some part of the BLM lease he hadn't fulfilled and might yet get in more trouble for, it still seemed a good season to him. Without the cattle around, his old man was doing more trapping, taking Wendell out into the mountains after school and on the weekends. And his mother was still janitoring four tens at the oven factory in Roundup, which meant there was money for new shoes and powdered Gatorade.

Evenings, Wendell would be out in the mountains with his father until sunset, and then his mother would wake him early the next morning, a soft hand on his forehead. Every day but Friday, when she was off work for the week and he took the south bus, Wendell and his mother rode into Delphia together as the sky from east to west tried on shade after shade of blue. They didn't talk much, or their talk was of schedules and essentials—when his basketball practice would be over, a new recipe she wanted to try for dinner, a low grade on a math test—but Wendell had loved those mornings. The quiet, the chill of sunrise, how after his mother dropped him at school she always honked the horn of the Cavalier twice as she drove away.

He was in the fifth grade then and liked his teacher, Mr. Whearty, whom most folks called a hippie or a tree hugger, and maybe he was, but he was a good teacher, the kind you knew you had to do your homework for. Mr. Whearty didn't abide laziness, wouldn't truck with attitude, but he was fun, too—he had a chart up in the classroom with little yellow smiley-face stickers for every book you read, and though Wendell wasn't much in math or science, he was the first to reach the top of the chart. Mr. Whearty made a big deal of it, even taped up another sheet of paper just for Wendell so he could keep track of all the books he read. And in April, as a final class project, Mr. Whearty had them put on an abridged version of *Macbeth* for the whole school. The principal thought Whearty was nuts, trying something like that with fifth-graders—the high-school drama club never put on anything more than silly one-acts—but Mr. Whearty insisted. So they all read the play and talked about it, and Mr. Whearty wrote the words *ambition, choice, violence, manhood,* and *morality* on the board, and they all had to go up and write quotes and scenes from the play beneath each. Wendell ended up playing Banquo—*What, can the devil speak true?*—and got to wander out onto the stage with red corn syrup dripping from his fingers and sit on the king's throne with a bloom of sweet blood above his ghost's heart.

That summer, though, the drought came crashing down, the sky wide and cloudless, the heat cranking up day after day. Not a lick of precipitation all June—just virga, those ropes of dry rain that fell with most every afternoon thunderstorm but burned off before they hit the ground. In July they fought two lightning fires, one of which charred half a section of their best range land.

Even as the grassy ashes of the second fire cooled, Wendell's father woke him in the night. They drove without headlights deep into the south pasture, parked above a dry cutbank, and scrambled down into the dark coulee, where the government fence, for the contortions of the land, was already loose, the wooden posts as wobbly as rotten teeth. With Wendell's baseball bat they beat the posts clean out of the ground, then took a pair of fencing pliers and snipped a couple of wires. It might look like elk had run through and knocked the fence all to hell. If the sheep were pushed even a little, they would find the break tomorrow. That way, his father explained, the woollies would get a week or so of good grass and water on government land, what used to be their land, what ought yet to be their land, before he and Wendell would pretend to notice, herd the sheep back in, and patch up the break. Then they'd find another bad stretch of fence a few days later and do it all again.

His old man was loose and happy on the drive back, cutting half-doughnuts in the dusty road, singing snatches of that Tennessee Ernie Ford song he liked: *You load sixteen tons, what d'you get? Another day older and deeper in debt.* He whipped his empty Rainier out the window and reached under the seat for another. He cracked it open and sucked at the foam. He winked, offered Wendell a drink. Wendell held the can to his lips, the beer fizzy and wild in his mouth. He couldn't square it. He knew he should be happy, but he was embarrassed. It reminded him of *Macbeth*. Of how wrong things could go. You don't just go around doing what you want in the night.

A third of a mile on from the junk coulee, they came to the property shooting range—just a waist-high sandrock to lean over fifty paces from an earthen bank onto which Wendell had pinned clean paper targets using pine branches. He breathed and fired and, depending on where the bullet landed, used a dime to click the scopes on the .243 and the 30.06 up or down, left or right, slowly zeroing them in. Rowdy watched it all and didn't put his fingers in his ears for the blasts, didn't even flinch. Didn't, Wendell noticed, do that thing with his fingers on his cheeks either.

Once the rifles were sighted in, he showed the boy how to firm the butt up against his shoulder, told him how to breathe and let the sights drift into alignment, and he let Rowdy pop off a few shots with the .22. His first couple of attempts were wild—the shots cracked and zinged through the sandrocks—yet he hit the target more times than he missed. One shot landed just up and to the right of the bull's-eye.

Wendell squatted down, his hand on the boy's shoulder.

—Look at that. You're a Newman, all right. A damn natural.

Rowdy looked at the .22 in his hands. Then again at the target.

Wendell walked out to the earthen bank and pulled out the two pine branches pinning the paper down and bore the ragged target back to Rowdy.

—Here you go, he said. Take this as a memento. And a challenge. Maybe next time you'll have a couple there in the red.

The boy handed the .22 to Wendell and took the paper. He held it to his face and peered through a shot hole right up at Wendell. Then made a popping sound, something like the .22. It was the first noise Wendell had heard him make other than his screaming in the field, and it sounded natural, just the sound a boy ought to make.

—That's right, Mr. Sharpshooter. Now, let's head on back. I'm about ready for some chicken noodle.

Still peering through the target, Rowdy spun on his heel and marched back through the sage and dry grass, back toward the trailer.

—*Pewwhg! Pewwhg!* The boy made the noise again.

—That's right, Wendell repeated.

He liked the high, scratchy sound of Rowdy's voice. He put his hand on the boy's shoulder as they walked. The social worker was coming out again on Saturday to see how Rowdy was doing, to see if he was ready to start school. Wendell thought he was, though he thought, too, that he'd better get the trailer cleaned up and pick up a load of groceries to stock the fridge with when he was in Billings tomorrow.

Billings. Lacy's sentencing. He hadn't said a thing about it to Rowdy, hadn't much wanted to think about it himself. Wendell figured the boy wouldn't mind spending the day with Carol again, as much as he loved those gummy worms she always had. But he still didn't want to go, though he knew he ought to.

Rowdy ran ahead of him, out from under his touch, and for a moment Wendell didn't know what to do with his left hand, which felt strange as a wing in the dry, piney air. He stuffed his empty hand into his jeans pocket, hefted the rifles farther up his right shoulder, and followed the boy on home.

VERL

Day Seven of the New Dispensation

If you saw five minutes ago a lean sonofabitch with a patchy beard scrabbling down a rocky ridge right in the smack dab middle of the Bull Mountains you'd have seen me boy. It makes hard going but I am sticking to the rocks in case they have dogs out or trackers who are worth a shit bucket. Seven days. If I have figured right. Which even for the running those first hours and nights I think I have. A full week of freedom. Day Seven of the New Dispensation. Which is what I am calling it. Dispensation means a new man in charge. I learned that at school. Learn what tools they will teach you boy but learn around the tools too. There is more out here in the mountains. Where your old dad is King.

The sky is coal dark now and no good for scrabbling around so a bit ago I sat down and began to write and thought this might be the place for sleep. This is not the place. Way off in the distance I shit you not I can see the highway. You wouldn't think you could be so far out in the Bulls and still see it. But there it is. Yellow drops of light edging the distance. I will go deeper into the mountains this night.

Later

Here in the night boy I hear things.

At my back the rocks. Before me a dark slope of sage and dry grass. And voices out there in the dark. Goddamn.

Maybe it is I hope some trick of the mountains. God I hope it is and they are miles off. The way coyotes sit themselves down to yip such that their calls sound through the canyons.

The moon this night enough to cast a shadow but I see nothing.

I hear them. I hold my rifle close.

Later

If this is to be it boy know I love you. Which I ought to have said to you when I was with you. You tell your mother too. She might yet be mad at me for what I've gone and done but you tell her. I am sorry about all this but there is a right way to live and a wrong way and never shall they meet. Never. Know this in your boy's heart and let it grow bright as this moonlight.

I will lift myself up now and go away from here. Into the night. The mountains.

GILLIAN

Tavin wasn't in school the next three days, but early Friday morning, with a day to spare before he could be failed, there he was in Mrs. Barnes's social studies classroom. Gillian could hardly believe it. Through the open classroom door she watched as the boy stared at the open workbook on his desk, fists mashed into his cheeks, then squinted up at the board. A shadow, a darker spot of sunburn maybe, was splashed across the right side of the boy's jaw and down his neck, disappearing beneath the collar of his T-shirt.

Dust-shot light fell from the high bank of rectangle windows above the blue lockers. Gillian's shoes squeaked on the scrubbed linoleum as she headed for Kent's office. She had a chance here, a real chance. The thrill and lift of it reminded her of her first years of teaching, when she was right out of college, those bright, crystalline moments when things in the classroom were going so well, when what you were doing without a doubt mattered—but Kent swung his glasses off his face and pinched the bridge of his nose, as if even the suggestion of meeting with the boy gave him a headache.

Kent Leslie was a florid, fleshy, well-dressed man whose carriage suggested he had more than a little money in the bank. Outside of Billings, the only city in the entire eastern half of the state, wage jobs were hard to come by, save minimum-wage gigs at interstate gas stations or seasonal

49

work with the highway department or, of course, farmwork, which often paid less than minimum but sometimes came with room and board. A teacher's salary, by contrast, was a comfortable living, and a principal's salary, well, even with his divorce, that was enough to make Kent Leslie—like Glen Hougen and a couple of other landowners with sufficient oil or coal under their acres to bankroll their ranching habits—royalty in the greater Bull Mountain area.

Kent clicked his tongue and scooted back in his chair, fumbling for something in his desk drawer. Gillian waited, studied the pictures on his desk. One of Kent standing in a mountain stream, holding a gaping trout and grinning maniacally. Another of Kent at the state Principal of the Year celebration, where he had been a finalist, though he hadn't won. A couple of family photos as well, which Gillian thought spoke well of the man: Kent, ex-wife, and three daughters at Mount Rushmore, at Disneyland, in front of the massive brick fireplace in their home on the bluff above the Yellowstone, the home that now belonged to Kent's ex-wife. Hung on the wall behind his desk were three enormous oak-framed pictures, each featuring one of his blond, big-haired daughters' senior photos. Poor things—they were all just about as homely as their mother.

Kent finally extracted a flat red tin and popped the lid, his fingers, despite his size, trim and sure. He held a little white mint delicately and, when Gillian declined his offer, tossed the mint into his mouth and slid the drawer shut with a bang.

—All right, he said, here's the deal. I appreciate you looking out for the school. A body is a body is a body, and God knows we need every body we can get, but you said something about the stepdad not being especially hot on education—right?

Kent paused and worked the mint around his mouth, his hands in the air before him.

—We can lose one and be fine, he continued, but what if we push too hard and this stepdad pulls his kid out and makes a stink and gets his redneck neighbors on his side, and a bunch of other families send their kids over to Delphia too—or, worse, start homeschooling? There's more than a few right here in town who think the same way. This whole Tea Party thing is downright scary. We elect a new president, and not two months later they're marching on Washington? Not even giving the man a chance. I mean, they want to get rid of the whole Department of Education! They're nuts! Completely nuts! But that's what we're dealing with here. Let's back off on this one.

Kent leaned back in his chair and threw one thick leg over the other, looking rather pleased with his reasoning. After his divorce last year, he'd asked Gillian out to dinner a couple of times. She had gone but kept her distance, kept things professional, friendly. Yet she wasn't above making him remember why he'd asked in the first place. She ran her hand through her hair, lifting the black wave of it behind her ear.

—I'm not thinking a body is a body is a body, she said. I'm thinking about Tavin. It's in the boy's best interest to stay in school. You'd think so too if you'd seen the stepdad's place. It's a mess. Who knows what he does to make ends meet. Maybe he gets a little CRP. Probably sells some of the deer and elk he poaches. Tavin needs to know that's not all the world has to offer.

Kent sagged forward, the great balloon of him losing air. She smoothed the front of her blouse. She had him now.

—Damn it, Gillian Houlton, why do you have to be right all the time?

—Just the way I'm made, I guess.

—You are well made. That is a fact.

She rolled her eyes at him but let the awkwardness of the remark pass without comment. She'd had a nice time when they went out. She liked Kent. She did.

—Okay, he said now, let's do it like this. Have the kid in, ask him how school's going, but don't push him on anything. Just see what he says. Sound good?

—Sure, I'll follow your lead.

—Well, I don't believe that for a second. But it's nice to hear.

* * *

Gillian had known he was big—had even joked with a fellow teacher that it must be all the growth hormones and antibiotics in the beef these kids eat—but still, standing to the side of Kent's desk, her back pressed into a shelf of old yearbooks, she was unprepared for the ovoid, hulking, vaguely armpit-smelling slab of boy-child filling the doorway. Tavin wore black sneakers, blue jeans, and a T-shirt with a picture of a prairie dog in a rifle's crosshairs on the front; on the back, that same prairie dog, still framed in the same crosshairs, but now blown into red, meaty pieces. The boy stood there, scratched his head, and sniffed.

Kent motioned to the chair by the door, and Tavin sat, slumping way down. Kent sat too and smiled and gee-whizzed awhile with the boy, who grunted in response, still scratching his stubbled, sunburned head. A scrape, Gillian decided. That was what hung on the boy's face and neck, the skin bruised to yellow at the edges, riven here and there with lines of scarring white and pink and, right along the jaw, in the center of the scrape, a dark splash of scab. Tavin shrugged in response to Kent's questions, and the colors along his jaw and neck twisted and rippled.

Tavin allowed that he wasn't doing so well in English, but he liked science, he said. They were looking at animals and plants and their systems. Ecosystems, he clarified.

Kent nodded along enthusiastically.

—Well, that's great! We're certainly lucky to live in a place like eastern Montana, aren't we? Ecosystems right out our front doors! The Yellowstone, and the Bulls, and the deer and elk and coyotes and whatnot.

Tavin scowled, scratched hard at his head, the burned skin flaking.

—We've just looked at the desert. And the ocean. I never thought about it, like, right here in the Bulls.

Before Kent could comment, Gillian cut him off.

—Tavin, I'm glad you're enjoying science. That's exciting. I used to teach it. We should definitely keep that interest in mind. You're a bright kid. As and Bs up until this year.

Kent leaned forward, ready to resume control of the conversation, but Gillian kept on. Science might lead him to new, exciting things, she said. Maybe he could study metallurgy and be a welder. Or electronics and be a computer technician. Or work with diesel engines. Ideas and jobs he hadn't even considered.

—The key, she said, is you'll need to keep applying yourself in school. And that means you'll need to be *in* school. Do you know how many days you've missed already this year?

Tavin sank farther into his seat, his gaze going flat and level.

—Nine. That's almost two weeks of classes. Your teachers tell me you're already pretty far behind.

She waited for either Kent or Tavin to say something, but Kent, apparently conceding that he'd lost this one, leaned back and pursed his lips. Tavin picked at the dirt and dead skin beneath his fingernails.

Gillian meant to wrap it up, to say something at once supportive and challenging, let the boy think on it, but as she started speaking, she saw again that hunting jacket, and in her mind's eye the dark stain at the bottom ran and dripped, thin ribbons of blood unwinding, pooling, rising around the three of them and spilling out the door—until she wasn't talking to Tavin anymore. She was talking to Brian, the boy's stepfather, and to all the other entitled, ignorant, violent men out there in the mountains, the ones who thought the whole of eastern Montana was somehow theirs to do with as they pleased, who conveniently forgot that their great-grandfathers were the ones given free land in the first place, that their grandfathers were the ones who had caused the dust bowl, that their grandfathers and fathers had poisoned the rivers and nearly decimated the elk, antelope, and grouse populations, and that the federal government had stepped in every step of the way—from rural electrification to cheap government grazing leases to generous rental agreements—to pay for this ridiculous *way of life* they were always going on about. She was tired of it. Save Billings, the whole of eastern Montana was a sinkhole for taxpayer dollars, a sick swirl of environmental degradation, lack of education, liquor, methamphetamine, and broken families. And people like her, the real working people, schoolteachers and social workers and BLM agents, were the ones who had to try to clean this mess up.

She leaned in close, her words sharp.

—The state limit is ten absences, she said. For the entire year. You miss even one more day, your teachers could fail you. No questions asked.

Tavin flushed, his face twisting, hardening. She'd gone too far. She tried to backpedal.

—I don't think they'd want to do that, but I'm saying—

—I don't give a fuck what you're saying, lady. Or what the state has to say. Or—

Kent leaned forward, pointed his thick finger right at the boy.

—You need to put the brakes on that right there, son. There's no room for that kind of language in here.

Tavin looked from Kent to Gillian, Gillian to Kent. Then he stood, reached out, and, in one motion, as he turned to push his way out the door, swept the framed photos off Kent's desk, sending the glass shattering to the floor.

When did she begin to distrust the shadows, the mouths of stars? When did she begin to fear the suck of mud, a cracked branch, the unsteady breath of the night wind?

There was a night in the Sipsey Wilderness of northwest Alabama, Kevin's first posting after Missoula. Old eroded hills and clear, curving streams burbling placidly along before falling from limestone cliffs, the pools below blue and deep, perfect for shucking off your clothes and diving right in. They'd hiked all day and set up camp near the head of Buck Rough Canyon. She set the chili to bubbling on the backpacking stove, and Kevin built a fire. Later, they sat knee to knee on stumps, the fire shadows at play on their hands and faces, and ate out of the same bowl, passed Kevin's little silver flask of bourbon back and forth. In the tent that night, as they made love, they heard it rise and break, the hoarse, unhinged shriek of a mountain lion, a female in estrus. Such a sudden, shocking sound. They were still. Then began again in the Alabama dark to move against each other.

It wasn't the lion. It was only that she remembered the screams, that the one burning memory always led to the next: They woke early, a thick light sifting through the trees. Gillian went to pee at the far edge of camp and found boot prints, a handful of heel-stomped cigarette butts. She called for Kevin. Above the prints, on the same tree their packs hung from, the scarred bark still bleeding sap, they traced their fingers over a knife-drawn approximation of the Stars and Bars. She couldn't imagine a man more capable or clearheaded than Kevin, and she knew herself to be fierce and insistent and ready to do what was necessary, but her breath ran anyway like water.

They never went to the Sipsey again, though they were in Alabama another eight months before Kevin got a transfer to the national wildlife refuge on Key West. Spring, then summer, and Gillian couldn't find work outside of tending bar and so wandered the island, talking to the wild, bright-feathered chickens and living off ceviche and sangria. Then there was a year in Nevada, where all the school districts were so desperate for teachers she was offered three positions the first day she was in town. In Colorado she worked, like Kevin, at Mesa Verde, teaching busloads of kids about the Basket Makers and the Ancestral Puebloans. Though the darkness was there, was growing, she found she could tamp it down, reason with it, as this was exactly how they'd dreamed their future lives those first years they were together in Missoula, while she taught at the middle school and Kevin finished his forestry degree. This was just how they'd planned it—here, there, and everywhere the wild land, all the many strange and delightful living things. Tulip poplar, key deer, sword-leaved yucca.

But still—that muddiness, that darkness.

* * *

At the Boiler Room, instead of her usual glass of chardonnay, Gillian ordered a vodka tonic and dispatched it in record time. She speared the drowned lemon wedge with a straw and lifted it to her lips, bit down on the sour rind. Kent had been furious, had spun elaborate scenarios of mass walkouts, smug Fox News anchors broadcasting from the empty halls of Colter Public Schools—but she eventually talked him down, and he settled into a wounded mope for the rest of the day, finally allowing that he'd call the boy's mother on Monday to see if there was anything that might be done.

Gillian clicked her fingernails against the bright copper of the bar top, considered the ice melting in her glass. She'd come straight from school and would miss Maddy, but she'd call later. Maddy was going out with her new friend anyway, the college girl from her Starbucks. Gillian knew she'd need to meet this Jackie one of these days, as much time as Maddy was spending with her. Tonight, she had more urgent matters to attend to. She shook the last of the ice into her mouth and crushed it between her teeth. If she waited, Dave Coles would buy her another drink. She couldn't wait. With a lift of her chin she caught the bartender's attention.

She was halfway into her second vodka tonic when Dave came careening between the tables, a half-shut briefcase smashed under one arm, a Colter Cougars booster jacket flopping across the other.

—Gillian! Hey, I made it! How are you? Wow, hey, what are you drinking there? Better have one myself—but only one! I've got to get back for the game tonight.

He ratcheted himself up onto the stool next to her and dropped an elbow onto the bar. Aimed his good eye at her, let the other, as it was wont to do, spin around the room. It was like he was made of Tinkertoys and bent springs. If there was an odder-looking man than Dave Coles, she hadn't seen him. Gillian couldn't help but smile and laugh.

Dave laughed right along with her, pushed his glasses up the bridge of his nose. He asked after Maddy and whether she still liked Central.

Ever since they'd left Delphia, where Maddy had started but not finished kindergarten, Gillian had kept her daughter in private schools. First Grace Montessori, then St. Francis Upper, and now Central Catholic. For the most part, her colleagues and friends understood; in the past decade, only a handful of Colter students had gone on to finish degrees at four-year institutions, while at Central, last year's graduating class alone boasted three National Merit Scholars and over two dozen students headed for top-ranked universities.

Gillian complained that between Maddy's job and homework and college applications, she hardly saw her daughter. And tonight she was out with a friend. Gillian glanced down at her cocktail, almost empty now.

—Say, Dave, get us another drink, would you?

After Dave hailed the bartender, Gillian got down to business. What did he know about Tricia Wilson? About this Brian?

Dave opened his briefcase, accidentally elbowing the man on the stool next to him and spilling half his papers on the floor. He gathered them, then shuffled through his notes and started at the beginning, as he always did, telling Gillian about the Wilsons, who by '17 were late for the homestead rush and so ended up settling deep in the Bulls, out by Bascom Creek, a sour, alkaline seep north and east of Colter. There'd been a lot of kids and not enough land, of course, and while there were a couple of Wilsons yet on the creek, Tricia's granddad, the youngest of five boys in the family, had ended up with the short end of the stick. For a time he managed a grocery in Big Horn, which was only a few tumbledown buildings off to the side of the interstate now, not even an exit, then a hardware store in Colter, though soon enough that went under as well. Tricia's dad, however, one of four boys himself, was right in time for the oil boom and got on with the company that ran the wells north of the Yellowstone near Vananda. He fell off a derrick and compacted his spine, but since it happened just before the oil dried up, perhaps it wasn't such a bad thing, as it meant he was eligible for benefits. By the time Tricia was in high school, her old man had pretty much settled into a life of collecting disability and drinking.

Tricia herself was actually on a half section of land that had come down through her mother's side, the Feeneys, and the Feeneys...

Dave kept on, but Gillian tuned the Feeney odyssey out. The bartender set the fresh glass down, and she swished her ice and took a long drink. Dave could likely keep worrying the history for hours, but it was all the same old dry-land-homesteading tragedy she'd heard before.

—But what about this Brian? she broke in. I saw a Delphia Broncs jacket there at the house, but I keep thinking I'd remember him. I mean, I taught there for eight years. The only Brians I knew would've been too young for Tricia. Or—and here Gillian leaned in and grinned conspiratorially—not quite her type. You know that Brian Martin, the youngest Martin boy? Well, he turned out to be gay. He's in Seattle now. I got a holiday card from him and his partner just last year. They've adopted a little boy.

Gillian straightened herself back up on her stool, enjoying the confused look on Dave's face. He wasn't a bigot by any means, just sheltered, isolated, nervous around anything new. Gillian let him wriggle another moment before rescuing him.

—But Tricia's Brian, did you find anything on him?

Though she expected Dave to launch right in, to prattle on about whichever train it was coming west in '08 or '16 or '23, he didn't. He took a big snort of his drink, coughed, wiped the wet from his broom of a mustache.

—Listen, I don't know how much you want to go into this. You're here in Billings, and it probably won't come to much. There's really no sense in getting worked up about this kind of thing. I'd say steer clear of it.

Something swirled in her, a suck-hole in a muddy river.

—Dave, come on. Just what are we talking about here?

—Ah, geez, I hate to upset you.

Brian Betts, it turned out, was not from Delphia or Colter at all, Dave told her. He was from Oregon. Had run with a group of free-staters there near the California border. People who wanted out of Oregon and

California, wanted their own state. And now Brian, who was calling himself the first general of the Bull Mountain Resistance, was planning some kind of gathering.

—It's all over the internet, Dave said. Or, you know, the places on the internet these types go.

The lights and shadows of the bar eddied, roiled. Dave's voice narrowed and flattened, disappearing into the high whine building in her skull. All those years ago, in her grief and terror, with nowhere in particular to go—her father dead by then, her stepmother a stranger—she had thought that moving to Billings, the biggest city by far in the state of Montana, with its private schools, wine bars, and theaters, its busy streets and great tall glassy buildings and more than a hundred and fifty thousand souls, would shield them from the idiocy and violence that had befallen them in Delphia. She had thought she and Maddy could both take her maiden name again, Houlton, and cut ties with most everyone back in Delphia, and the city would surely deliver them from the scraped distances of the plains, the god-bent Bull Mountains.

Dave pulled his glasses from his face and frowned, his bad eye drifting, and his voice began again to match the flapping of his lips. He was sorry as hell to spring this on her, he was saying, but everything he was finding out about Brian Betts had to do with the wolf hunt next month and with what had happened back in '97, with the killing of her husband.

VERL

Day Ten of the New Dispensation

It has been some time since I wrote. Those voices put the fear back into me. I ran through the night. God I thought any moment to feel a bullet in my thigh. My shoulder. The back of my neck.

Just the end of October but it is colder than you might think at night when you are out like an animal in the night. I camp hidden away in jack pines. Or settled in some cave in the rock. Still. The wind finds me. Here is how it is. I lay my head on a pillow of sand. I shiver. I feel like a little child to shiver but anyways I shiver. I guess I cannot help it.

I have thought of slipping up to some house and stealing. There are not many but a few houses out here in the Bulls. A few ranches and hunting cabins and log houses with big windows which are owned by goddamn Californians or some such.

But those voices have me thinking twice. I know I talked big earlier but you know me boy. I talk. If I steal a hen or clothes off a line someone might notice what is missing and make a report and the feds would be on my trail. To shiver is better than to run. To let my belly growl is better. I will shiver and wolf growl for now.

Later

Also I do not like to think I am some thief. That is another thing that keeps me from it. I am no thief. (Not like the goddamn government taking my right to live the way I please to shoot what I please on my own land. The banks taking folks' land. Goddamn.) If I do have to steal you will have to tell them boy how it was them that made me do it. What is a man to do with only a thin shirt on his back in the cold? They do not think on that when they think on thieves.

I write this to you boy in the middle of the night. It is too cold to sleep. How are you boy? I hope you are warm. Even if your old dad is cold clean to his rib slats I hope you are knowing your old dad is a free man and chose to be a free man. I hear now a coyote call from the ridge over Lemonade Springs. Some others off south yip back. I cannot place where from.

WENDELL

Fʀᴏᴍ ᴛʜᴇ ʜɪɢʜᴡᴀʏ, ᴀʟʟ ᴛʜᴀᴛ ᴀɴɴᴏᴜɴᴄᴇᴅ ᴛʜᴇ ᴘʟᴀᴄᴇ ᴡᴀs ᴀ sᴍᴇᴀʀ ᴏғ neon in the dark, the quick glare of bare bulbs. But Wendell knew where it was. He pulled the LUV up out front of the Antlers, an old roadhouse between Roundup and Delphia, and killed the engine. The truck ticked and settled. A knot of moths cut and spun. Above the muted, tinny music coming from inside the bar, a coyote howled. Another answered the first.

Wendell had ironed his blue jeans last night, left Rowdy with Carol early this morning, and driven along the river valley and through the mountains and then south across the Comanche flats—sage and bunch-grass bejeweled with the season's first frost, the blue leaves and dry stems sharp and bright in the rising light—and down through the heights, around the Rimrocks, and onto the gray one-way streets that always made him so nervous, hands hard and slick on the wheel, before finally pulling into the lot behind the sandstone courthouse in downtown Billings. They hauled Lacy in wearing an orange jumpsuit and handcuffs. Didn't take their time at all sentencing her to three years for possession of methamphetamine and one year for child endangerment and willful ne-glect. Lacy never once looked at him. Never once even looked up that he could tell. It was another person sitting there was all he could think. The Lacy he knew would have raised hell. Would have pleaded not guilty, would have cursed them, demanded to see her son.

Ever since she'd come to live with his mother and him, she was the one out front, the one no one could catch. Her senior year, at the district track meet, there were only three girls running the eight-hundred, so they'd lined them up with the boys. Wendell watched from the sideline. He'd been running first in the district, had even had his eye on State, but then he'd turned his ankle and torn some ligaments, and now he was just hoping he'd be all healed up by next year's basketball season, his senior season. In the noon light the boys and girls stood there together, quiet, focused, nervous—everyone but Lacy, anyway. She was all spit and giggle, winking at the boys and poking fun at the other girls, and 2 minutes and 9.23 seconds after the gun sounded, she broke the ribbon, besting every boy in the race and setting a district record. There was even an article in the Billings paper, a picture of her making her hand into a pistol, shooting someone outside the frame of the photo. That's me, Wendell remembered thinking, though he wasn't sure, couldn't picture who it was Lacy had been shooting at.

A few days later, just before the divisional meet, Lacy jumped into the silver Mustang of her new boyfriend—a thirty-year-old down from Roundup—and didn't come home that night. Didn't show for school the rest of the week or for the divisional meet, and the day she should have been competing at State, Wendell loaded his rifle, stowed it in the rack in his LUV, and drove to Roundup. He felt betrayed, as if what he'd thought mattered hadn't, as if the years spent pushing each other on the court and on the field were only years and not a kind of promise. At a gas station he ran into the boyfriend, who was buying Doritos, Mountain Dew, and Sudafed. Wendell waited until he was crossing the lot and then dragged him behind the building by his long, ratty hair. When the boyfriend tried to run, Wendell slugged him one, two, three times. While he rolled and bled in the weeds, Wendell got his rifle, chambered a round, and stuck the barrel into the hollow of the son of a bitch's neck. He blubbered and told Wendell he didn't know where Lacy was, that he was looking for her too, that she'd stolen his car. The cops found the Mustang weeks later, abandoned on the side of a highway between Billings and Laurel, but Wendell and his mother didn't see Lacy again until the next winter, in the middle of his last, disappointing basketball season, when she came walking down the gravel road to the trailer with her hair hacked short. Came walking down the gravel wrung out and half starved and three months pregnant, and without an explanation for any of it—not her disappearance or the pregnancy or the gummy squiggle of scar beneath her right eye.

Thwap of pool balls, gravel of men's laughter, smoke of a woodstove, sour warmth of beer and bodies—all of it washed over Wendell as he stepped into the Antlers. He paused a moment in the doorway, and it felt good and right, even necessary. He took his bearings and slid onto an open stool and ordered a shot of Beam with a beer back. The whiskey rolled through him and bloomed in his gut. He closed his eyes with satisfaction. After his mom's death, he'd made his own trouble in bars and had to stop frequenting them for a while. But he had to pick up Rowdy later and didn't intend to start all that again. For now he just wanted to enjoy the burn, wash it down with a couple big, cold chugs of watery beer. Lean into the three-drink swirl that might swirl his last glimpse of Lacy away.

—Wendell! Wow! Fancy meeting you here! How are you?

Wendell turned to find Jackie Maxwell smiling at him. Jackie Maxwell wearing a sleeveless, Western-style blouse and tight Wrangler's, underage but trying hard to look the part of an Antlers-going rodeo gal. Jackie Maxwell lightly touching her hand to his shoulder.

—Gosh, you ever think two south-bus kids would end up way out here at the Antlers on a Friday night?

Jackie lifted her drink, Coke and something, and sipped at it through a small green straw.

Wendell couldn't help but think how nice she looked, how damned nice it would be to settle into some easy bar banter and see where the night might take them. Yet even if Jackie, the pleasant daughter of pleasant hippies and goat farmers, was new to all of this, he knew it was about as likely as the sun coming up—that a couple of south-bus kids would end up riding the night down at the Antlers. Why start driving that bad road? Wendell knew all the dead ends it led to. He was just about to claim an early workday tomorrow and take his leave when another girl joined Jackie. She was tall, nearly as tall as he was, hair long and midnight dark, bare shoulders bony and wide. She too wore boots, jeans, and a low-cut blouse, but Jackie could pull it off. Not this one. No, she looked like she was from another country, another planet—like he imagined Cherry from *The Outsiders* must have looked. She moved toward Jackie, and he was reminded of the way the silver leaves of cottonwoods shift in the wind along the river.

Jackie looped her arm through her friend's and introduced her to Wendell as Maddy. Then she looked about the bar conspiratorially and leaned forward to whisper. Maddy was just a baby, she said. Still in high school! That private school in Billings—but *shhh*, don't tell! They worked together at the Starbucks on Grand, and—let's see, what else could she tell him?—they were both about the biggest Avett Brothers fans in probably the whole state of Montana. Anyway, when Jackie heard that Maddy had never, ever, not once, been to a bar, well, she knew just the place to take care of that!

Jackie ducked her head for a sip of her drink and poked herself in the nose with her straw. She snorted, giggled, and buried her face in Maddy's neck for a moment. Then she breathed, fanned herself with her splayed hand.

—And Wendell here, gosh, okay, Maddy, let me tell you something about Wendell. When I first moved to Delphia, Wendell was Mr. Big Basketball Stud, and I was such a little nerd, wore these goofy glasses and stupid braids, and one time on the bus Wendell flicked a wad of bubble gum that hit me right in the back of the head—I was so, so, so embarrassed! I mean, it's the kind of thing my mom would have told me to take to my therapist, but my therapist was back in Boulder, and my parents were too busy with their goats, and I really think that's why I'm exhibiting so many unsafe behaviors right now, you know, like being underage and drinking in a cowboy bar out in the middle of nowhere.

Jackie affected a wounded look, dropping her chin and sighing, sipping at her drink, but Maddy looked genuinely angry on Jackie's behalf, as if she understood something about the story that Jackie was missing. Wendell leaned back against the lip of the bar and pulled his good, going-to-town cowboy hat from his head.

—I was hoping you didn't remember that, he said. I was more than a couple parts asshole back then.

Jackie pretended to pout a moment more, then bounced up on her toes and beamed.

—I know how you can make it up to me! Get me another rum and Coke?

Wendell took her glass and turned to Maddy.

—Fair enough. You want one too?

Maddy looked Wendell full in the face, studied him. She reminded him for a moment of Lacy, a certain tilt of the jaw, the hard brightness in her eyes.

—No, thanks, she said. I'm driving.

The hours slid away. The room filled with the spicy-sweet smell of pine smoke. Someone lined up a run of George Strait songs on the jukebox. Two men Wendell didn't recognize, probably laid off from the Klein Creek Mine for the season, pulled off their shirts and started slugging each other, though they broke off after only a couple of blows, and one of them grabbed his own shirt to stanch the blood from the other's nose. Wendell drank more than he'd meant to. Another couple of whiskeys before he switched over to straight beer, and even then he found himself staring at the sudsy bottom of a bottle with seemingly every other swallow. No one had been dancing, but when the songs Jackie had put into the jukebox started up, she squealed and pulled Wendell to his feet, swung him around the woodstove. She scooted right up close to him.

The other men in the bar looked on with a mixture of derision and jealousy building behind their eyes. Jackie kept hold of his hand as they wandered back to their stools and then lifted his arm over her shoulder. It felt good and easy—his hand on the bare skin of her arm, the small weight of her against his ribs.

It wasn't until Jackie asked about Rowdy, and Wendell told her that Rowdy was eating chicken noodle like it was going out of style and would likely be heading to school next week, that Maddy leaned in. She and Jackie had put their heads together now and again, and he'd caught her staring at him a couple of times, though she'd always turned away quickly and begun singing along to whatever was on the jukebox. But now here she was, listening.

—This is your son? she said.

—No, my cousin's boy. She got arrested. Sentenced today. And turns out I'm the closest relative. It's either me or the group home.

Jackie made a soft, sad sound in the back of her throat and hugged his arm all the more tightly.

—I'm so glad he's with you. Poor thing must have seen some awful stuff already. You should see him, Maddy. He's as skinny as a stick but awful cute.

Maddy frowned, shook her head.

—Maybe it's not what he's seen but what he hasn't. What he's missing out on.

Through the blear of beer and whiskey, wood smoke and country music, Wendell tried to unwind the threads of her comment. Was she saying he'd already somehow let Rowdy down? That no matter what he did it wouldn't be enough? That people like him—his mother, his father, Lacy—simply didn't have it in them? He felt his jaw tighten. He tried to let it go, but the world burned now at the limits of his vision. That same old shame, that fear and rage at being examined, judged, found wanting. Like in the days and months after his old man had taken off, like the night of the divisional championship game, like the last months of his senior year, after Lacy disappeared for the final time, like whenever he had to go to Billings to talk to some guy in a suit at the bank, like every other night he'd been in a bar since he'd found his mother slumped in the front seat of her Cavalier with a garden hose running from the tailpipe to the window.

—And what do you know about it, Miss Private School? What do you know about my meth-head cousin, her boy that won't say a goddamned word? You got lots of experience with that? Maybe you saw it on TV? An after-school special? I guess since you're the fucking expert I ought to start calling you when I got questions.

—Wendell, stop. She didn't mean it like that.

Jackie still held his arm but had put her weight on her own two feet.

Wendell jerked his arm away from her and knocked over a beer bottle that clanked, rolled, and fell to the floor with thud. He flipped open his wallet and threw a wad of bills at the bar, then spun around and bumped another table. The spill and shatter of cans and bottles. The lights bright and hard in his underwater eyes. He nearly fell over a chair but finally reached the door, which someone opened for him, though that only made him all the more furious.

When he was eight he had stolen another boy's replica flintlock pistol. God, but it was a pretty thing.

The boy, a town kid named Daniel McCleary whose hair was slicked and parted not far above his right ear, had stood up front by the chalk-board and passed the flintlock around for show-and-tell, told about his family's vacation to the Black Hills—the reptile garden, the water slides, the souvenir shop where his mom had bought him the pistol and a coon-skin cap. Wendell ran his fingers along the gleaming wood, the cool, smooth black barrels. He cocked back the hammers and aimed at the chalkboard. Pulled the trigger. *Snap, snap*. The dual hammers fell like that, one after the other. The girl in the desk behind him poked his shoulder. Wendell gazed a moment longer, then passed the gun to her.

He hadn't planned to take it. He'd just gone in at recess to use the bathroom—and there it was, in Daniel's cubby. His muscles seemed to work at his bones of their own accord. He slid the pistol into the waist of his jeans, pulled his T-shirt over it. Outside, for the rush and noise of the recess yard, no one even noticed when he tossed the pistol into the evergreen bushes in front of the school, which was where, hours later, after the last bell had rung, as kids ran here and there and loaded themselves onto the buses, he slipped it into his backpack.

That was after a whole day of anguish, though, because when they had all gotten back inside after recess, Daniel—whose father was the Congregational preacher and whose mother was president of the PTA and the Republican Women's Club of Delphia—had blamed Freddie Benson for the theft. Freddie's folks had come to town a couple of years before, moved their four boys and half a dozen caged birds and collection of lamps into one of the rotting Victorians that eighty years ago had been some railroad baron's place. Freddie's mother, who dyed her hair a startling orange two or three times a year, tended bar at the Snake Pit, the one bar left in Delphia proper, and his father, an enormously fat man, spent most of his days sitting in an easy chair on their front porch, where he smoked cigarettes and read Westerns and romances and sometimes fell asleep with his mouth wide open for everybody to see. Freddie often hooked the romances and brought them to school. All the boys would crowd around him at recess, beneath the jungle gym, where they collectively tried to puzzle out the sex scenes. Freddie pilfered his old man's cigarettes, too, and had been caught stealing candy at the drugstore a couple of times. And once his folks had left him in the care of his older brother, always tinkering with his Trans Am in the front yard, and Freddie had put out bowls of raw hamburger to lure in a bunch of neighborhood cats. The local deputy finally came by and put things to rights, yet rumors swirled about what Freddie had done to those cats before the deputy arrived. Tying them up in pillowcases and dunking them in rain barrels. Duct-taping them to one another. Lighting them on fire.

That morning after recess, Daniel cried and howled and pointed at Freddie, and the teacher called Freddie out into the hall and questioned him and eventually sent him down to the principal's office. Freddie didn't protest. Didn't even look scared. Wendell was terrified. He couldn't concentrate for the rest of the day and ended up with his name on the board and two check marks by it. His old man had whipped him with a leather belt once—whipped him so hard he had to sleep on his stomach the next two nights—for pocketing a dollar and change left on the kitchen counter.

That afternoon, with the flintlock heavy in his backpack, Wendell got off the bus, waited for it to disappear down the county road, then hiked into the Bulls. On top of a butte, on a great slab of sandrock, he took out the pistol and laid it in the center of the stone, like an offering. He'd never had a toy as pretty, was sure he never would again. He knew—by his thrift-store jeans, the thin walls of their trailer, the generic potato chips his mother bought—that his family was one kind of poor. He knew, too, that the Bensons were another kind of poor—a sadder, meaner kind. He wasn't sure what the McClearys were, if they were rich or not, but they sure weren't poor. They had a maroon minivan and a green lawn, and Daniel got new gym shoes twice a year. They could pass for the kind of people you saw on television. Wendell knew he and his old man couldn't, likely not even his mother, not even with her shiny hair and recipes from the morning shows. Whenever they drove down to Billings for groceries or to sell a load of culled ewes at the livestock yards, Wendell felt exposed. Scoured and windburned, angled and stiff. He'd been to the mall a couple of times, and he'd seen other kids his age, city kids, and they'd seen him. There were some distances you could not cross, those geographies intricate, shifting, unmappable. That afternoon, atop the butte, Wendell stood there in the wind and touched once more the polished curves of the pistol, then built a cairn over it, placing the rocks just so.

Years later, after Freddie quit the basketball team and grew his hair long and pierced his ears, after everyone started calling him Fudgepack

Freddie, out dragging Main along with everyone else one night, he drunkenly smashed his brother's Trans Am into and through the front of the school building at fifty miles an hour. Freddie lived, but the shock of it loosed something in Wendell. The next day he tried to find the cairn. He and Lacy hiked around all day, and she kept asking him what it was he was after, and he wouldn't tell her, and they never did find it. Lacy was pissed. That evening, even though he had a home ball game, she took the LUV into town without him. He had to wait for his mother and was nearly late. On the drive in, he wondered if he'd made it all up, if he'd somehow misremembered. So many things had begun to shift and swirl that he was having a hard time sorting the world into reality and dream, into things wished for and things witnessed. Had he really stolen that pistol? Had Daniel McCleary, now the starting point guard and class president, really cried like that? Was it true that Toby Korenko's father was about to lose the family ranch? If he drove to Billings, would Freddie be in the hospital with a collapsed lung and alcohol poisoning? Were they really going to win the state championship this year?

He'd touch his mother lightly on the shoulder as they cleaned up after dinner. He'd bump into Lacy as they hiked the Bulls, their elbows and hips knocking, their fingers brushing. He'd wait for the pass from Toby or Daniel, feel the whap of the ball in his hands, hear the ball snap through the net, the roar of the crowd. And for a moment he'd know it was the truth, and the world would stop its swirl. But it always faded, the knowing, the roar, the touch. The twin barrels of the pistol slick and gone beneath his fingers.

Days after that night at the Antlers, Wednesday afternoon, as the wind whirled devils of dust, Wendell leaned against the LUV. He rooted in his back pocket for his Copenhagen. Got ahold instead of the silver medallion he'd found in the middle of the kitchen table the morning after he'd run into Jackie and her friend. In his bleary rush to pick up Rowdy at Glen and Carol's and get the boy back to the trailer before the social worker showed up that Saturday, he must have pocketed it. Now he turned it this way and that in his hand, this silhouette of a howling wolf in a quartered circle. He didn't recognize the medallion and had the strange thought that someone must have come into his trailer when he was gone and left it there for him. A cool film of sweat broke out along his neck, the length of his spine.

No, no one would break in just to leave this trinket, and he hadn't noticed anything missing. The rifles, the only things worth much in the whole place, were all still in his closet—he'd seen them there this morn-ing. Maybe the boy had rustled it up from some corner of the trailer. It might have been his old man's, or even his from when he was a boy, some-thing he'd traded for on the playground. It was a pretty thing. Wendell rolled it between his thumb and forefinger, the wolf turning over sage and greasewood. In the distance, dust rose from the road, the first orange glint of the south bus out of Delphia, ferrying Rowdy home from his third day of school.

The social worker had emphasized that this was a critical time. Rowdy had transitioned well, better than she might have guessed, to living with Wendell, but starting school, while necessary, would put renewed stress on the boy. He'd need Wendell to be steady, to be there for him. Wendell had jammed his hands in his pockets and nodded along. He didn't men-tion that the very night before, blackout drunk, he had forgotten to pick Rowdy up from Glen and Carol's. Or that when he finally got there in the morning, Carol had met him in her bathrobe and told him that Rowdy, once he realized he wasn't going home, had begun to knock things over and hit himself, that the boy hadn't screamed himself out and fallen asleep until well past midnight. Carol looked Wendell up and down and smelled, he was sure, the stale booze rolling off him. She held her robe closed at her throat and turned and went back in, sent Rowdy out. The boy stood there on the step in his stained T-shirt and blue jeans. He blinked up at Wendell and shivered for the chill of the morning. The boy seemed fine, seemed as he always was, and the whole of Wendell's chest seized and all but cracked open for the sadness of it, for his own shame. How many nights had Rowdy waited for Lacy to come home? How many nights had Wendell himself wished his own father would crawl out of the mountains? Not one more night, he swore to himself, standing in the pale light as the boy drummed his fingers across his cheeks. Not one fucking more.

In a fist of dust the bus ground to a stop before him and the doors folded open. Rowdy came hopping down each step and raised his own little cloud of dust as he hit the ground and ran for the LUV. Wendell turned to follow, but the bus driver—bald now and even fatter than Wendell remembered from when he'd been a south-bus kid—called to him, heaved himself partway out of his seat, and held out a folded sheet of paper. The principal wanted to make sure Wendell got this, he said. Wendell stepped up into the bus, that same old smell of Naugahyde and sweat, took the note, thanked the driver.

The bus groaned away, and the wind came hard across the road, lifting bits of gravel. Rowdy was already bouncing up and down in the pickup bed. Wendell opened the note.

At dinner Rowdy drummed his cheeks, jerked himself around in his chair, knocked his milk over. Then he closed his eyes, screwed up his face, and commenced screaming. Screaming and rocking back and forth and kicking.

—Hey, it's just milk, bud. Just an accident.

Rowdy pulled his fingers from his cheeks and began slapping the tabletop. Knocked his plate over and spattered ketchup on the wall, spilled tater tots across the floor.

—Ah, Jesus. Christ Jesus.

Wendell scooped the boy up and fell into the easy chair with him. Rowdy screamed some more and bucked against him. Wendell held him hard. Rowdy battered at him with his elbows, slammed his small, sharp heels into Wendell's shins. Wendell sat there and rocked and held the boy.

He was supposed to go to Delphia tomorrow to meet with the principal. That was what the note had said. Some boys had been teasing Rowdy at the early recess, and at the noon recess Rowdy had snuck up behind one of them and pushed him headlong off the jungle gym. The boy broke an arm, and before the teacher got there, while the boy was crying on the ground, Rowdy straddled him, cocked his finger, and—*Pewwhg! Pewwhg!*—pretended to shoot the boy in the face. In the office, he'd done it again. Looked right at the principal and fired. You couldn't do a thing like that these days. Not even way out here.

Rowdy's breath slowed and his hands stilled as his thousand small, furious muscles began to relax. Wendell rocked the boy. He wished he didn't know how a thing like this happened, but he knew exactly how. A teacher needed a cigarette or was getting a divorce or just didn't want to deal with it and turned away, let a bunch of kids tease a boy like Rowdy because it was easier in the moment. But the easy thing was damn near always the wrong thing. His old man used to say that. He recalled his father looking him right in the eye, and, in a way, Wendell was proud that Rowdy hadn't taken the easy way out.

But how was he supposed to go into town to meet with the principal when they'd suspended Rowdy for the rest of the week? He couldn't ask Carol to look after the boy. Not after what had happened last weekend. And he couldn't leave Rowdy alone. That's what Lacy had done.

Wendell rocked and rocked, and Rowdy fell into a deep, thrashing sleep, his small body jerking through dreams. Wendell found himself reciting in his head the two lines from *Macbeth* that he remembered best. *How goes the night, boy?* Banquo inquires of his son Fleance, who is at the watch. And Fleance responds, *The moon is down; I have not heard the clock.*

How goes the night, boy? The moon is down; I have not heard the clock.
How goes the night, boy? The moon is down; I have not heard the clock.
How goes the night, boy? The moon is down; I have not heard the clock.
The way those two lines clicked and clacked, the way the father asks

not after the son but after the night, and the son offers exactly that, the night—it all crushed down on his heart so wonderfully. Nearly a decade and a half had passed since Mr. Whearty had staged the play with them, and in that time Wendell had often chanted those lines to himself as he fixed the fence or drove the combine or rode for strays. It was Freddie Benson who'd played Fleance, and in both shows he'd mumbled and tripped over those words—*The moon is down; I have not heard the clock*—and Wendell had been angry. Still was, in a way. After the show, on the dark drive home, he had complained to his mother about Freddie. He had tried to explain how much those lines mattered to him, and though she listened, she just smoothed her hand over his head, told him not to worry, that he'd been such a good, scary ghost.

He hadn't seen Glen or Carol since picking Rowdy up last Saturday morning. He'd set it up with Glen the week before that he'd be doing fence work close to home, which meant he could meet Rowdy at the bus after school the first few days. Tomorrow, though, he was supposed to help Glen ready the corrals for the roundup and the sale. Wendell thought about calling him to say he was sick and heading out into the mountains tomorrow to set a trapline with Rowdy. He thought about calling the school at Colter and enrolling Rowdy over there, which would probably be easier, true, but it was all he knew to do. He thought about sad, thrashing boys and sad, hard words and the sudden guns we make of our fists.

The chair groaned beneath them. Motes of dust sifted through the lamplight. The mountain dark pooled at the windows.

VERL

Day Eleven New Dispensation

Have walked and climbed maybe six miles in the early dark but stopped here now in the light by these sunwarm sandrocks and leaned my back up against them because it is nice to do and also I have thought of something. It is getting to be a decent stretch of time I have been out here. They are after me yet but by winter the feds will think I am dead and rotting somewhere and stop looking. Then I will be free. (Of course I have been free and that is why I am hunted.) Anyways after they have gone home I can live like this is my true home. Then I can shoot a mulie deer through the heart and not worry about the noise. I can smoke deer chops over a pine fire. I can dry hides and wrap them around me like an old Indian. Oh I will live big then. Do not worry about your old dad then.

Must make it through these cold weeks though. These cold weeks they are looking for me.

Or you can leave something for me. Yes fuck yes I see it now boy you could leave me long johns and lined pants and gloves and sweaters and a good stocking cap. God but I might give a knuckle of a finger for a good wool stocking cap. Here is what you do. Leave a wool hat and a flannel jacket in the cab of that old three-wheel Ford in the junk coulee in the south section and give me a signal like a bit of baling twine tied around the side mirror that all is clear and no surprises and I will go get that hat and jacket and the feds will wonder how I am doing it in the snow and

77

cold and not know I am doing it because of you boy. Yes I will not wait. I'll live big right now.

But goddamn.

How will I get this to you? How would I send this page to you? You must read this if you are to know. This page I am writing on. It is a school notebook of yours I grabbed thinking to use for starting fires but I was not thinking straight. I can have no fires. I should have been as prepared in my head as I was in my hands. Let that be a lesson to you boy.

Anyways how to take a sheet of this paper with my instructions for you all the way to you? A boy should be able to hear always his father. Know always his father's mind. But I am all the way out here and you and your mother are in the trailer. The feds between us.

Goddamn them.

A man cannot even lay for the night next to his woman. A man cannot even give his voice to his son. I think of them now closer to your bodies than me and see red. I pick up my rifle and figure to sneak up on them and end it. But that is what they want goddamn them I cannot think on that.

How will I get this to you? How will you know me?

Later

I mean to tell you boy I was yet thinking on how to get this to you for it is yours and I am yours and I found where you had written your name on the back cover of this notebook. Your name. The name I gave you the name your granddaddy carried. Wendell. I tell you it fired me. I felt it in my tired bones and I was not tired then and got up and walked a mile along the dark ridgetop not fearing to be found or to slip or anything. Just your name boy. I stop here in the night and write this to you by starlight.

GILLIAN

When Maddy was in the eighth grade, at St. Francis Upper, she won the blue ribbon at the intercity science fair. Through the late winter and into the spring she'd ridden her bike every afternoon to Two Moon Park, on the east edge of Billings—a wide peninsula jutting into the Yellowstone. The park was a teardrop of gravel bars and grassy wetlands, of willow, cottonwood, and wild rose, and Maddy would hike to its far point and, with the bluffs to her back, the river widening into a rapid before her, sit on a fallen cottonwood and catalog the birds. The project required that she compare her findings each evening with a list compiled near Two Moon in the early 1950s by the elderly daughter of a long-dead railroad magnate. Gillian had insisted on going with her the first couple of trips and after that rode along whenever she could, usually on the weekends. Upriver, oil refineries roared and belched, and the sweet, chemical stink of processing sugar beets drifted with the wind. Yet Two Moon chirped and burbled—the afternoon light hazed with cottonwood fluff, gnats, the quick, iridescent wings of birds—and as the days lengthened, the park went riotously green.

When she accompanied Maddy, Gillian would lie back in the grass and nap. Maddy sat forward, binoculars about her neck, pencil in hand, and attended to her list. She had noted, by the time of the science fair, more than a hundred species. Compared with the earlier Two Moon catalog, more birds of prey plied the air above the river, though fewer herons stalked the waters, fewer larks called, and only a very few grouse beat the ground with their wings. Maddy worked up possible reasons for each of these observations and put together several conservation recommendations. At the science fair, standing off to the side of Maddy's poster display, waiting and listening, Gillian marveled as her daughter spoke with the judges, as she pointed to her graphs and even disagreed, respectfully, with something one of the judges said.

Afterward, in celebration, they rode the glass elevator to the top of the Crowne Plaza, where they had drinks in the dining room—cava for Gillian, club soda with lime and a shot of lemonade for Maddy. They clinked glasses and grinned and talked about birds, politics, the general raise for the staff that Gillian had recently pressured her school board into. Later, they made dinner together—salmon with lemon and the first of the season's fresh herbs, potatoes whipped with butter, roasted garlic, and Parmesan, and a green salad. They ate out on the back deck, reliving Maddy's science-fair win and listening to Lightfoot. After the dishes, Maddy asked to stay up late to see what stars they could see, for the city lights, and though it was a school night, Gillian said yes. As the dark came down she brought out a blanket and wrapped it around the both of them. And when she held her tall daughter in her arms, she thought they'd come through it all, finally, that like the hawks and eagles at Two Moon—despite the ashy air, the waters now and again rainbowed with discharge—they'd ridden out the hard winds and could drift the big, wide sky together, that they could live safely and well once again.

With Dave Coles calling after her, Gillian stumbled from the Boiler Room in a blur of vodka tonic. She missed a stop sign on the drive home and got honked at twice. She didn't bother to check if Maddy was back, just shut herself in her bedroom with a bottle of wine and binge-watched episodes of *The Wire,* the sorrows and injustices of inner-city Baltimore carrying her away from Montana, away from those dark times a dozen years ago in the Bull Mountains of Montana—until she woke. Woke in her clothes bleary and chilled, an empty bottle on the bed stand, the brand name of the DVD player sliding silently across the dark television screen.

She shivered and swallowed. A headache cracked across her temples. Maddy was already up and moving around in the front room, humming, breaking into a few lines of song now and then. Right, Saturday. Gillian forced herself out of bed, splashed water on her face. Pulled on her running gear. They had a standing date, every Saturday morning, as long as the weather allowed, to run for an hour. They'd started with routes through their neighborhood, sometimes stopping by Maddy's Starbucks for a bagel on the way home or dipping downtown for a slice of quiche at the new place Gillian liked, but lately Maddy had convinced her mother to start running the many park trails below the Rimrocks, the eighteen-mile-long wall of sandstone rising a thousand feet above the Yellowstone Valley and slicing through the city of Billings. Even if the houses and streets quickly disappeared, Gillian reasoned, the trails were well used, were, for the most part, in cell-phone range. Still, whenever they came on meth-heads zonked out in the sagebrush or derelict, muttering men shuffling through the scree, she gripped Maddy's hand and held on tight. Maddy seemed to understand and most days let her mother's worry go without comment.

The morning was bright and cold, the sky white-blue at its heights and stone blue along the horizon. They ran, talking at first as their breath allowed—the chances of Obama's new health-care bill passing the House; Maddy's latest thoughts on college, Gonzaga, Lewis and Clark, or Linfield—but both mother and daughter, it seemed, had other things on their minds, and as they bounded off the sidewalk and onto the dusty trails below the Rims, their talk fell away until the only sounds were their breath and the crunch of rock and dirt.

Gillian's head throbbed. Her arms felt made of granite. She began to flag. Maddy didn't slow or wait, as she usually did, but kept on, her stride lengthening the distance between them, her shadow long and slim and shifting as she disappeared over a yucca-pocked hill. Gillian slowed on her way up and stopped at the top, laced her fingers behind her head and blew. The trail bent left, then right, winding through sage, sandrock, and bunchgrass before climbing another dusty hill. Maddy was nowhere to be seen. Likely she was over the next rise and halfway to Starbucks by now. Gillian couldn't summon the energy to be angry with her, or even annoyed. Anyway, she'd rather be alone this morning, rather be in her own itching skin, let her bad thoughts pound around her pounding skull. Hands on her hips, she started down the trail, the chill wind drying the sweat along her neck and back.

She knew Dave was probably right: this business with the wolf hunt most likely wouldn't come to much. There wasn't a thing those redneck morons could do to her or her daughter. And if she didn't pay attention, if she just turned away and refused to look, it would probably be as if it never even happened. She knew this. Still, she couldn't help but imagine the river below their old house, that same river turning north toward the rodeo grounds on the outskirts of Delphia. She could see all their old neighbors gathered there for some idiot's idea of a patriotic rally, full-ton pickups parked at every angle, Western-style shirts made to look like flags, folks spouting lots of drivel about standing on your own two feet, about hard work and private property. Pam and Larry, Kevin's sister and her husband, would be there, she was sure of that. God, but she didn't want to think of Elner there. She wouldn't go, would she? And would they say Verl Newman's name? Would the vowels and liquids of his name crackle and spill from the tinny speakers—and no one even blink? No one dare to be so good as to say, *That's not right, not right at all?*

—Hey, lady, got a buck?

Gillian startled, tripped, and her right knee came down hard on the packed dirt and gravel of the trail. She caught hold of a wiry knot of bunchgrass to keep from slipping farther down the hill and pulled herself back up to her feet. A thin line of blood traced the bone of her shin. The man, or boy—she couldn't quite tell for the saggy layers of dark clothing and the stained American flag bandanna tied tightly around his skull—picked his way among the rocks and cactus in the lee and shadow of the Rimrocks. He stepped into the light and rubbed his eyes. He was skinny, unshaven, his face all blades and angles. A meth-head, she thought. Maybe twenty, maybe thirty-seven. It was hard to tell. Stooped, skeletal, the bones of his wrists pronounced. He took another half step toward her.

—Hey, sorry. It's just I haven't eaten in a couple of days.

She reached behind her, reached for the belt she wore around her waist, up under her running shirt. The man cracked a weary, thankful smile and continued toward her, lifting his cupped hand.

From maybe three feet away Gillian hit him full in the face with a blast of pepper spray. It was cartoon-like, the way his whole body, leaning toward her a moment ago, pivoted the other way around the fulcrum of his feet as the first shot knocked him onto his back. She hit him once more with the spray, a quick, whistling blast. He screamed and curled into a fetal position, pawed and kicked, rubbed his wet eyes, twisted his face right into the rocks and scrub and dust.

Gillian stood above him. At one point he struggled onto his hands and knees, his black jeans twisting down to reveal the pasty white skin of his backside, and began to cough in short, chirrupy breaths and to throw his head from side to side. Gillian had the urge to kick him in the stomach, even felt her muscles ready themselves, but his hands slid out from under him, and he fell again to the ground.

She slipped the canister back into the holster on her belt and turned and ran down the trail—away from the Rimrocks, back into the city.

Alabama, Key West, Nevada, Colorado, and their longest stint was their last: Alpine, Texas. Kevin was stationed at Big Bend, down along the border, and she was teaching at the high school, just three blocks from the small adobe house they rented on the edge of town, the Davis Mountains rising to the north and the Chisos like dark, dusty rumors in the frame of the south-facing kitchen window as shoulder to shoulder they scrubbed the evening's dishes. One sunset they drove south, turned off on a dirt road, then another, and finally pulled to a stop near a barbed-wire gate that led to a remote spread of BLM land administered by the park service, a wildlife migration corridor recently declared off-limits to grazing. They left Kevin's green work truck and hiked the dry washes and creosote hills. Kevin kept reaching for her hand. She was four months pregnant. They spread a blanket on the brittle desert ground and lay back as the stars sharpened in the dark. Though Kevin swore the stars of eastern Montana were just as bright, just as numerous, Gillian had never seen anything quite like it, the way the land beneath seemed to lift them toward the perfect black bowl of night. Such a spill of sugar, salt.

Hours later, after picking their way back by flashlight, laughing, planning, throwing out baby names both beautiful and ridiculous—Evelyne, River, Gracie Ann, Cuthbert—they found all four of the truck's tires knifed, the headlights shattered. And scratched into the driver-side door: *Fuck you fed. Ill kill you dead fed.*

She couldn't keep herself from spinning—around and around. Someone was there, she was sure. Someone was watching them, advancing each time she turned her back.

These threats weren't new—but this was the most brazen. In one way or another they'd been dealing with the slow erosion of respect for NPS, Forest Service, and BLM employees for the past ten years, from Reagan's embrace of the Sagebrush Rebellion to the relative respectability of the now ascendant and even more radical wise-use movement. And there'd been trouble before, of course—a red-faced governor calling for privatization of public lands, ominous letters to the editor after the arrest of a rancher who refused to pay his grazing fees, and just recently the trash cans out back of the ranger station lit on fire. But now they were stranded on a gravel road in Texas, stranded in the purest dark she'd ever known, and there was a violent idiot out there with a knife, and maybe worse.

Kevin tried to take her by her shoulders. She cursed and pulled away.

He tried once more to hold her, and she spun and fell. On her knees in the gravel, cradling her belly, she wept. She loved this life. But she couldn't live this life anymore.

Kevin stood above her, spread wide his useless hands, said sorry. Sorry, sorry, sorry.

On the ride home that night, they talked—they had to leave Texas; they had to find a place they could imagine raising a child. The next day, Kevin started looking for work. The best of what was available was Montana, where she had kept up her teaching credentials, where they had felt, if not at home, then at least reasonably safe. There wasn't anything near Missoula, which would have been their first choice, but there was an opening for a game warden out of Roundup, just west of Delphia, where Kevin had grown up. Kevin's mother was still on the homeplace and, though he wasn't especially close to them, so were his two older sisters, their husbands, and a handful of nieces and nephews. The county school wasn't much, but Gillian could supplement their child's education. While game warden was still a government position, it was a state post rather than federal. And Kevin knew most everyone living out in those mountains. There wouldn't be any surprises. Even though he'd gone off to college and turned his back on ranching—let alone farming that dry country—it was still where he was born and raised. It was home.

They sold most everything, packed what was left into their two-door Tercel, and drove forever up through the scrublands of Texas, across the Oklahoma panhandle, along the achingly flat eastern plains of Colorado, over the sloping land and past the sudden river canyons of Wyoming— so much Wyoming—and then they were sliding through the shadows of refinery stacks and bulbous, spiral-staired oil tanks along the ragged edge of Billings. It was spring, the high flats green and rolling, blue flax flowers brightening the ditches. As they drove north into the Bull Mountains, with their ridges and box canyons, their yucca and knots of prickly pear, Gillian was reminded, sharply, too sharply, of the big desert country they had left behind. Something hollowed around her heart.

Then Kevin began to tell the stories.

Hands on the wheel, turning them this way and that through the mountain curves, he narrated the history of most every little homesite, told her who lived here and there and for how long and what funny thing some grandmother or uncle had done—for the view down the valley, he put a glass door in the outhouse!—and as she listened, the hollow filled with his sure stories.

They pulled into the Kincheloe place, a great sprawl of alfalfa fields and pastures south and east of Delphia, near the north bend of the Musselshell River, in among the foothills of the Bulls. Kevin cautioned her once again not to talk politics or religion, though he insisted, too, that they'd be welcomed, that his people were good and reasonable and kind.

And he was right. His sisters, Billie and Pam, were cautious but warm, fussing over them and pushing glasses of iced tea on them immediately. Their husbands, Roy and Larry, were round-faced and shy and handy, both still somewhat sheepish about the fact that Kevin had let his sisters, their wives, have the Kincheloe land after his father's death some years ago. Without a word, Larry hauled out his air compressor and filled their back left tire, which he'd noticed was a little low. Kevin's mother, Elner, whom Gillian had met only briefly at their courthouse wedding ten years earlier, was a fiery little Irish woman who preferred horseback work to laundry. Gillian liked them all, liked Elner immensely.

When she and Kevin found an old farmhouse to rent off the Delphia-Colter Road in a stand of cottonwoods near the river on land belonging to Glen Hougen, the whole Kincheloe clan pitched in to gut and scrub and paint and generally make the place livable again. They cut the weeds down out front, blackjacked the holes in the roof, painted the kitchen a canary yellow. After Billie and Pam's picnic lunch—cold sliced roast beef, brown bread, garden radishes and cucumbers, and squares of dark sheet cake with burned-sugar frosting for dessert—Elner hauled an old rocking chair from the back room and carried it to the front porch, where she dusted it off and pushed on all the joints, just to make sure. She found

Gillian in the kitchen, scrubbing out the cupboards, and took her by the hand, led her to the chair.

—You just sit on down, Mama. Put your feet up on the rail.

Some hundred yards below the porch, along a foot trail that bordered a tangle of chokecherry trees, an opening in the cottonwoods and willows framed a bend of the river, a shallow, gravel-bottomed rapids. Across the water, the forest thickened and the Bulls rose up humped and sloped and broken, the nearest peak washed with the blue-green of the trees everyone called cedars but that Gillian was sure were actually a kind of juniper. She sat gladly down, and the chair creaked beneath her weight. She closed her eyes, tipped her head back. How tired she was—she hadn't even realized.

Elner put a hand on her shoulder.

—That's right. Take it easy for a spell. We'll get this here place whipped into shape. It'll be a home before you know it.

The fridge light cut through the night shadows of the front room. Gillian studied the many slick packages, the bright bottles and bins. Finding nothing, she shut the fridge and pulled open the freezer, that little pop as it came unstuck. There—a plastic cylinder of frozen orange juice. If Maddy came out, she'd say she was getting ready for Sunday breakfast. How about French toast? But save for the dim strip of light from under Maddy's door and the low music, the hallway remained dark and quiet. Gillian plopped the concentrate into a pitcher and added water and mixed it all, then poured a tall glass half full and dropped in two ice cubes. From the cabinet on the other side of the fridge she lifted out a plastic handle of vodka—she'd drunk her last bottle of chardonnay earlier in the evening—unscrewed the lid and tipped it into her glass. Let it glug one, two, three times.

She held the glass up and out, so as not to spill, and padded down the hall to her office, where she closed the door behind her, making sure it latched, and settled into her high-backed chair. Her first sip was mostly vodka, which watered her eyes and set her to coughing. She took another drink to clear her throat and clicked the computer screen to life again. Against a black background with a splash of camouflage flashed a banner taking up a quarter of the screen: ***JOIN THE BULL MOUNTAIN RESISTANCE***

With the shades drawn against the streetlights, against the great black shadows of the Rimrocks, Gillian leaned into her computer, careful not to bump her scraped knee, and tried again to make sense of what she saw before her. It was like another language. The tyranny of the EPA, the IRS, and the BLM. The lie of ecology and the primacy of wise-use. Allodial title and sovereign citizens. Christian identity, Adamites, and kind after kind. The original ten. The liens to be served at gunpoint on the federal government and Barack HUSSEIN Obama for unconstitutional takings. The seal of the Bull Mountain Resistance was a howling wolf touched by crosshairs set inside a silver circle. There were links to other groups as well: Posse Comitatus, the Three Percenters, the Pacific Patriots Network, the Militia of Montana, the Idaho Militia, the Jefferson Free Staters. And a dozen links to gun shows and gun stores, with strings of bullets bordering both sides of the website. Gillian read about the coming land war, the time of trial, the suffering and the blood that must be let, about the sure victory of free and pure and godly people, of the new dispensation.

The shifting lights played across her face. She took a swallow of vodka and juice, scrolled, and landed on a picture of Brian Betts, the first general, wearing black boots, baggy camo pants, and a tight khaki T-shirt, some kind of assault rifle cradled in his arms. His hair was buzzed, his mustache dark and sharp, which was expected, yet he was short, his arms stubby, his belly soft. Tavin might even be his height. How had Tricia ever ended up with such a chinless little sausage of a man? How could she have let him poison her boy?

When Gillian clicked on the link below the photo, she found the call for the gathering that Dave had mentioned. All *Free and Sovereign*

Citizens were invited to join the Bull Mountain Resistance on October 25, the first day of the first legal wolf hunt in Montana in over thirty years. Yet in an act the flyer termed *Patriotic Resistance to* TYRANNY, no one was to buy a wolf tag, as that would only legitimize the government's supposed right to keep free people from defending their property from vicious animals. With no authorization other than their own will and their own rifles, they planned to gather at Betts's place and move into the Bull Mountains, slaughtering every wolf, coyote, and other nuisance animal they might find.

Gillian scrolled down to the bottom of the web flyer, and there, under a slash of cursive purple script that read MARTYR, was his picture. Verl Newman. Kevin's killer. She tried to stand, tried to get away, but banged her hurt knee on the bottom of the desk and fell back into her chair, knocking over what was left of her drink, sending the ice skittering across the desktop, shushing wetly to the carpet. Before she could even read his name, she clicked the mouse. The little wheel spun, and she zoomed in— zoomed until his face began to pixelate, explode.

Which reminded her of the cloud of pepper spray, the boy's face obliterated like that. Of how good it had felt. How good it would feel to do that to Brian Betts.

VERL

Day Twelve

They are not even close. I shook them days ago and circled back. You
want to know the godhonest truth I am not so far from you boy. It makes
me smile to think on that. I have taken to sleeping in the afternoons when
the sun is round and warm. Writing these words in the evening. Traveling through the night and early morning when it is cold and my heart
thumps and thumps to keep me warm. This afternoon I snoozed like a
big old bear only rolling over to get the sun on the other side of me. Are
there bears here in the Bulls anymore? I do not think so. Those like my
old granddaddy killed the wolves and tried for the bears though the bears
got away up into the Rockies. I believe I am the only old bear up in these
mountains now.

The eastern sky this evening blue and dark as your mother's eyes.
On one side of me there is that nightward blue. On the other the far
mountains red and gold in the setting sun. Did you know there is a
whole box of colors between red and gold? I never knew. Or maybe
I knew but forgot. Anyways I see now some dozen shades between
the two.

Later

I am thinking of things. Here in the night. It was seeing the sun set like that over the Rockies which I know are real mountains and not just twisted hills like these Bulls. But these here are where I am. These I call mine.

How does a body come into country? Sure these Bulls are mine because there is no other way things are but only this way. What I am after is would I have chosen this country? I am thinking if I was a homesteader on a train or even earlier some fur trapper like in the Louis L'Amours. If I come strolling through would I say yes this is for me. That is what I am wondering. Things are a sight prettier once you get farther west nearer the Rockies. And it is goddamn dry hereabouts. Windy and hot in the summer. Windy and cold in the winter. West of here the mountains snag the rain and they put up three cuttings of hay without a drop of irrigation. Might I have spat and gone on? Might I have passed through? What I am saying is maybe I have just gone and gotten used to this country?

No. I tried it for a spell but that kind of thinking does not sit right with me. I do not like to think like that. Do not like to think this country I call mine is just a crapshoot chance. There is a country for each of us we might in our bones call home. The shape of the land what fits us to ourselves. These plains and hills. That snarl of chokecherries down the draw from the house where we pick until our fingers go blue. Meadowlarks singing because they are lonesome and scared and the sun is about for the night to burn down. Does some bear up in the Rockies remember he walked these hills and plains and pine for them? I say yes. They are all a part of it. Like me. Like you boy. Like your granddaddy my daddy and our granddaddies down the line. The country is us. We know it from time before. Like a hand we would miss and feel ghosting us if it was gone.

Or maybe that is backwards. Maybe we are but an organ of the land. Maybe we are the ghosts and when we go the country mourns us. Is that right? Does the country grieve my old granddaddy? The gone grizzly bears? Does it sorrow the both of them?

WENDELL

They left the trail. The pines tightened about them. Wendell had to get down on his hands and knees and shoulder through tangles of honeysuckle and wild rose, little weepings of blood along the backs of his hands. Rowdy came behind, in the space Wendell made, having to crouch only now and again. On a shelf above the ravine they found a small clearing with a gnarled jack pine near the edge to serve as an anchor, and Wendell stood back up, slapped the dust from the knees of his jeans. He set Rowdy to digging near the pine, then stepped down on the springs, the trap's jaws lolling open, and placed the pin beneath the shaft of the pan.

—That's it, good job. You've got it deep enough now.

Wendell set the trap in the shallow hole Rowdy had dug and showed the boy how to sprinkle enough dirt back around it to bury it, but only lightly, and they took turns sifting dust and grass over the trap, and Wendell drove a spike through the trap's chain, deep into the roots of the tree, and buried the chain as well.

He pulled his ball cap off and wiped at his forehead. Rowdy wore no hat but he wiped at his head just the same. They stood there and admired their work. It was clear there'd been some disturbance, but you'd have to know where the trap was not to step in it. Wendell had gone ahead and skipped out on work, held the boy out of school for the day—he'd called the district in Colter and gotten Rowdy enrolled over there—and he was awful glad about it all now.

—We need a bone, he told the boy.

Rowdy blinked up at him and took off along the lip of the coulee, shoulders bent toward the ground. There were always bones about—in ditches along the roads, in the dead pile near the house, here in the mountains. As a boy Wendell had gathered bones and brought them back to the old farmhouse, to the bone shrine his grandfather had started in the basement. His mother, fearing the unoccupied house might collapse, hadn't wanted him in there, but she didn't want all those bones in the trailer either. As a compromise, she let him build his ossuary on the screened porch of the old place. It had been quite a collection. The fragile straws of bird bones. The thin, sickle moons of prairie-dog skulls. The quick, hard curves of coyote. The mandibles of a mountain lion, teeth like ragged knives. And cow and sheep bones too. And yellowed bones, impossibly thick, from the last bear his great-grandfather had killed out in the Bulls. His favorite was the great long hollow skull of a horse, which he'd found, crumbling and sun-bleached, miles out in the mountains. He would often dream the thing back into flesh and sinew, hide and hair: a Crow warhorse or a seventeen-hander in the Seventh Cavalry.

Rowdy came pounding back through the trees with a small white femur clenched in his fist.

—That's the ticket. Here, let's have that.

Wendell took the bone, likely deer or antelope, and broke it. One piece he handed back to the boy and the other he buried, with just the torn end showing, between the trap and the tree. Then he took a small glass vial from his pocket.

—This here's a stew of piss and what all else my old man milked from the insides of a coyote. It'll about knock you down. Go ahead, take a sniff.

The boy's eyes went wide. He reached out and clutched the amber vial, waved it under his nose. Blinked, pulled a face.

—Yeah, it's nasty stuff, but coyotes love it.

Wendell dribbled a few drops of the tincture into the broken end of the bone, then capped the bottle and stowed it.

—All right. Four more to go. What d'you say? Being a mountain man work for you?

Rowdy grinned, toothy and lopsided, and took off running, angling through the pines.

He hadn't seen his mother much that last year.

Wendell had left the community college over in Glendive after a semester and a half to come take care of her after her first surgery. He'd thought she'd get better. Thought he'd go back and take up his basketball scholarship again. He never did. He worked odd jobs for a few years until Glen hired him on steady, which then meant Wendell left in the early dark and didn't get back to the trailer until the day's last light leaned on the trees. More and more often he found her zonked out on pills in front of the television. She was only forty-three, but she'd been in pain for a long time. He could remember evenings from way back when he was just a kid that his father would work at the knots in his mother's shoulders while the two of them sipped beer and listened to the classic-country hour on KGHL. It would flare up like that, and she'd take a couple of months off work, go on temporary disability. By the time she quit working at the oven factory for good, the winter after Wendell graduated, she could barely sleep for the pain. They said something was the matter with her synovial joints, then she was diagnosed with lumbar spinal stenosis, but Wendell wasn't sure any of the doctors really knew what was wrong. She had a string of surgeries, each more extensive than the last, and they seemed to help at first, though each time, just as Wendell was starting to think about heading back to Glendive, there was some new complication. Eventually, she stuffed her workout videos and exercise equipment in the closet. Shuffled from bed to couch to bed. Every once in a while drove into town for her prescriptions.

When Wendell got back from work and found her passed out on the couch he'd get ahold of her and help her down the hallway to her room. She'd stumble and slur, sometimes thank him, sometimes curse. Often she called him by his father's name. Once, as he lowered her to her frilly bed, she kissed at his mouth, reached for the crotch of his jeans. He pulled away, nearly dropped her, embarrassed to find himself swelling at her touch. She said his father's name again—*Verl*—and then parted her robe to reveal an old sports bra, her loose white stomach. When she reached for the straps of the bra, he turned and rushed down the hallway, grabbed his hat and slammed the trailer door behind him, jumped in the LUV. He reached under the bench seat as he drove and lifted a fifth of Jack by the neck. An inch of amber liquid sloshed around the bottom of the bottle and he tipped it up and up, then slung the empty out the window. Watched it shatter against a fence post. An old girlfriend, Starla Collier—though she was married by then to Toby Korenko, even had a kid at home—was tying one on at the Antlers. They closed the place down that night and ended up fucking in the parking lot up against his truck. Some old bulb-nosed drunks stood around watching, cheering now and again, and Starla bit at his neck and said she'd always loved him.

Wendell felt so shitty afterward—like he was up to his ears in shit, had been sinking in it so long, he saw the world through a scrim of it, felt the muck in his lungs—that the next week he asked for even more hours. He started taking some of his meals with Glen and Carol and had a good run of months away from the bars. Those times he did come home to find his mother on the couch, he just threw a blanket over her, turned off the TV.

A little less than a year ago now, October, with the evening's freeze ghosting the dry grass, he got back from work and saw her Cavalier idling out front of the trailer, the windows fogged, dripping. It was dark enough that the hose confused him, though when he pulled open the driver-side door and a wave of exhaust rolled out, he knew what it was all about.

She was in her robe, had brought a pillow and reclined the seat. He reached over her and shut off the engine.

***

They made their second set of traps along the bank of a blind creek, the third near a game trail in the pines, and the fourth above a steep-sided box canyon. Though Wendell hadn't thought of it, he was soon nervous, as high up as they were, as interested in the cliff edge as Rowdy was, but the boy was careful for the most part, and once they'd set the trap Wendell let him lie on his belly and hang his head over the edge, like a plumb bob. Wendell lay beside him and did the same, and with just their round heads out there in so much air, they grinned at each other. Wendell called a few hellos, which knocked around in the canyon, and as if it weren't anything at all Rowdy called out a hello as well, his high, thin voice echoing faintly.

Wendell's heart beat against the ground. He thought to say something, to make a big deal of that hello, but then thought better of it. He pulled himself back from the edge, onto his knees, and Rowdy did the same. He smiled and took the boy's hand, and they stood there like that, hand in hand. Wendell gestured toward the head of the canyon, where the wind sheared and flattened the grass.

—Used to be a spring down there. Lemonade Springs, they called it. My old man said the water was sweet and sour at the same time.

It was dry now, he told the boy. A good snowpack in the winter might make for a little creek in April and May, but not much more than that. Rowdy studied the canyon, the dry watercourse, and leaned into Wendell's arm, laid his head against him. Wendell could feel his own pulse sounding the boy's skull. Against his hip the boy's more rapid, wingbeat pulse was the lightest feather.

Then, above their own hearts, above the wind, came the gravelly sound of an engine. Or engines. Wendell turned. In the valley behind them, beyond the canyon's mouth, two four-wheelers roared on fast and growling and skidded to a stop at the fence line. With the engines still running, one of the drivers fumbled for something holstered at his waist. As he lifted the black device toward his eyes, Wendell understood. Binoculars.

He grabbed Rowdy's wrist and pulled him to the ground, down behind a small outcropping of rock.

—Stay down. Stay close.

Wendell counted to thirty and inched back up. The other driver had gotten off and walked over to the first by then, and the two of them parleyed. The one yet on his machine was a man, given his mustache, and the other a boy, Wendell thought—a big boy, but a boy—judging by his roundedness, his clean cheeks. The man grabbed something—a pair of fencing pliers—from the tool case wired to the back of the ATV, just in front of a gun rack that held at least three rifles.

It's that Betts, Wendell thought. *And Tricia Wilson's boy.* What was his name? One of those newfangled names he could never seem to keep in mind. Tricia, though, he remembered. She was older than he was, had been a varsity cheerleader when he was just in fifth grade, and whenever Delphia played Colter, he'd spent more time watching her than the game. He'd met Betts, too, maybe six months ago now, at the barn raising they'd had for Cotton and Donna Pinkerton, after Cotton, who'd only just turned forty, had been diagnosed with cancer.

Three property lines came together down below, and none of them was Betts's. To the south, where Betts and the Wilson boy had come riding up, was Glen Hougen's land. To the west was all BLM, much of it leased by Glen. And Wendell and Rowdy were on the far edge of their land, what was left of the Newman spread, which was also leased by Glen.

The Wilson boy strode right up to the four-strand barbed-wire fence between Hougen and BLM land and cut his way through, the wires whanging, looping up, and snaking as he went. Then he walked on down the fence and cut the next section too, and the wires fell stiffly, with the tension already released. Wendell watched as he cut close to a quarter mile of fence, all told. You couldn't mend that; you'd have to refence. It'd be a whole day's job. This wasn't about driving stock through. This was about something else altogether.

Once the boy was done, he handed the pliers back to Betts and got on his four-wheeler and rode on into the BLM land, where he disappeared around a ridge. Betts pulled out his binoculars and glassed the countryside again. Wendell dropped back down behind the rock, held Rowdy by the wrists. He breathed and waited. The clouds, massing in the north, swept over them, high and wide and white, and Rowdy shivered.

Wendell inched back up and peered over. Nothing but a mess of cut fence and tire tracks in the grass, narrowing off to the west. He let go of Rowdy and straightened up.

—Sorry about that, bud. I got a little spooked. I didn't expect company, but, hey, we're all right.

The boy sat where he was, rubbing his wrists. He was so thin that the wind must cut right through him, Wendell realized. They'd left in the relative warmth of the noon sun. The boy wasn't even wearing a coat.

—You a little chilly? We got one more trap yet. You want to set it or hike on back?

The boy stuck his hands in his armpits and shivered again. Rocked where he was in the pine duff and dust.

Wendell said that was probably enough for today. They'd head on back. The boy had school tomorrow anyway—first day at his new school. Wendell helped him up and they were on their way.

Wendell leaned over and plugged in the space heater—the wall unit in the boy's room was out—and the thin coils reddened. He tucked the covers in tight around the boy and sat on the edge of the bed. They'd have to drive about ten miles to catch the north bus out of Colter, he told Rowdy, but even with that trouble he thought he'd have a better time at this new school. He hoped he would. The new school could be really good, it could, but he had to try to get along. If someone teased him, he had to go get the teacher. He couldn't pretend to shoot anybody again.

Rowdy lifted his hands to his cheeks. There was a bruise already beginning to show on the underside of his left wrist. Wendell touched the soft skin there.

—Sorry about that, bud. Those fellas made me nervous.

He knew too many men like Betts. Twitchy, sneering, always eager to prove something. He had worried what a guy like Betts might do, his rifles in easy reach, if he suddenly saw someone poke his head up over the rocks.

Rowdy blinked, and Wendell thought for a moment the boy might say something. But he didn't. Just yawned, swallowed. The boy's face was at last beginning to fill out. Plenty of butter crackers and chicken noodle, Wendell thought. Well, good.

—Here. I got something for you.

Wendell dug the silver wolf medallion from his pocket and held it out to Rowdy. Told him to keep it in his own pocket. If he was ever scared or worried all he had to do was reach down there and get ahold of it to know that he was okay, that his uncle Wendell would look out for him.

Rowdy sat up and took the medallion, studied it, brought it right up to his eye. Then smiled and closed the medallion in his hand and lay back down. He settled his head on the pillow, tucked his fist underneath.

The space heater clicked off, and Wendell picked a book up off the floor. He had finished reading him *Bless the Beasts and Children* and was just getting started with *A Tree Grows in Brooklyn*. He didn't know what he'd read next. Most of the books he'd taken from school didn't seem appropriate for seven-year-olds. Wendell wasn't sure what Rowdy was getting from the books, beyond his voice and presence. But the boy had begun to insist on these readings before bed. Maybe the story itself didn't matter. Maybe it was just the fact of a story—any story—that made the difference.

The space heater clicked on again, and Wendell found his place and started reading:

There was a special Nolan idea about the coffee. It was their one great luxury. Mama made a big potful each morning and reheated it for dinner and supper and it got stronger as the day wore on. It was an awful lot of water and very little coffee but Mama put a lump of chicory in it which made it taste strong and bitter. Each one was allowed three cups a day *with milk*. Other times you could help yourself to a cup of black coffee anytime you felt like it. Sometimes when you had nothing at all and it was raining and you were alone in the flat, it was wonderful to know that you could have *something* even though it was only a cup of black and bitter coffee.

Wendell was surprised by how much he remembered all these years later, how the stories seemed so close to him, how they seemed to be his own life, his own language. Rowdy shifted and sank that much deeper into the bed, his eyes falling closed. Wendell pulled the quilt up around the boy's neck once more and his fingers grazed the small whorl of his ear. He had been trapped in that apartment alone, Wendell thought. Christ Jesus. He swallowed. There was a lot the boy had suffered that he would never know, but he took some comfort in the thought that at least the boy could get himself some butter crackers now. Like Francie Nolan, he could at least have *something*. Francie had always seemed to Wendell simultaneously close and impossibly distant. She was a poor girl, someone he knew through and through, yet she was all the way to New York City. She was like Lacy. Or his own father. He could close his eyes and conjure the exact slopes of their shoulders, the feel of their hands in his, yet in his life in the world, his life of work and bills and a beer or two in the evening, he didn't know either one of them anymore.

Little puffs of breath slipped from between Rowdy's open lips. Wendell read on a few minutes more before dog-earing the page and setting the book on the floor. He unplugged the heater and quietly stepped out of the room, pulling the door closed behind him, the windowless hallway inky dark. He made the front room and was feeling for the light switch when the phone rang. That loud, jangling ring. He rushed toward where it hung on the wall by the front door, nailing his shin on an end table and nearly running his head into the cupboards. Just as he grabbed at it, the phone rang again. When he answered, his voice was sharp.

In reply, a fumbling voice, a girl's, asked for Wendell.

—You're talking to him.

A pause.

—This is Maddy. We met the other day at the Antlers. Jackie gave me your number.

Wendell started to hang the phone up but caught himself. The last time a girl had called him on the phone was just after his mother had died. Lacy hadn't said much, had mostly just cried. What had he said to her? Had he told her to come home? That whatever had happened didn't matter? He couldn't remember. He wished he could remember.

—I wanted to say I'm sorry, Maddy continued, about what I said. You're right. I don't know anything about you or your little cousin.

Beyond the surprise of the call itself, and of the apology, there was something about being in the dark, in the utter dark, and her voice traveling the many prairie and mountain miles across the lines right into his ear. Wendell got the same feeling he'd had hiking through the mountains with Rowdy—a relief falling down through him like rain, a sudden gratitude at being so unguarded, so exposed.

—It's no problem, he said. I was drunk. I shouldn't have got loud like that.

—Is Rowdy in bed?

—I just put him down.

—I hope the phone didn't wake him.

—I don't hear him.

There was a moment of silence. Wendell leaned into the door frame.

Maddy went on. She was wondering if there was any way she could help, she said. Not that he needed her help. That's not what she meant. She was sure he was doing fine. It was just that her school was having a toy, book, and coat drive for Catholic Charities, and she could get a box of things—nice things—for Rowdy, if he needed them.

The receiver hung in Wendell's hand. He knew just what his old man would say to something like this, and he could feel the words of refusal already assembling themselves in his throat—but then he saw Rowdy shivering in the wind, thought of his own small shelf of pilfered books.

—I could maybe even bring the stuff down some weekend, Maddy offered, her voice nearly trailing away.

Wendell imagined her, tall and striking, among the pines.

—Rowdy could use a winter coat, he said, swallowing. And some kid books. He likes me reading to him.

—Oh, great! Maddy said, her voice bright with relief. She could do that, no problem. She asked him what size coat Rowdy wore. Wendell faltered. He hadn't thought to check.

—Shoot, he said, I'm not sure. When they brought him out, they just had his clothes in a couple of plastic grocery bags. I'll have to look.

Wendell flushed as he admitted this, his body readying for judgment, but Maddy's voice was warm, understanding. She told him to go ahead and check and get back to her, and he scribbled her number on a piece of junk mail on the kitchen table.

Out the thin window in the front door a few stars sharpened in the dark, the silhouettes of rocks and pines. He wanted to tell her about Rowdy talking today, the first word he'd heard him say, but held back. Later, he thought. He'd save it for later. They said an awkward good-bye and she hung up. The line clicked and buzzed in Wendell's ear. He stood there staring out the dirty window, studying the same extravagant stars, the same stark ridges and trees he'd known all his life.

VERL

Fourteen

Eating hamburgers and hotcakes your mother fries you would not believe it boy but this very day your old dad licked the inside of a pear cactus for dinner. (I am holding back some jerky and candy bars in case.) Anyways it was pulpy and green and sweet. I would not say it was bad but a sure sonofabitch to get at. I don't know how much energy and vitamins and things I took from it. Your mother would know. She watches those day-time doctor shows.

I will tell you this. To eat cactus meat and chew only a handful of dry jerky is a sight better than welfare or that disability. I will damn myself to hell before I take any of that again. I know your mother feels another way. Feels she was owed what came to her as she worked hard and that janitor work bunged up her back. Still. We must live how we say we live. She signed on. She was paid for the work she did. Yes I know she will say they signed on too. But who is they? I mean your mother is on one side that's clear as a summer sky but it's not even the same boss that hired her on the other side and is the new boss to blame or the oven company that works the both of them? These are things I don't know.

Anyways I walked all morning and holed up here most of the afternoon and napped and drew pictures of this country about me. Before me is a space of grass and sage. Off in the distance is Bald Knob. You know how

105

it is with that lean fist of rock up top. It sweeps out. As if blown. As if there is a wind rushing across it even when there is not. I tried to get at that in the pictures. That feeling of wind. I think the likeness is not bad. I would like to show you someday.

Later

How are you boy? How is school? Are you into your basketball season now? Tell me about your days boy. God but I would like that. To hear about your days. To step out of my own. I walk and walk and my breath is easy that is true but my old heart still charges off with whatever I am thinking. I thought for a time I might somehow send you these notes. I thought on it hard but know now I would have to send them in the wind. Or if they would ride the light.

Goddamn but there are things I want to tell you boy like remember the colder it gets to chop the ice for the yearlings in the morning like I wear this wolf's tooth at my throat ~~but goddamn I can tell you nothing now you will have to wait for~~

Later

I am thinking of why it is I am out here. It is time I tell you. Listen to me boy. I had been saying one thing with my mouth and another with my two hands. I had been cashing your mother's disability checks and buying feed and gas and whatall. I had been collecting CRP on that old pasture near the creek. I had been taking grass that was not mine. I had been lying to myself. It is easy to do. Here is a hint boy. When things are easy they are most often wrong. Most often dishonest and cowardly. That is why I am out here. Because I would not lie anymore.

Would not be a coward anymore. Would not abide the cowards and fuckers those fuckers.

I imagine you are hearing all kinds of lies and should hear the truth of it from your old dad who made you. It's true I killed a wolf. I do not deny that. Don't do me boy like Peter did Jesus. When a friend asks you tell him. I am not ashamed. They let those wolves loose down there in Yellowstone and did not think of us. Did not think of us here trying our best raising cattle and sheep and families on the land. There was a wolf on our land. My land. A wolf will thin a lamb crop down to nothing. A wolf would thin us down to nothing. What does it matter we didn't have any wolf kills yet? It was only a matter of time. I tell you when I had the time I took it. I spotted that wolf down by the hayfield where the elk and mulie deer come to munch alfalfa nubs in the morning and shot it through the heart. I saw later by the blue of its teats it was a she-wolf.

To kneel down by her there. That was something.

We speak of wolves. You hear about them in the news and everyone jawing at the café and who has ever seen one? Not me. Until then leastways. I was shaking. I remember I was shaking. Was it because I had done a thing they could jail me for? No I have done more than a few of those in my years. I am telling you boy a wolf is a thing to look at. I think now if I only had fur thick as a wolf I'd live out here and not be cold when the sun goes down.

But the wolf was on my land. That is the beginning and the end. That she-wolf may as well as have come up and ate a hole in my heart.

That right there is enough. But that is not all. The wolf is more than the wolf. One thing the wolf is is laws. What I have much hate toward are laws that make a man a slave on his own land. If I wanted to let that wolf champ and slaver then fine. If not then fine. But that is not what the law says. The law says the wolf can only be shot after confirmed livestock kills and the right paperwork and whatall. The law says I have no choice. Marks me ignorant. Makes me a coward. The law is a goddamn crime. This land is mine. God give it to me through my old dad and his old dad through him.

Kevin ought to have goddamn known.

He may be the government's man but he is a man. Before he is a game warden he is a man. Some few days after I killed the ~~world~~ wolf and took only two claws and a tooth which I have on this loop of fishing line about my neck and buried the rest of her in the junk ravine and hauled an old frigidaire up over the turned dirt Kevin Kincheloe came by knocking on our trailer door and scared your mother half to death. When I come home that evening I swore Kevin a blue streak up and down but she said it wasn't Kevin's fault. Why'd you have to do it she asks me. Why don't you for once do what's best for your family. Verl what in the hell will we do if they haul you in. All this she asks me. Then she up and starts to cry.

I imagine you heard. Those trailer walls are thin. There was a time when you were just a little green-nutter I did not think on what you heard. When I come home drunk. When your mother come home drunk. When she sat on the couch for days not saying a thing to either one of us and I cooked and cleaned without knowing why she was sitting there. I imagine you know. I knew about my folks. I did.

Anyways I thought to argue but answered her nothing. What kind of an answer could I give to all that? How can she say what is best for me isn't best for my family? I answered her nothing. I only opened a can of beer and sat down and read my Louis L'Amour.

The next morning I go out to pump water for the yearlings and here comes Kevin in his green government pickup and out he gets and plucks a length of grass and commences to chewing like I don't know what he's come for. Can you believe it? Maybe that was when I decided. When he didn't have but cowardice in him. Once I finished watering I set myself to loading bales and finally Kevin walks over and says I found the wolf. Says I don't want to do it but Verl I got to take you in.

And the whole time he was saying these things he was acting like he was real sorry hanging his big head and such. And I almost believed him. Was almost a fool. But I am not a fool. I looked in the eye Kevin Kincheloe who I have known years and years and wanted to tell him you ain't got to do a damn thing you don't want to do because in your heart you are a free man Kevin. In your heart you do not have to turn against one that has been your brother and balled up his fists with you on the recess yard. That's what I was thinking but I only stood there. I said nothing. I shot him.

It was easy. My .270 leaning there against the truck cab.

I pick it up. Kevin flaps his mouth like a fish says Verl what the hell. Verl it's my job. Verl I knew your daddy. First I shoot him not really aiming and hit him in the guts. Then shoulder and aim and shoot him in the jaw.

There was about ten gallons of blood in the grass. I hope you did not have to see it. Or your mother. It was not a good thing to see though I did it and am telling you I did it. I don't know how to square that. But I know I am a man who will not be pushed one inch farther. They have pushed and pushed on me. I have kept it from you and your mother thinking I could figure it on my own but I will just go ahead and say it.

They are trying to take our land.

That goddamn bank. I wish Daddy never mortgaged for machinery. Goddamn. When we lost your uncle's section that was almost too much. To see that sonofabitch from California with his brown loafer shoes move in and pull out the fences and not graze a single goddamn sheep or cow and say around town he is letting the land heal itself. What does some long-haired dough-faced sunfucker from California know about this land? We are in this together. The land and us. If you take one from the other that is when we hurt. I am hurt and you are hurt and I do not know what will happen now with the loans and the back taxes but they just can't keep taking it away. Someday there won't be any left. What then? What of us? What of the land? Where is it all going? You would think it would stay where it is. It does not. Of a sudden it's gone. The government or the bank or some such says a word and it's gone. Goddamn goddamn goddamn I do not understand a goddamn thing about any of this.

GILLIAN

In the chill dawn air the boys jostled and cracked jokes, the clouds of their hot breath massing and thinning above their bare red ears, their ball-capped heads. In twos and threes the girls circled and whispered, cut their shadowed eyes at the boys. A handful of couples were paired off as well, holding hands or leaning hip to hip against the brick wall of the school. It was the first cold morning of the changing season, the grass out front laced with frost. Gillian closed her eyes, rubbed at her temples. She'd already turned away one request from a sophomore girl who claimed it was abuse on the level of torture to keep the students outside in this cold. But it was only the end of September. It wasn't truly cold yet, at least not by Montana standards. And Gillian knew, too, that just as soon as she stepped into the warm, stuffy school building her headache would ratchet up another six notches. She wasn't about to open the doors a minute before eight thirty.

As she'd done most of the last week, she'd woken hours before her alarm, mouth dry, sour heart thudding, the spike of a wine headache just beginning to hammer at the base of her skull, and hadn't been able to get back to sleep. She hadn't slept more than a handful of hours the past six days. This morning she'd burned a piece of toast and left a note for Maddy, then taken off for work early.

Now the north and west buses rumbled up, sighing to a stop at nearly the same time, the one behind the other, and the yellow doors folded back. The Bull Mountain kids came bounding off the north bus, grinning and hollering. They wiped their noses on the sleeves of jackets that were too thin and nearly to a child lacked stocking caps, their hair nesty and wild. The kids living in the ranchette communities and suburbs halfway to Billings came off the west bus coats puffy and bright, backpacks decorated with popular cartoons and superheroes, the girls with ribbons and clips in their hair, the boys stocky, shining, those little red lights running around the edges of their tennis shoes.

The Hougen boy, Tyler, jumped off the bottom step of the west bus and strutted toward the playground. As if he owned the place, he surveyed the jungle gym, the tetherball, the little girls shrieking on the swings. With his round head, his big chest and bandy legs, Tyler looked so much like his grandfather Glen that Gillian often had to remind herself that the boy's last name was actually Meredith. His father, Timmy Meredith, was a former star running back for Colter, yet that hadn't done him much good. His parents had lost their land in the '90s, and only by staying in his father-in-law's good graces did Timmy keep himself afloat. For a time he had tried his hand on the Hougen spread, but he hadn't proved much of a farmer, and Glen set him up at the John Deere dealer, where the owners were smart enough to know that it was customers like Glen Hougen who really ran the place.

Gillian had long resented the outsize sway the big farmers and ranchers held in Montana. She wasn't a class warrior, not exactly, but still, she hadn't inherited a thing. No, she'd put herself through college, working in the library during the school year and waitressing during the summers. She had saved and bought the house in Billings on her own, managed to save as well for Maddy's college tuition and her own retirement. Yet all these ranchers lived on land that had just been given to their grandparents or great-grandparents, and they somehow thought they were the only ones working hard, their way of life the only one that mattered when it came to making decisions about the state of Montana.

To hear the stories, Glen Hougen ought to have been the worst of the lot. He'd inherited a veritable kingdom, nearly fifteen sections—each a full square mile, 640 acres, as Kevin had once explained to her—but like everyone else, Glen had landed in financial trouble by the mid-'70s: too many loans for machinery, too many dry acres plowed into corn and wheat, one too many years of drought. That was just when they found oil on his place, the lucky son of a bitch. But she had to admit that Glen had been good to her and Kevin when they first moved back to Montana and rented that farmhouse down on the Musselshell. He'd charged them only half the rent the first year as they fixed the place up, and Carol, Glen's wife, had made Maddy a cream-and-red star quilt for her first birthday. It was often hard for her to square the facts that one of the richest landowners in the Bull Mountains was also, in many ways, one of the kindest, though maybe it was just that he didn't have anything to prove, that he had so much, he could afford to be considerate.

Gillian closed her eyes and pressed at her temples again. The first bell jangled through her, its long, loud electromechanical ring occasioning a circus of shouts and hurried steps from the students, the *whoosh* of the glass double doors. Gillian kept her back to the ruckus. The cold, as the noises faded, again enveloped her, and she opened her eyes. Before her stood a small boy. No, not small—scrawny. His legs thin, arms awkward, neck jutting at a funny angle. Ears bright red in the cold, eyes wide and dark. No proper winter coat. No stocking cap. He tapped his hands at his cheeks.

Gillian put her hands on her knees and leaned down. That was the bell, she told him. He ought to be lined up with the other kids over by the playground.

The boy looked up at her, fingers still drumming his face. Eyes jittery, scared.

—All right, Gillian said. I'll walk you over.

She reached out her hand. The boy stopped drumming a moment and squinted. Then took her hand.

* * *

Kent popped three mints into his mouth, crushed one between his teeth—Gillian could smell the damp peppermint—and banged his drawer shut.

Gillian had wanted to ask about the new kid, the one who didn't talk, but now here she was, not fifteen minutes into the school day, and Kent was telling her the special-ed teacher had quit. Gillian would have to take the elementary kids in special ed, and Mr. Stormer, the football coach, would take the high-school and junior-high kids.

This was a whole new class to prepare for, Gillian protested. Kent was sorry, he was. He knew it would mean more work for her, but there was no one else. Another wave of headache crashed across Gillian's vision, and she breathed and pinched the webbing between her thumb and forefinger. Pinched hard.

—Let me get this straight, she said. We've burned through three special-ed teachers in two years, and putting this onto Stormer and me is your grand plan?

Kent leaned forward. Even smiled. She didn't allow him to say a word.

—Even though neither of us has a special-ed degree or any special-ed experience?

—I know, Kent said, but Coach Stormer will at least be able to keep order, and you're about the best teacher on staff. Sometimes I think it's a shame you have as many administrative duties as you do.

Gillian shoved her way up from the chair.

—Oh Jesus. Save the patronizing bullshit for your ex-wife. Really.

—Gillian, hold on.

But she was gone, slamming Kent's door and brushing past the peroxide-blond school secretary, Miss Kanta, who stared at her wide-eyed and open-mouthed, wad of gum forgotten on her tongue. Gillian was surprised to find, as she hurried down the hallway, that she was close to crying. She swallowed and wiped at her eyes, then slowed at the door to the special-ed room. Stormer stood up front, his massive shoulders framed by the chalkboard, and slapped a ruler into his palm. The junior-high and high-school students, absolutely silent, bent to some worksheets on their desks.

Her hands began to shake. She tried to still them but couldn't. She crossed her arms, trapped her hands in her armpits. What was wrong with her? Lack of sleep, too much wine, this whole mess out in the mountains. She needed to get ahold of herself. She needed—Jesus, what was it she needed?

Maddy had been born in June, a summer of drought, the days hot and curtained with hard, white light, the nights hot as well, though more bearable, save for the hour after sunset, when mosquitoes swarmed. Even for the heat, the first two weeks had been an exhausting delight, as she and Kevin passed this tiny red-faced baby girl back and forth, reading to her, cooing at her, spending nearly every minute, waking and sleeping, together. The three of them.

But then Kevin ran out of vacation and had to go back to work. As if on cue, Maddy's colic—the fussiness before bed, after naps—cranked up another notch. At first, the baby swing was enough. Gillian would turn it on high, and Maddy would nap in there for twenty blessed minutes, enough time for her to shower or make a phone call or just have a cup of coffee and collect herself. When that quit working, Gillian discovered the only way she could get her daughter to sleep was by holding her, bouncing her, walking with her. She would swaddle Maddy and tie her to her chest with a sheet, then take off for the river—which by then had dried to a chain of fetid pools, a few carp thrashing in the still water, scaling themselves on the rocks—and the jounce of her walk would eventually put Maddy out.

Grasshoppers flung themselves through the dry grass. The seconds cracked and ticked. The bleached sear of them always on her back, in her scorched lungs. Soon she'd be sweating, Maddy a hot, wet stone at her chest. After fifteen minutes of hard walking, she'd loop back, hoping

Maddy wouldn't wake until she made it to the house, where she could sit in a chair to nurse her. Sometimes she timed it right. Other times, before she made it home, Maddy would begin to wail. She'd lift her head away from Gillian's chest, hold a moment, scream, then slam herself back down, the little slit of her lips like a wound. Once, tired, hot, half a mile from the house and half out of her mind from her daughter's piercing squall, Gillian pulled Maddy from the sheet, tore off the swaddle, and just set her on the ground, on the shaling mud and river gravel, as if she were a red, raging fish, and stood there and cried.

She had thought motherhood would be easier for her. She'd been a teacher for ten years, had worked with all kinds of kids, even been named teacher of the year in her district in Alpine, and she and Kevin weren't like so many other couples they knew. He cooked dinner all the time, and when it came to fixing a broken toilet flapper or rewiring a lamp, she was the handier one. They had spent years traveling, hiking and fishing and exploring, the two of them, always in it together. She thought all this would somehow matter, that motherhood wouldn't look on her the same way it looked on Kevin's sisters, with their loose jeans and stained sweatshirts, the stink of potato salad, day after day given over to the whims of an infant, a toddler, a child.

It infuriated her that Kevin didn't seem to notice her struggle. When he was home, he got right down on the floor with Maddy, packed her everywhere in the crook of his arm, swung her about in the air. And she squealed, grabbed at his beard, smiled for him like she never smiled for her mother. Gillian was glad for the break, but it meant that while Kevin played with the baby, she was the one who had to cook dinner, finish the laundry, the dishes. It meant that each hot night lying in bed, only a thin sheet over them, Kevin was the one who prattled on and on about some funny little thing their daughter had done while she drifted near sleep, knowing she'd have to feed Maddy soon, knowing she didn't have the luxury of attention, of delight. She envied the distance Kevin had, the perspective. He could dive in and pull himself out while she thrashed forever in the muddy water. She was too tired to love, she thought, too worn out.

That fall Kevin went hunting with some old friends from high school, way out in the Bulls, and he came home on the far side of a six-pack, full of piss and vinegar, having gotten a nice cow elk. He strung it up from the big cottonwood behind the house and was planning on butchering it the next day out at his mom's place, where they had a cold room. He followed her around that evening as she did the laundry, telling her, in the grim, serious, declamatory voice he used after a few drinks, that he thought he'd seen some evidence of poaching out at his buddy's place, that these guys needed to be reminded that he was their friend but he was the game warden too, that there were good ecological reasons for hunting regulations. That it didn't matter your political affiliation—if you loved elk hunting, then you had to do right by the land and listen to what the science said. He cracked open another beer. Behind the bones of her chest Gillian felt the pop of that can, felt her blood fizzing in the tiny arteries that wrapped her heart.

Right then she didn't give a good goddamn about ecology and reason, about poaching, about anything his idiot, unreconstructed friends did. She shoved through the screen door and stepped outside into the late heat, into the hum and hive of mosquitoes rising from the river.

With Kevin calling after her, she got into the Tercel and drove away.

She turned west down Highway 12 and was miles past Roundup before her blood began to settle, before she realized where she was, the high plateau country rising to meet the Rockies. The river curved to the south, and the highway lifted ever higher onto the dry plain: long golden wheat fields interspersed with strips of fallow, the rangeland pocked with sage and greasewood. Off to the west, over the Crazy Mountains, thunderheads massed—anvils, horseheads, stacks of black rock. She drove into that darkness, and the rain came pounding down. It steamed on the highway, veined the windshield. Wind screamed through fence wires and hammered at the car like invisible fists. Lightning cut here and there. Great claps of thunder sounded. Soon, she couldn't see a thing but dark sky and rain. She slowed, pulled off the highway and onto a gravel road. The storm shrieked and beat its wings and just as suddenly passed over.

She cranked down the windows to clear them and up the gravel road spotted a sign, one of those brown tourist-information signs: DEADMAN'S BASIN 1.5 M. She drove north, toward the earthen wall of the reservoir, with the windows down and the smell of ozone, grass, and cow shit in her nose. She parked and got out. It was still hot, though more bearable now, a rain-rinsed heat. The ground was wet, yet each of her steps ground down through the mud to dust. Always the dust. In the basin, which was nearly dry, the mineral wrack of the receding waterline had painted the dirt bowl in concentric stripes. Far below, near the last of the water, a man splashed in the shallows. He had a long stick—no, a net. He stropped it through the water, this way and that, and suddenly lifted it into the air. A carp or a catfish twisted in its ropes. He walked up the bank and dumped the fish in the dirt, where it smacked its slick tail in the mud and dust, flipped itself six, eight inches off the ground, and fell, then lay still, working at the raw air.

She was crying now. She got in the Tercel and drove back to the highway and sat there for a time. Then turned toward home.

Kent had knocked on her office door just after lunch with an iced tea—a wedge of lemon, just like she liked—an apology, and all the files on the elementary-school special-ed students. Gillian had gotten herself together by then and offered her own apology in return. Kent was right about one thing: She was a good teacher. She could do this.

Gillian went over the files on her new students once more and then set out for the elementary wing. The elementary special-ed students spent most of the day in their grade-level classrooms and were pulled out in the afternoon for a couple of hours of what the district termed "enrichment." For those who needed more one-on-one time or fewer distractions, this made sense. But there were others for whom no amount of enrichment would help, children with issues so involved it would take a truckload of resources to reach them, to perhaps tilt their coming years toward a path, if not better, at least less mean. For instance, the fifth-grader who couldn't read, who had burn scars licking up his neck from a house fire, likely meth-related. And the third-grader who couldn't keep a book or pencil or homework sheet, who lost everything she was given, who sometimes showed up to school without shoes, who kept sneaking away and hiding in small, dark places—beneath tables, in supply closets, behind the hedges on the recess yard—and wetting herself.

When Gillian knocked on the door to the second-grade classroom, Miss Allen poked her head into the hall and ushered out three children. Gillian looked at her form and said she was expecting only two students.

—That's these two here, Miss Allen said.

She motioned to a moon-faced girl with a bowl cut and an incredibly obese, brown-haired boy.

—But you're going to want to take this one too.

Miss Allen put her hand to the third child's small back and pushed him forward. It was the boy from this morning, still tapping at his cheeks. He was new just today, she explained. She'd heard that he'd been fostered out. Then Miss Allen leaned in toward Gillian.

—Definitely autistic, she whispered, but probably some trauma too. Doesn't say a word. Not. A. Word.

Gillian studied Miss Allen's thin face, the flyaway hairs at her temples, the yellow of her blouse. She knew what it was like, the immense work of a classroom, of keeping everything together and, hopefully, moving little by little forward.

—I don't have any paperwork yet, but, sure, he can join us in the afternoons.

Miss Allen put her hand to her chest.

—Oh, thank you. These past few days have been a bit rough.

Gillian smiled at Miss Allen. Then leaned down to the boy.

—And what's your name, kiddo? Is it Ricky? Bartholomew? Oh, I know. Eustace. I just bet you're a Eustace.

The boy paused his fingers in mid-tap and gave her a lopsided grin.

—I'm Rowdy, he said.

His voice was cracked, sandy, clearly not much used. But high and sweet too. The boy swallowed, knotted his hands at his chest, and looked up at Gillian, who reached out and touched his shoulder. It was like the wings of moths all through her, and she had the sudden idea that this classroom itself might be the thing she needed.

VERL

17

I have had hard times lately boy. Writing the story out for you I saw red and cut north to the river and shot a mulie deer come down for water just to show them I was not afraid. You have probably heard about it in the papers or on the radio news. Them almost catching me. Goddamn. I ran. Ran in the night and through the night. Slept only minutes here. Minutes there. I do not even know now where in the mountains I am.

WENDELL

He cranked the heat in the LUV, but in the predawn chill Rowdy shivered anyway until the Colter bus came groaning up the hill. It was an older style than the one from Delphia—faded yellow nose curved, windows low, clear, and wide—and Wendell felt bad about that. The bus driver, a woman with a tight helmet of tiny red-brown curls, squinted at the two of them and told Rowdy to look lively, that they had more stops to make. The door folded shut behind the boy, and the bus heaved and sighed, then disappeared south down the road. Wendell studied the dark gold hills and the dry grass, the blue shadows pooling in the cutbanks. Land he'd known all his life. And he wished Rowdy a good school day, a good teacher, maybe even a friend.

The early light came bright and sideways, from east to west, and in that cold, distant brilliance Wendell shivered himself. He thought of the winter coat Maddy had promised. He had called her back with the boy's size yesterday, after he'd put Rowdy to bed, and she'd asked if Rowdy had a favorite color. He felt bad that he hadn't noticed that either—hadn't considered it, to be honest—and didn't want to admit a second such failing, so he just said red. He could hear her writing it down, the scratch of the pencil all the way through the phone lines, and it pained him to be lying like that, on top of taking a handout. Still, he didn't know the next time he'd get into Billings for a coat. And he wasn't sure if they carried picture books at the Walmart. He'd never had occasion to look. That was if he could even afford it, after groceries, after the next payment on the back taxes. Whether it was red or any other damn color, Rowdy needed a coat. That was the simple fact, no matter what his old man would have made of it.

Wendell drove north again and at the timbered gateway turned off the county road and drove west into the Bulls, toward the Hougen ranch. He parked near the shop, by the gas tanks, leaving plenty of room for Glen's flatbed and Carol's Buick to get out. He tucked his T-shirt into his jeans, made sure his fly was zipped up, then pulled the can of Copenhagen from his back pocket and tossed it on the dash of his truck. Though he figured his reputation was more or less shot from the stunt he'd pulled last weekend, he knew Carol frowned on chewing tobacco. No need to keep digging when he was already in the hole. He crossed the gravel and came up the curving sidewalk through a front yard that was green even this late in the season and knocked on the door.

Carol answered in a housedress and slippers. She eyed him a moment, then waved him in. Wendell pulled his cap off and stepped into the mudroom. Carol didn't wait but went ahead, and he took off his flannel jacket and boots. He took his time in the hallway, studied the Western art—a lone Indian slumped on a paint horse above a deep canyon; a bull elk posing on a mountaintop; three cowhands crouched around a breakfast fire, the sky stained with sunrise. He liked the feel of the soft cream-colored carpet beneath his socked feet and the rich brown paneling of the walls and the way the ensconced fixtures filled the house with thick, buttery light. He could smell bacon. He hadn't realized how hungry he was. He'd handed Rowdy one of those breakfast bars in the truck but hadn't grabbed one for himself.

Glen was at the kitchen table, slurping coffee, jotting something on the little notepad he always kept in his shirt pocket. He looked up at Wendell, gave a chuckle. Since he'd given Wendell a couple of days off and then Wendell had been working on the fencing nearer his place, they hadn't seen each other in more than a week.

—You dry out yet? Glen asked him. Carol said you were just about pickled the other morning.

Carol banged a spatula and brought out a plate of bacon and toast and without even looking at Wendell set it at the table.

—Sit on down, son. We've done forgiven you.

Glen glanced at Carol.

—Mostly, anyway.

As Carol turned back toward the kitchen, Glen continued.

—I tell you, it weren't so long ago I used to get to feeling itchy now and again myself. Once slept the night on the pool table there at the Antlers. Woke the next noon to old Dean Feeney pumping quarters into the poker machine.

Carol dropped a cup of coffee in front of Wendell, the black liquid sloshing. Wendell thanked her and turned to apologize again about last weekend, but she was already gone. Back in her bedroom or somewhere. Glen chuckled.

—She don't much like it when I tell war stories. She thinks the church cured me of all that, but mostly I just don't get so itchy as I used to. That happens if you get old enough, trust me. Anyway, don't just sit there looking hungry. Makes me uncomfortable. Eat up.

Wendell laid two slices of bacon across a piece of toast and folded it into a sandwich and took a bite. Butter, salt, bacon fat—Wendell wasn't sure the last time he'd had something this good. He'd have to pick up some bacon for him and Rowdy. That'd be a treat.

Glen slurped his coffee, slurped again. He closed his notepad and dropped it into his shirt pocket. Trained his eyes on Wendell.

—Listen, Wendell, I'm sure you had a reason, and you don't even have to tell me, but on top of getting shit-faced and leaving that poor little bastard here all night, you cut out of work yesterday. That's one thing I can't have. Just can't. I needed you on those corrals.

Glen toyed with his coffee cup. Wendell's guts churned.

—You know there's plenty of boys over in Delphia or down in Colter that'd like your job. Lanter ain't the brightest bulb, but I could pay him half of what I pay you and bunk him out there in the shed, and he'd be happy as a buck goat.

Glen allowed that Wendell was the best goddamn hand he'd had, and he knew Wendell had a kid to raise all of a sudden and that was tough. But he'd let Wendell off early the whole week to meet Rowdy at the bus stop, even though Carol would have been happy to pick him up. And he'd let Rowdy ride with Wendell in the truck that day.

—I ain't being no son of a bitch about this, Glen said. You just got to get it figured out. You maybe got a kid to raise, but I got a ranch to run. And goddamn but I'm going to run it right.

Wendell glanced over at Glen and turned back to his plate. He could feel each little wing of bone in his neck shift and creak as he nodded.

—All right, that's enough out of me. Finish up your bacon.

Glen pushed up from the table, slapped his hat on his head, and was out the door. Wendell washed his last bite down with a swig of coffee and ferried his plate to the kitchen sink. He felt plain pinned to the wall about last weekend, but though he'd hung his head and nodded along, trying on the guilt, Wendell couldn't find his way to feeling bad about yesterday. In truth that had been a good goddamn day, setting a trapline out in the Bulls with Rowdy. Wendell smiled to himself, and he hoped Rowdy might think on it and give a smile today at school. He turned for the door and nearly ran over Carol, who had a pair of Rowdy's little white socks in her hand, was holding them out to him. Wendell made himself look right at her as he took the socks.

—I'm sorry, Carol. I'm awful sorry.

They spent the morning shoring up the corrals—hammering loose boards, replacing the rusted hinges on the cutting gate, and against the dust laying down a load of straw all through the pens and chutes. On Monday, they'd start the roundup, start bringing in Glen's herd of red

Angus and polled Hereford. Most would be shaggy and half wild, and it'd take the better part of three days, hunting the cattle out of the draws and hills and trailing them all back here to the homeplace, back to the corrals. Babe MacDonald, the cattle buyer, would roll in with his stock trucks on Thursday, and they'd cut, weigh, and sell the calves on Friday, which would make it a full week of cattle work. They'd need help. They'd get Glen's daughter, Rochelle, and son-in-law, Timmy, to come out. Wendell mentioned that Freddie Benson was almost always looking for work and so Glen said all right, give him a call, but make sure he knows he's got to show up sober.

With the crew accounted for, Glen and Wendell set themselves to readying the tack, checking the oil and the tires on each of the dirt bikes and four-wheelers. As Wendell lugged a gas can over and began filling the tanks in turn, he thought he might as well ask and so he did.

—You ever had much to do with that Betts?

Glen was bent to a four-wheeler, checking the tire pressure.

—Brian Betts. Now there's a hardscrabble son of a bitch. He'd know his way around the mountains. And I don't believe he drinks at all. A religious type. Carol'd like him. Maybe we ought to skip Freddie and get Betts to cowboy for us.

Glen straightened up and leaned this way and that to stretch his back, his work shirt sliding up over his hard, round belly.

—Yeah, I know Betts. What's your business with the man? I didn't figure the two of you'd cross over much. Now, your dad, he and Betts would've been thick as thieves. They'd've talked all manner of subjects up and down.

The stink of gasoline watered Wendell's eyes. He blinked, and in the dark behind his lids he felt wires snap and whine. It all came back—those long-ago nights his father had taken him out to cut fences. He tried to harness in his mind's eye the starlight such that he might see his father's face—tried to pull that faint light down around him like a shawl—but the night proved too black, the dark complete.

He glugged a tank full and capped the gas can and set it down. Wiped at his face with his shirtsleeves.

—He was out with Tricia Wilson's boy yesterday cutting fences.

Glen paused his stretching.

—Well, that's downright interesting.

—Between you and the BLM. Maybe a quarter mile of fence, near Lemonade Springs.

—And he had the boy with him?

—It was the boy who cut the fences. Betts just sat there on his four-wheeler.

Glen spit, kicked at the oil-stained floor of the shop.

—Christ Jesus. Betts ought to think a little harder on that. The boy ought to be in school.

—You're all right with him cutting government fences, then? Just not having the boy out there with him while he's doing it?

Glen looked at him hard. Spit again.

—I ain't got no love for the federal government, Wendell. You know that. The EPA, the BLM—I've had run-ins with the lot of them.

Then began the familiar litany of complaints. First they couldn't spray this or that on account of some damn butterfly that needed protecting. Then they couldn't keep cattle on land they'd rightfully leased on account of "proper range-management directives" or some such shit. Then, in the '90s, it was wolves, which Wendell more than anyone knew all about. On its own, any single thing might not have seemed like much, but ranching was a tight business. He knew he didn't have to tell Wendell that. He'd seen as well as Glen had the banks taking enough farms, enough ranches, to know. It was the little bits here and there that would grind them down.

—Us Hougens been out here three generations, Glen said, raising cattle and hay and cutting wheat, and now it's like they want us out. It's like if they had their way there wouldn't be no ranchers at all, and just where do they think they're going to get their beefsteaks and hamburgers then?

They'd rather have wolves and buffalo and a bunch of half-naked hippies dancing around?

Well, he didn't mean to preach. Wendell knew as well as he did how they whittled on them. Glen took a breath and ran his hand over his bald head. But this Betts had ideas, he said. Just like Wendell's old man. Betts figured the wolf hunt coming up would be a chance to show them. With this Obama in the White House they didn't have time to waste. Glen had considered bringing Wendell in on it, with Verl being who he was, but the timing was bad. It wasn't so long after Wendell's mother had passed that they first started talking, and now he had a boy to look after, and Glen would just as soon he stayed out of it and let the rest of them deal with the feds.

—Who's in on it? Wendell wanted to know.

Glen grinned. Just about everybody! Young folks, town folks, even respectable folks like him. They might not all be as full of piss and vinegar as Betts was, but they'd had enough and knew it was time. Glen cocked an eyebrow at Wendell and waited a moment, as if to let him weigh in with his approval, then squatted down by the four-wheeler, busied himself with the valve cap, the tire gauge.

Wendell took in the dusty air, the motes of dust riding the slanted light toward his lips as he breathed in, then whirling away as he breathed out. He could, if he wanted, take two quick steps and launch his boot into the side of Glen Hougen's head. Did he want to do that? He wasn't sure. He turned and left the shop, crossed the gravel.

How did Glen Hougen get to be the one to decide what Wendell ought and ought not do? How did Betts get to be the one to ride four-wheelers with his boy all day? How did he, Wendell Newman, end up the one who couldn't fuck up or take a day to set a trapline for fear of losing his job? Was his father's face long and lean, like his own? Or was that from his mother? He had her stone-blue eyes, he knew that much, but her face had been so bloated with medication by the end he wasn't quite sure anymore. What had come down to him from his mother? From his father? What had come down to him at all?

He wandered down to his truck and reached through the open window and grabbed at his can of Copenhagen. Popped it once with his finger and pinched up a chew, all those little glistening strands of cut tobacco. He'd picked up the habit when he was thirteen or fourteen because why not, because the only boys who didn't were made fun of, because the only men who didn't, he'd once heard an older boy say, were schoolteachers or worse. Wendell flicked the tobacco to the ground now and wiped his finger and thumb clean on the thigh of his jeans. Winged the half-full can off into the weeds beneath the gas tanks.

One winter when his mom was laid up—medical leave without pay, they called it—he and Lacy took their rifles out into the mountains and each shot a cow elk. This was after the new year, months after the close of the legal season. They worked their knives up the bellies of the elk, pounding and sawing through hide and rib and chest bone. Lacy levered herself against the great cave of the ribs to hold it open, and with both his hands slippery and numb and steaming, Wendell got hold of the trachea—so wide and springy, still half alive beneath his fingers—and pulled. It ripped free with a scissoring sound, and he kept on pulling, all the way down through, as the guts spilled into the snow, which reddened and melted and ran beneath them. Because the elk were too heavy to drag, they went for a chain saw. They quartered both animals and hauled the quarters to the LUV and drove back home. In the barn they set about boning and cutting and wrapping the meat. It was hard work, and they hadn't ever been taught correctly, and their knives weren't sharp enough—the steaks and roasts hacked at and ugly. Still, late in the night they finished two quarters and strung the others up from the rafters. For a midnight dinner they fried onions and potatoes and elk steaks in a cast-iron pan. The meat lean, herbal, dark.

Wendell dreamed again that night of wolves, wolves mewling and circling the barn, scratching and gnashing at it, until finally they clawed the door to pieces and rushed into the barn and leaped up and tore down the hung quarters.

They had planned to butcher out the rest after school the next day, after Wendell's basketball practice, but when they got home, the winter evening already black and bitter cold, there were tire tracks in the snow by the barn, a note pinned to the door. It was from the game warden out of Roundup. He'd seen them the day before, had caught them in his binoculars, but didn't have time to make it out that night and so had come out this morning and confiscated the remaining quarters. Considering the circumstances—he'd heard Wendell's mother was laid up—he was letting them off with a warning. That's what the note said. But just this once. Next time there'd be a fine. Next time they'd lose their rifles.

Lacy was pissed. She wanted to go out again, spotlighting in the dark. But reading the note just made Wendell tired. Tired of so often wanting things to be other than they were. Lacy lit up a cigarette. She was only sixteen, a sophomore, just a year older than he was. He didn't know where she was getting her smokes. She swung her arm out and the cigarette's coal inscribed a red arc across the Bulls.

—Your dad's still out there, you know. He'd want us out there too. He'd want us to put our thumbs right in their eyes.

Wendell thought of his mother hurting in the trailer, waiting for dinner, waiting for him to bring her a glass of water and her pill. But he could feel the pull of the hills.

—How do you know what he'd want? he said.

—I just do. So do you, if you don't pout about it or think too much, if you'd just let yourself do what you ought to.

The night was so starry, so cloudless, that Wendell could make out the exact profiles of the mountains, the buttes, right down to the knobs, ridges, and canyons. He turned away, away from whatever ghosts haunted those hills, and left Lacy smoking in the dark.

Maddy came out that evening, after suppertime. It was already dark, but she insisted his directions had been super, that the drive had been nice, with the sun setting and all. She was carrying a cloth bag, and she held it out to Rowdy, who looked up at her and drummed at his cheeks.

Wendell patted him on the back.

—Go on. She brought it for you.

Rowdy reached his thin arms out and took the bag and, bumping it on the ground, peered inside at all the books. Looked up smiling.

Maddy smiled back, then motioned to her car with a mention of the clothes and took off before Wendell could offer to help. He felt unsure, wooden in his movements. Rowdy, though, sat right down in the dirt by the stairs and paged through a book about a boy and a penguin.

Maddy returned from her car toting a cardboard box. She set the box down near where Rowdy was reading and pulled out a puffy red and black winter jacket, which she held out by the shoulders, the zipper open. When she asked Rowdy what he thought, the boy was so absorbed by his penguin book that at first he looked at her with some irritation, but he got to his feet and slid himself into the jacket and let her zip it up. Then sat right back down and picked up his book.

Wendell reached down and squeezed the boy's shoulder.

—It's real nice. Just what he needs. This is awful kind of you. Really.

—Oh, good, she said, and drew a swing of black hair behind her ear.

She was pleased, Wendell could tell, and maybe a little embarrassed.

—I mean it. It's been hard, taking care of a boy all of a sudden. This helps a lot.

He paused, tried to gauge her reaction.

—You want to come in, warm up? I've got a can or two of pop in the fridge.

Maddy took a half step back. Ah, he'd gone too far, misread all of this. It was about charity, pure and simple.

Then a meadowlark called, and Maddy turned toward the rise and fall of sound and reached out, just touching Wendell's arm.

—A meadowlark! We don't hear them often in Billings.

She lifted her hand, and where she'd touched him at his elbow was warm, alive.

—Used to be even more, he said. But there's some yet. They like the dry creek bed there along the road.

Despite the shadows, the deepening night about, Maddy studied the creek, the woods, the ridges beyond. She asked Wendell if he'd lived here all his life and he said he had.

—What's it like? she asked.

—Like anywhere, I guess. But farther away.

Maddy cocked her head at him, like she didn't quite believe him. He wasn't sure he believed himself. But how could he answer a question like that?

—There used to be some towns out here in the Bulls, he went on. Mining towns with hotels and saloons and such. They're all gone now. Just falling-down shacks. Bits of blue and purple glass in the washes.

She was staring right at him, wide-eyed, unguarded. He turned away, checked on Rowdy sitting there in the dirt. When he glanced back up, Maddy had finally caught herself. She swallowed, shifted on her feet.

—I'm glad the coat fits, she said. And that Rowdy likes the books.

She started toward her car, then turned back. For his awkwardness, he hadn't really been able to see her until now, and he took her in. She was wearing fitted jeans and a black blouse, a silky, blue-green scarf about her neck. She was nearly as tall as he was.

She had to go, she said, but wanted to come back the next Friday, if that was all right, and bring some more books. She had a half day at school—she could get there before dark.

—You could show me around, she said.

The light fell from the windows of the trailer, from the stars. With her dark clothes, her dark hair, Wendell could barely see her.

—Yeah, you bet, Wendell said, and grinned despite himself. That'd be all right. That'd be good.

She took her leave, calling out a good-bye to both of them, and as she pulled away, Rowdy looked up, blinked a few times, and went back to his penguin book.

The next days, the wind stilled for a time. And the hills and old scarred trees settled down into the unyielding densities of themselves. Then the wind came again, harder and from the north, carrying the smell of ice and minerals.

The bite of it was at his wrists, his neck, the quick of his eyes. They'd been at the roundup three days now, since Monday morning, and only a fraction of the herd was left to gather. Wendell rode the dirt bike north and west, zigzagging up and down the broad valleys, hunting the draws and box canyons. At tight stands of chokecherry, cedar, and jack pine, he dismounted and thrashed his way through. Here and there he turned out a few cows and calves and got them moving south toward the bulk of the herd, then rode north again himself.

He came to the cut fences late in the afternoon—the heaped wires now snagged with cheatgrass and elk hair—and killed the engine. He and Rowdy had tromped out to check their trapline over the weekend in those windless hours that were almost warm, and he'd checked the line each day since. They hadn't gotten ahold of anything. It had been a long time since he'd run a line, and he didn't know the mountains quite like he had as a boy, when he was still his father's son. Maybe once the calves were sold he'd take the boy out and pull up the sets, try somewhere deeper in the mountains. He wanted a chew and reached for his back pocket, forgetting it wasn't there, forgetting he'd decided something, though what that was, exactly, he wasn't sure.

Wendell kicked the dirt bike to life and rode on. The ghost of Betts's tracks narrowed into the hills before him. He drove slowly, considering each box canyon, each valley mouth and rising ridge. He crossed the dry run of Hawk Creek, where the mountains rose in earnest, their high spine visible in the distance. The wind whirled and gusted, spit snow that stung his eyes and cheeks. A bit early, the first of October, but not unusual. He turned up a wash and kickstanded the bike and scrambled twenty feet up the blind ridge to a mass of sandstone, then skirted the rocks, the footing precarious in places, to the yawning opening of a cave. He ducked in, crouched a step or two, and straightened up.

They'd scraped out the floor and put beams across the rock-and-sod roof. The cave proper, a stretched rectangle, shadowed and dank, had space for maybe ten men to sleep out of the wind. At the far end, a few steps were hacked into the wall, with scattered shafts of gray light leaking in from where a man could haul himself up and out onto the ridgetop. A second entrance, or exit. Along one wall stretched a section of metal shelving filled with traps, snares, water jugs, gas cans, maps, shovels, tarps, tools, and whatnot. There were three steel trunks as well, below the shelves, the first two crammed with canned and dried food, the third bristling with rifles and pistols and boxes of ammunition. Wendell hefted one of the more ridiculous-looking guns, some kind of air-cooled assault rifle, the metal black and oily. Still holding it, he peered out of the cave mouth. The freezing wind tore at the pines along the ridge, lifted the dead, dry branches, even bits of rock, and sent them crashing into other trees and rocks, scraping along the face of the flats.

VERL

18

I have slept some and feel better. But sleep has been hard. I wake every few minutes to listen for engines. Voices. Helicopter blades. For the last days I have heard nothing but wind. My bootfalls on the cold hard ground.

I guess I should tell you boy. I am okay. Hungry but okay. I ate only a few small bites of that mulie deer. Even as I pulled the trigger. Even then I knew it was a bad idea. Knew someone would hear and word would get around and soon the fuckers would be crawling all over. I hurried. Butchered out a back leg and cooked some in the ground like I told you and ate some blood raw while I ran like a wolf. It tasted good. I sit and rest now and wish for more. There is no more. I heard hunger stories from my old granddaddy but did not know hunger. Nothing but a howl in the belly.

Later

Saw the frost come down this morning. That was all right a thing to see. Was tired was walking to warm myself through the cold early dark when the sky lifted. As if a man shrugged a weight from his shoulders. The wind came a notch warmer then and like that the grass broke with frost under my boots.

GILLIAN

T HEY WERE OUT BACK OF THE SCHOOL, IN THE SCRUB HILLS WEST OF THE
dirt football field and the scoria track, hunting specimens—empty egg
sacks and cracked chrysalises, the desiccated bodies of beetles and flies.
Cold wind gusted across the hilltops, swirled down the draws. A front
had moved in, and the kids hurried here and there, winter jackets flapping, notebooks tucked up in their armpits, as they knelt down in the
greasewood and dry grass and held magnifying glasses up to their watery
eyes and chapped noses.

After just a single day in the enrichment room Gillian had seen that
working her way from child to child, helping each of them finish
homework sheets from their regular classes, just wasn't going to cut
it. That was probably why the last special-ed teacher had struggled so
much—she, like too many other teachers, had thought kids ought to be
able to sit still for twenty minutes. Of course they couldn't. They'd get
fidgety and bored and turn to the quick delights of mischief. No, Gillian
knew she had to get the whole group involved in something. Hence this
unit on bugs—on where they go in the winter and what they leave behind.

On Monday, they'd brainstormed a list of all the things they knew
about bugs. Yesterday she had the older kids do some online research
and the younger kids draw pictures of what they found. They were collecting specimens today. Tomorrow, they'd count and graph and see if

their results matched the research. And Friday they'd write and illustrate small reports. She was thinking of having the kids present their reports as well. She could probably drum up a small audience of teachers. She could even call Dave Coles, have him cover it for the paper. It was just the kind of feel-good, small-town story he'd love. She was having a bit of her own feel-good, small-town story, she thought now, and laughed at herself for thinking it. But it was true, the classroom gave her something necessary and absolutely real to focus on. And she and Maddy had had a great run last Saturday, making it all the way to Zimmerman Park. Then, Sunday, she'd met Kent for brunch, just to clear the air, and they'd ended up talking for hours. As they gathered their things to leave, she told him it was her turn. Her turn for what? Her turn to ask him out to dinner, she said. He grinned and accepted.

The wind gusted now, canting the yellow grass, and Gillian turned on her heel, tallying—*six, seven, eight, nine*—her motley crew of entomologists. The light this afternoon came in swaths, the wind hauling great high clouds across the sky, and she squinted into a brilliant slice of it to see Rowdy Burns come running up to her, breathless, something held before him in both hands. He hadn't said anything more after that first day, as if he'd already covered what was important—that he was Rowdy—but he'd listened devoutly, greedily, and had done everything she'd asked, as best he could, anyway. He recognized only half the alphabet. He had some number sense but seemed to have been given little arithmetic instruction. He was likely on the autism spectrum, though because of his selective mutism, it would be difficult to tell the extent of it. Yet the boy had shown up on Monday with a new coat, which was a good sign, and he'd tried hard the last three days, screwing his little face up as he drew his bugs. Over the years Gillian had had a few foster kids who'd done well, who'd landed in decent homes, were reasonably cared for, and had the time and space then to be kids again, to let down their defenses and learn. She didn't yet know Rowdy's home situation—Kent said the paperwork was in process—but a new coat, along with how well he listened, made Gillian think the boy just might get lucky.

He stood before her now, eyes wide, and slowly opened his hands into a cup. Gillian leaned down. He'd found a grasshopper in torpor, she told him, and reminded him that *torpor* meant its body was shutting down for the winter. That's why it wasn't jumping out of his hand. This grasshopper had probably already laid eggs or fertilized eggs, and those eggs were in the ground now, safe, and in the spring they would hatch a bunch of new little grasshoppers.

Rather than bring it inside, Gillian suggested that he draw a picture of this one that the class could use as a specimen. Rowdy pulled out his notebook, pushed his coat sleeves up his arms, sat right down in the dirt, and commenced drawing. Gillian watched him for a time, smiling. Just as she was about to look away, to check on the other students, the light shifted, a cloud far above whirling away in the wind, and something caught her eye—a butterfly wing of bruise, yellow with a bit of blue, on the underside of the boy's wrist.

That afternoon, as the buses queued in front of the school—diesel engines grumbling, exhaust swirling up and reddening in the brake lights—the snow began. A hard, thin, spitting snow. The kind that freezes ruts, ices windshields, and leaves a scrim beneath loose windows and doors.

With Kent busy most of the afternoon mediating a disagreement between Coach Stormer and two sets of parents who both thought their respective sons should be getting more playing time at running back, Gillian had offered to take afternoon bus duty for him. The highschoolers shivered and milled in the foyer, complaining about the snow, checking texts, until finally they ducked their heads and raced to the parking lot. The grade-school kids ran delirious circles on the small lawn out front. They gathered little handfuls of the dry snow and threw it in the air like confetti and tried to catch the snowflakes on their tongues.

The town kids filtered off in clumps down the dirt roads of Colter, and the country kids eventually sorted themselves onto the buses.

Gillian watched for Rowdy, and when he came loping across the yard in that little sideways gallop of his, she squatted down to intercept him. She told him he'd done an awesome job collecting specimens today and asked if she could get a high five. He grinned and ratcheted his small shoulder back and slapped her hand. She touched his arm and held him lightly by his elbow, asked if everything was all right at home, if he was safe. Rowdy screwed his face up in confusion but nodded emphatically, mashing his knob of a chin against his chest, then tipping it up into the air.

Gillian let him go then and the boy hopped up into his bus. She looked for him to sit and wave at her, but he must have chosen a seat on the other side. The buses groaned, sighed, and one by one turned down Main Street. The scent of diesel swirled away with the wind, and Gillian took a deep breath of what would soon be winter air, the burn of it sharp and cold and clean inside her.

Back in her office, after readying the enrichment room for the next day, she brushed her hair and changed blouses and slipped on heels, dabbed perfume behind her ears. In the past year she'd been out for drinks and dinner with a lawyer, a contractor, and a software engineer, and while she'd enjoyed herself, she always found it hard to explain what it was she did. She'd say *teacher* or *assistant principal,* and they'd nod, but she knew they were seeing the private schools their own kids went to in Billings. There'd be wine and vinaigrette and small talk about interesting magazine articles, and she knew their world. They didn't know hers. Colter, Montana, was beyond them. But Kent, Gillian thought as she pulled her phone from her purse—Kent understood.

She called Maddy and left a message, told her there was lasagna in the fridge, ice cream and a pan of brownies in the freezer, that she'd be home late so not to wait up. She left a message with Dave Coles, too, inviting him to the presentations on Friday and asking him what he knew about a new student of hers, a Rowdy Burns.

With Miss Kanta gone for the day, Gillian slipped around the front desk and peeked in Kent's office. His tie was loose, and a tin of mints lay unhinged and empty atop his desk. The two sets of parents sat there almost knee to knee, still arguing. She caught his eye, but Kent shook his head, mouthed, *Ten minutes*. She grinned, mouthed back, *Meet you there*.

A short while later she pulled up to the old brick false-front of the Grand and parked her Prius next to two mud-splattered flatbeds. The freezing snow bit at her face, her neck, the tender place on her wrists where her gloves didn't quite meet the sleeves of her coat. She wobbled on her heels in the gravel and the wind but got her purse situated and the car door closed and stepped up onto the old boardwalk. She put her shoulder to the heavy wooden door. It had been years since she'd been to the Grand—some teachers' night out when she'd first started at Colter, she thought—but when the door swung open, it all looked just like she'd expected. Nothing in the entire place tracked the passage of the past ten, twenty, even thirty years. Not the bare lightbulbs hanging from the ceiling on dust-furzed cords, the round-bellied woodstove, the low bookshelf of Westerns and romances, the mismatched folding chairs, or the pool table with a long, dry rip in the green felt. The bar itself—cherrywood, intricately inlaid and filigreed, with a heavy lead-glass mirror reflecting all the clear and amber bottles—harked back even further, to the mythologized years before barbed wire, to saloons and cattle barons and cattle drives, a time when the land and the law were what you made them.

Gillian strode across the raw boards of the floor and took a stool right in front of the mirror, right in the middle of the bar. The two men already there, the pickup drivers, were either laconic or cowed. They stared down the necks of their beer bottles as if they might discover something they didn't know in the sudsy depths, then tipped the bottles slowly to their lips. The bartender—one of those bony, hard-living women who looked sixty-five but was likely thirty-eight, all squint and sunburn and cigarette—fumbled a bit with Gillian's cocktail, but in the end delivered something that resembled a vodka tonic. Gillian ventured a sip—her first drink in six days, since last Thursday—and it was fizzy and sharp, the rim salted like she'd asked. On the far side of the bar, nearer the two men, a blow-up sheep was stuffed behind a two-gallon jar of pickled eggs. On the other side, above the pool table, hung a massive elk-head mount with a cigarette stuck in its dead, velvet lips. She almost laughed out loud, almost choked on her drink. It was too much. Like some ridiculous country-music video.

Kent threw open the door, stamped his feet.

—Jesus, I thought I'd never get out of there. I need something stiff. Barkeep, get me a Jack and Coke! Make it a double!

Had she ever actually heard someone use the word *barkeep*? Or say *Make it a double*? He's performing, she thought. She didn't mind.

Now Kent draped his booster jacket over an empty stool and got out his wallet, set a twenty-dollar bill on the bar, tapped it with his finger as he again addressed the bartender.

—Let me know when we've drunk that up. I've got another one spends just the same.

Gillian laughed and shook her head, and Kent grinned in turn.

—I'm surprised to see you so rambunctious, she told him.

—Meetings like that will make anyone a little rambunctious. Jesus. You'd think their boys were playing for the Denver Broncos and not the Colter Cougars. Anyway, here we are, cheers.

They clinked glasses, drank. Gillian licked at the salt on her lips, ran her hand across the dark polished wood of the bar top. This was nice. It was.

—You know, I'm really enjoying my time with the enrichment kids.

Kent, assuming sarcasm, apologized and said that just as soon as the school board approved it, they would advertise for a full-time special-ed teacher.

Gillian laughed, touched his shoulder. No, really, she meant it. He was right. She had no idea how much she'd missed the classroom the past few years. It was good to be reminded of why she'd started doing this in the first place.

—You might want to try it, she said. If nothing else, it's a little less time stuck in meetings.

—Well, when you put it that way. Here's to less time stuck in meetings!

They clinked glasses again and drank. With their second drink, they ordered steaks and moved to a table in the back. In ones and twos men filtered in. A group of women came in and scooted some tables together. They ordered wine coolers and fried appetizers and loaded the jukebox up with pop country songs. Miss Kanta, the school secretary, was right in the middle of them. She winked at Gillian. Gillian waved back. She knew she'd hear about this tomorrow, but that was fine. She could handle it.

Kent leaned in and told her his ex-wife had offered to sell him back their old house, which seemed both hilarious and sad, though what was perhaps more hilarious and sad was that he was seriously thinking of taking her up on the offer. Gillian commiserated, then told him Maddy had maybe finally hit her rebellious phase, that she'd been hanging out with this college friend of hers till all hours of the night. Kent laughed. This was the 4.0 girl they were talking about? Right. Rebellious. She studied too hard as it was. Kent's youngest daughter was still in Portland, he said, still trying to break into the theater scene, which he admired—her persistence and tenacity. His oldest had gone back to school for a master's degree in engineering at Washington State. And his middle daughter and her husband were expecting their first any day now. He wasn't sure he was quite ready to be a grandpa, but he'd already bought tickets to Denver for the holidays.

—Oh! Here we go, he said as their steaks were placed before them. Now, I solemnly swear to you, Gillian Houlton, there is nothing in all of Billings, even Seattle and San Francisco, that matches Prime Rib Wednesday at the Grand in Colter, Montana—I mean, look at this!

Gillian inspected what had been set before her: a massive steak, a foil-wrapped baked potato, a bowl of shredded lettuce slathered in ranch dressing. She picked up her fork and the gleaming, black-handled steak knife.

—Well, I'll give it a shot.

In the months after Kevin's death she'd slept with a succession of men. She found the first few of them just days after she'd fled to Billings, in bars downtown, late at night. The last couple in hard joints on the south side of Montana Avenue, where she had begun ending up after the other, more respectable bars closed for the night. Not a one of the men was someone she would've wanted to spend time with in the clean light of day. She wouldn't even bring them in the house until she'd paid the sitter, a girl down the block, and sent her home. So what was it about? She wasn't sure until Maddy, seven, wearing pink, long-sleeved pajamas, woke her one noon asking for cereal, asking who that was beside her. Gillian rolled over to find in her bed a hatchet-faced, ponytailed man with cigarette burns studding his upturned arms. That's when she knew. It was about oblivion, the swirling pain we embrace hoping to eclipse the greater, harder pain of loss.

Things hadn't always been perfect with Kevin. They'd struggled those first years in eastern Montana. But as Maddy grew out of her colic and as they were reminded again and again that the place they'd made their home didn't have much room for people like them—liberal, college-educated, not particularly interested in high-school sports or religion—they turned, as they had often done while living here and there across the country, ever more toward each other. They both still went to work, of course, while Elner looked after Maddy, but when they came home, they stayed home. They gathered wild asparagus along the river in the spring. They broke more than an acre of ground out back of the house for a garden, where they grew tomatoes and peppers and sweet corn. In the fall they picked chokecherries. The cellar brimmed with mason jars of chunky, basil-studded tomato sauce and smooth, tart chokecherry syrup.

Kevin taught her to hunt, and between the two of them the freezer filled with white-wrapped packages of elk chops and deer sausage. He built a sandbox for Maddy and hung a board swing in the cottonwood. He took his daughter's hand as they splashed through the river gathering purple and mother-of-pearl mussel shells. Gillian painted the study a sage green, the front room terra-cotta. She wired speakers through the house so that wherever they were they could listen to Dylan, Charley Pride, Joni Mitchell. Of an evening, they ate simply and well—deer sausage and greens over grits with sliced tomatoes—and watched for blue herons and golden eagles rising from the river.

But that life was behind her now. That was the damnable part of it. When her daughter woke her that morning, Gillian hadn't sworn any oaths or made any promises. She'd gotten out of bed, lifted Maddy into her arms, locked herself in the bathroom, and waited for the man to leave. Sitting there on the edge of the tub, holding Maddy, she understood—clearly, starkly—that this wasn't the way to honor her grief. And that's when the real pain came. She had cried in the beginning, of course, but now, months on, the sobs brought her to her knees. He was gone, gone, gone.

The pain then was a dull saw working up through her, slicing tendons, splitting ribs, until the dry air hissed all through her. She'd get home from work, put Maddy to bed, and then give herself over to jags of ragged crying. She came to depend on it, to define herself by it—I grieve, she told herself. That's what I do and who I am.

For years there was no one, even when more reasonable suitors came along. Kent Leslie was one, and there were others—good, kind, sometimes even half-handsome men who could have loved her, whom she most likely, given time, could have found a way to love in return. But for a long time it was easy to say no. Easy as could be. She would turn forty-nine this year, and her knees hurt her after she ran, her hips were a little wider than she'd like them to be, but Kevin would always be thirty-seven, always sandy-haired and broad-shouldered, always slyer, kinder, quicker—as good as he ever was. And whenever she was with him in her mind—remembering Key West or Texas or a summer evening on the porch, the meadowlarks calling up and down the Musselshell—whenever she closed her eyes and let that staggering, welcome grief come washing over her once again, she, too, felt like her best, fiercest, most beautiful self.

She woke in the dark to the soft green light of an alarm clock, a slow drip somewhere echoing in the pipes. Kent, huge and warm, snored lightly beside her. She got up, slowly, carefully, so as not to wake him, and went into his kitchen. Found a glass and filled it from the tap. Out the window wind-drift snow swirled through a streetlight, though not much of it had stuck. A frozen rime here and there in the gravel, in the dead grass of the yard. She wanted to let whatever feelings might rise in her simply rise. So far—no shame, no regret. Some tenderness. And, if not happiness, at least a kind of contentment, a bit of warmth.

She rooted in her purse and found her phone. She'd left two voice mails for Maddy, both from the Grand. She'd texted as well when they got back to Kent's little rental house. She saw a new voice mail and was hoping—but it was Dave Coles. Couldn't Maddy reach out just this once? The old loneliness gusted through her. All these years without Kevin, raising her daughter alone. Why did she always have to be the one making sure, taking care, keeping them safe and together? Maddy was too old for it to still have to be this way.

The oven clock read 4:52 a.m. She could probably grab another forty minutes of sleep—but no. She'd drive home now to be there for Maddy, to make eggs and toast and orange juice, to touch base. She'd leave a note for Kent—see if maybe he wanted to have dinner at her place tomorrow. But for now, despite her annoyance with Maddy, she needed to get home.

All that day at school Gillian was distracted. When she had told Maddy about Kent, her daughter had smiled and said she was fine with it, was really happy for her. But then the girl ate only a bite of toast and a couple of forkfuls of scrambled eggs before rushing out. After the front door banged shut and Maddy's car turned over, in the silence that followed, Gillian studied the table she'd set—scrambled eggs with chives, buttered sourdough, orange juice, coffee, a bowl of just-washed grapes—and felt tired. The thinnest edge of anger knifed its way in. Lately she had to reach so far just to catch the most precarious hold of Maddy.

She also didn't want to think about the implications of the message from Dave Coles. Halting, cryptic, it had played in her head as she finished breakfast alone, as she drove to work, as she sat through the morning meeting about the possibility, due to state budget cuts, of moving to a four-day school week. He had found out some things about this kid, this Rowdy Burns, but he thought he should tell her in person. That's what Dave had said. *I ought to tell you in person.*

Now the fluorescent lights of the enrichment room whirred and snapped. Gillian straightened up from where she'd been bent over helping a group of kids work on graphs for the bug project and massaged the ache in her lower back. She had felt a headache coming on too. Then Rowdy caught her eye. He had scooted his chair out of the circle and was toying with something, holding it up to his eye and then zooming it out and back in. She asked him to put it away, which he did, or tried to. But he fumbled, and the object struck the linoleum with a tinny sound and rolled beneath the table. Annoyed, Gillian retrieved it. Some kind of medallion, silver, warm, a little sticky from the boy's hand—roughly the size of an old dollar coin. As the image on the medallion clarified and Gillian recognized first the outline of a wolf and then the crosshairs, she felt she might be sick.

The nausea crested and faded and in its place rose rage, flapping through her as if on black wings. That son of a bitch. Kent had known all about this boy. There was no way he couldn't have. The medallion in her fist, she turned and left the room. Each square of linoleum seemed to float in the dusty light, and yet her every step was hard and sure.

At the front office Miss Kanta spun her chair toward Gillian and grinned, no doubt ready to make some comment about the previous evening at the Grand, but Gillian strode past her and threw open the door to Kent's office, where he sat in the midst of a phone call.

—That boy, she said. The one who can't talk. You know something, don't you?

For a moment Kent's mouth hung half open, unmoving. Then he apologized to whoever was on the phone and asked Miss Kanta to get the door.

The interstate unrolled in a blur of concrete and cold, blue-white light. She'd stopped once, for wine at Albertsons, and sat now at her kitchen table, hands like quaking birds, and poured a glass. It wasn't the boy's fault. She was trying, at least, to remember that Rowdy had done nothing wrong. It was rural poverty, it was lack of education, it was fundamentalist religion and reactionary politics, it was the mountains themselves—and the family, the uncle, that Wendell Newman.

She remembered him from the few months she'd had him in seventh-grade earth science, before she'd left Delphia for good. Or anyway, she remembered the boy he had been—quiet, polite, often reading or day-dreaming. A memory of a newspaper picture flashed behind her eyes then, replacing this earlier, kinder vision—a lean, sharp, messy-haired boy wearing a T-shirt and patch-kneed jeans and staring out past the camera, out into the mountains.

It was the second anniversary of Kevin's death—his murder—that she was remembering. She had just picked up the *Billings Gazette,* like she did every morning, and there on the front page was Wendell Newman, wind-tousled and lonely, the story all about how they'd never found his father's remains. For half a moment she had felt a kind of sympathy, a certain kinship. Here was another child, like Maddy, without a father. His mother was a widow as well. But then she read on, in astonishment, as the article mentioned Kevin just once, saying only that he'd been killed, and the airy door in her heart slammed shut. All these years on, she could still hear it, like an actual physical happening: that whoosh and rattling bang. It didn't fucking matter that Wendell Newman had lost a father. It was already in him. She could tell even from the picture, from the mountain light on the line of his jaw, from the way he jammed his hands into his pockets.

She had known it then. She knew it now.

Wendell Newman was the heir of it all. He was even still living in that same godforsaken trailer. He'd made his choice. He was in league with Betts, was part of the same sick cycle, was poisoning Rowdy as he'd been poisoned himself—filling the poor boy with all kinds of racist, sexist, ultraconservative junk. Violent, truly murderous shit. He had to be stopped.

She drained her glass and refilled it. And Kent had known just where Rowdy was staying but had kept it from her. Had sat there behind his desk and nodded—just like he did with all those idiotic, irate parents—and said he'd done it for her, that he was thinking of her, that he hadn't wanted to upset her. Bullshit. She'd held up the medallion to him and told him about the connection with Betts. This was the seal of Betts's group of crazies, she said, and Wendell Newman must have given it to Rowdy. Tavin was only the beginning. There would be more trouble for all of them up ahead.

At least, she thought, Kent hadn't known this. After she told him, he sputtered, flapped his mouth like a fish. She didn't stay to talk it out, though, or wait for him to suggest how to deal with it. She knew how to deal with it.

She poured herself a third glass, poured and poured and was surprised to empty the bottle and see that the glass, an upside-down bell of bloodred wine now, held everything that was left. She got out her phone and looked up the number, called Child Protective Services. Told them about the boy, about the bruises on his wrist.

VERL

20?

How many days now running in the dark? I stop and reckon the sun in the sky and hours later reckon again and am yet not sure. I have eaten the last snickers bar though I don't remember when. Today gnashed only a little jerky. It tasted so good I held it a long time in my mouth to keep tasting it.

Later

I have found a great pile of bones. All kinds of bones. Coyote. Skunk. Horse. Some I don't know. Some wider than a man's big leg bones. Bones shot through with cactus and yellow grass and wild rose. I can't explain. They are not exactly white but the color of old light. A strange sight. A wonder.

Later

I will not stay here with these bones. I will keep on into the mountains.

WENDELL

They ran the cattle through the chutes, cutting the calves into the sale pen, the cows into the corrals. In the raw air of early morning the cows bawled for a time at being separated from their babies but eventually trotted off to the feeder and commenced to chewing the good alfalfa hay.

Wendell was working the cutting gate. Timmy Meredith, Glen's son-in-law, stood at the end of the chute with his lariat just in case Wendell accidentally cut a sale calf into the corral, which he wouldn't, though Glen liked to cover his bases, and Timmy, the former football and rodeo star, liked to stand around not really doing anything but swinging his lariat and showing off. Glen and the cattle buyer, Babe MacDonald, watched the action from just past the end of the chute. MacDonald's gut strained the pearl snaps of his shirt, and his nose and cheeks were spidered with broken red vessels. He had a boot on the lowest rung of the sale pen, his elbows resting up top, right near Glen's. They were near enough that Wendell could at times—over the bellows and stamps of the cattle, the hard thwack of the cutting gate—hear the two of them, their conversation rhythmic and practiced and full of silences, though they were never fully silent, always nodding or shifting or scratching or spitting. They talked Obama and swine flu and the best steak houses in Billings. They talked the wolf hunt up and down, and the recession, and just about everything under the low, gray sky except cattle buying. Yet

Wendell knew they were both taking careful stock as each calf bucked and shied into the sale pen. It was a kind of dance, and Glen was the man for it. Wendell would rather keep sharp on the cutting gate.

Freddie Benson had shown up today with his shirt tucked in and his hair buzzed short. For a long time he'd been telling everyone he was going to be a drummer in a heavy metal band, so that haircut surprised the hell out of Wendell. Freddie had come right up this morning and shook Glen's hand and then nodded to Wendell and Timmy. They'd laughed and clowned around, Wendell and Freddie, back in high school, and Wendell had expected Freddie would know he was the one who'd spoken up for him. Maybe he didn't, though. Maybe all that was just long enough ago. Wendell had nodded in return, reached once again for his back pocket, for the can of Copenhagen that wasn't there.

Now Freddie and Rowdy stalked the dusty, shit-spattered alleyway that circled the sale pen and narrowed into the cutting chute. Their job was to keep the herd tight, pointed forward, and not allow them to bolt or stampede. Wendell hadn't been sure it was the right thing to do, keeping Rowdy out of school, but it was a Friday and when he'd asked the boy about it this morning, Rowdy's eyes had gone wide, and he'd hurried to pull on his work jeans. What's more, he'd already proved himself a good hand. Tyler, Timmy's boy, had tired after twenty minutes and gone in to play his video games. Rowdy, though, had kept at the herding, despite the cold, despite the choking dust, the green fountains of shit, the bawling and walleyed slaver of the calves. Rowdy carried a ring of wire strung with old tin cans. Every now and again he gave it hard shake, and the cattle in the alley bunched up all the tighter. Wendell snapped the gate this way and that, separating the cows and calves as they streamed through, and above the din rattled the rusty music of the boy's tin cans.

They finished the cutting and turned the cows out, and there was more bawling, though it died away again as the cows found the thick grass in the near pastures. Now Glen readied the scale in the southwest corner of the sale corral, with Babe looking over his shoulder and making his own marks. The corral was a large round-cornered square, which meant there was no natural way to funnel the calves to the scale. By this time they were red-eyed and shifty, dirt ringing their lips and nostrils. The wind ratcheted up another notch, and dust and bits of straw swirled through the air. Wendell sent Rowdy to the left side of the pen and Freddie with his cattle prod around to the right, and he and Timmy walked up the middle, all four of them clapping in time and talking to the calves, massing the animals on the west side of the pen.

Timmy smacked his boot leather with the end of his lariat, and Rowdy jangled his wire ring of cans, and together they pushed the calves toward the scale. A first few piled in, their hooves loud and hollow on the boards of the scale floor, and when Wendell whistled through his teeth and clapped his hands, a dozen or more followed, and Glen slid the metal gate closed behind them. Wendell told Freddie, Timmy, and Rowdy to hold the rest of the calves where they were, and he came around wide and joined Glen at the scale to help count. With the calves piled in there nose to ass, it would be easy to miss some. Wendell took his count and waited as Glen and Babe finished theirs. The counts came out even—seventeen all around—and they took the weight and opened the other side of the scale and let the weighed calves bound out into the alleyway.

It took some time, counting and weighing bunch after bunch, and Wendell, as always, kept his eye on Rowdy. The boy held his ground, rattled his string of cans. On Wendell's other side, though, Timmy twirled his fancy lasso and sang snatches of some song. Glen pulled the scale gate back for another load, and they all *hey*ed and *hiya*ed, and just as Glen was about to slide the gate closed, three big winter-born Angus calves bolted between Freddie and Timmy. Timmy stood there wide-eyed, his lasso thunking in the dust. Freddie spun on his heel and tried to follow. Running hard, one of the calves crashed into the far side of the corral. Its skull cracked against the boards. In a whirl of dust, the other two turned sharp and charged back, heads down and swinging—aiming right at Rowdy.

Timmy and Glen shouted, Freddie stooped and chucked dry cowpie at the calves to try to turn them, and Wendell took off sprinting. Hearing the commotion, Rowdy turned, and turned again, and finally saw the calves. Just as fear broke across the boy's face, Wendell hooked him beneath his armpits and swung him out of the way.

The calves pounded past and a kicked hind hoof caught Wendell in the thigh. He fell to his knees with his arms still wrapped tight around Rowdy. They were still for a moment in the dust and shit, their two hearts banging each against the other, before Wendell relaxed and slid back onto his haunches. Set the boy's feet on the ground.

—You okay, bud? You all right?

Rowdy's hands were light and shivery at Wendell's shoulders but he looked him in the eye and nodded.

—Okay, then. I don't guess my leg's bleeding. I believe we're all right.

Wendell rose, touched the back of his thigh. No blood but he'd have a hell of a bruise.

The two loose calves had run hell-for-leather into the herd and broken it up. The calves were scattered all over the corral now, and Freddie and Timmy chased after them flapping their arms as if it might matter.

Glen came huffing up. He tousled Rowdy's hair, clapped Wendell on the shoulder. Rowdy breathed, and breathed again, and Wendell kept his hand on the boy's back, but light.

—Damn. If you boys was looking to wrestle, you could've picked some smaller calves. You all right?

Wendell said they were. Rowdy, for his part, swallowed and nodded.

—Would've hated to lose my two best hands this late in the game.

Glen motioned toward Timmy and Freddie, both still darting this way and that.

—Once you got your feet under you, what say you get these yahoos lined out again. We got more calves to weigh.

They worked straight through lunch and finished in the afternoon, just as the low ceiling of gray clouds thinned and broke and winter light rained down. They made the last count, summed the numbers, and opened the gates, then herded the calves the other way down the alley and up the loading dock and into Babe's big silver livestock trailer. Babe cut Glen a check, and Glen folded it and put it in his shirt pocket without even looking at it. Then the two men shook hands and it was done. As the trailer pulled away, Glen grinned and slapped his cowboy hat against his thigh and said it was time to eat.

Carol and Rochelle, Timmy's wife, had set up two folding tables in the yard and loaded them with platters of roast beef and mashed potatoes and green beans boiled with ham hocks, along with a couple of loaves of white bread and a dish of butter. The men lined up and filled their plates, and after they'd eaten, Glen hauled out a couple of coolers of pop and beer. They all hung around drinking and talking then, save Freddie, who left right after lunch, which again surprised Wendell, Freddie passing up free beer.

Wendell punched open a Budweiser and handed Rowdy a clear glass bottle of strawberry pop, which Rowdy turned around and around in his hands, marveling at its cold, dripping curves. Glen came over and slipped Wendell an extra fifty dollars on the sly, then made a big show of giving Rowdy a crisp new five-dollar bill. Rowdy took the bill and folded it and stuffed it in his shirt pocket, then stuck out his hand to shake, just like he'd seen Glen and Babe do. Glen laughed out loud. He told Rowdy he'd make a fine rancher someday and took the boy's hand and shook it good. Wendell leaned back in his lawn chair and smiled. He wasn't even that pissed at Timmy for his inattention. Things had turned out all right. Even with the hard, dirty snow earlier in the week, the light on this day— the second of October—was dime bright and nearly warm.

Wendell snagged a road beer for himself and another bottle of strawberry pop for Rowdy, and on the drive home the light was sharp and clear for miles, the mountains blue and dark and knotted as they'd ever been. Cool wind spilled in through the open windows. Wendell took it slow. It was nice to be driving the hills, sipping beer, talking now and again about something from the day to Rowdy, his boy. Wendell had been thinking that phrase more and more often—*He's my boy*. They pulled up out front of the trailer, and with neither of them wanting to go inside and clean up just yet, Wendell let down the LUV's tailgate, and they sat there swinging their legs and sipping their drinks. Wendell leaned back on his elbows, the better to reckon the sky. He tipped the Budweiser to his lips for the last swallow and stowed the empty in the five-gallon bucket of cans and bottles behind the wheel well, then lay down in the truck bed and laced his fingers behind his head.

—It's a sight. A pure sight.

Rowdy scooted up into the bed and lay down so he was shoulder to shoulder with Wendell. Looking over to see how it was done, he laced his fingers behind his head like his uncle, and he, too, commenced staring at the sky. The high, horsetail clouds.

They lay there like that a long time, with the steel ridges of the truck bed cold and hard beneath their bones, the tatting of cloud and light brilliant above them, and all about the sounds of the dry washes and yellow hills, the mountains nigh on winter—susurrus of wind and sere grass, tick of dry needles, hacks and warbles of magpies and larks. They might've even slept for a time. Wendell wasn't sure. Some span of minutes later he opened his eyes to find the sky, of course, and the light, and his boy, Rowdy, right beside him.

He leaned up on one elbow, put his hand on the boy's chest.

—I wonder if we ought to have a fire. What d'you say? That girl's coming out again today. Maddy. The one who brought you the penguin book. Once it starts getting dark, it'll be cold, and I was thinking it might be nice to have a fire.

Rowdy blinked and sat up. Then hopped down from the truck bed.

Wendell sat all the way up just in time to see the boy disappearing into the near woods, gathering sticks as he went.

—I guess that's a yes.

He smiled and stretched and got down himself. From the shed he fished out the lawn chairs and opened them up around the fire ring, then rolled a stump over, figuring Rowdy would like that better than a chair. There'd been a woodstove in his grandfather's house, though it hadn't ever been used as far back as Wendell could remember, and there was still half a cord or better of cedar and pine stacked on the porch, near where Wendell kept the bones he'd scrounged as a boy. He hauled over a couple of armfuls of wood, the logs light and dry, absent the blue stains and squiggling trails beetles cut into the wood. Everything you'd fell now would be stained and chewed, and there were more beetles every sum-mer, it seemed, and they started chewing earlier in the spring and stayed longer into the fall. From any Bull Mountain ridge these days you could see forests shot through with orange-needled, beetle-killed pines. In a strong wind you could hear them shatter, like a dry sneeze. How old was this good wood in his arms? And who had cut it? And where in the mountains had it come from? How grand all those years ago were the trees as they stood on the ridges? Wendell dropped the load and brushed the wood dust and bark from his chest and arms. He thought for a mo-ment of the lines he'd had at the end of the play as Macbeth's messenger, long after Banquo has been killed: *As I did stand my watch upon the hill, / I looked toward Birnam, and anon, methought, / The wood began to move.* It was moving now. Falling down around them.

Wendell knelt to stack the haphazard pile. Hearing something behind him, he looked over his shoulder, expecting to see Rowdy. Instead, a long cloud of dust rose from the road. There she is, he thought, and smiled. He made for the trailer, where he washed his hands and face and neck and changed into a nicer pair of jeans and a clean shirt. He'd have liked to shower, but a clean shirt would have to do. Although the back of his leg was tight where he'd been kicked, the rest of him felt light and strong. Jittery but good. Air funneled in and out of his lungs. He pushed open the trailer door.

And there was Maddy, all right, standing in the space between her car

and the open driver-side door, her hair as long and dark as he'd remembered. The sky spread an ocean of light above, and the wind carried notes
of salt sage and pine. What confused him, though, was that Maddy had
her back to him and was watching two pickups—a diesel and an S-10—
pull in right behind her.

VERL

21?

Not even that much below freezing. And still so cold. Goddamn. How I would like a fire. I cannot have a fire. They are after me. Here is what I do. I dig down as deep as I can which is not too deep for soon there are roots and rocks but no matter I burrow in there like an old bear and heap sand and leaves and needles over me. It helps. Some. The rocks are hard beneath me and give me back some portion of my heat. I only wish against the wind. The trees in this dry country are scrawny as mutt dogs and the night wind scrapes along the top of me like a dull knife down my bones.

   I am sorry to go on like this. I should not complain. It is my own god-damn doing. I should have brung more clothes. More food. Should not have shot that deer. Should not have done so many things.

   I took this wolf tooth like it mattered.

Later

I think now we would get along. The wolf and me. It would be nice to hear her howl at a fat moon when I too am holed up beneath the moon. My belly howling.

Later

Her tooth at my throat. The lengths of her claws.

GILLIAN

She dreamed that night they were in Texas hiking the Chisos, she and Kevin, the south-rim trail, moving from high desert ever higher into subalpine forest and from there into alpine meadow, until they arrived at the rim, with a view a hundred miles or more south across the badlands of Mexico. When they could, they hiked side by side, holding hands, touching shoulders. Other times he took the lead. Or she did. They both knew the way, both loved this trail in the Big Bend, the many delights and surprises of the red desert land.

Though, as happens in dreams, the familiar route became ever more sinuous, dark, twisted. Suddenly she was on her knees, crawling through juniper and desert willow. They needed to fill their canteens and she was sure this was the way to the creek. But when they got there, the creek was dry, a chalky track of dirt and gravel, and the boy, Rowdy Burns, was sitting there in the gravel. The only thing to do was pick him up. He didn't weigh a thing. In fact she felt lighter as she hiked back up the trail, as if with the boy in her arms she might leap off from any rocky promontory and fly.

We've got to help him, she said.

Kevin shook his head. His jaw was gone where it had been shot off.

Oh, Kevin, she said, *I forgot. I'm sorry. Here, I'll put him down right here. Someone will come along.*

Kevin shrugged and buckled. She reached for him just as he collapsed and disintegrated in the wind. The silty ash of him spilled through her fingers. She rubbed the dust of him across her face, ground it down into her eyes. Now she didn't know where Rowdy had gone. Hiking back the way they'd come, down the rim, she could see farther than she'd ever seen, for miles, right through spars and washes, right into the hearts of red-tailed deer and lizards, and she saw now someone hiking with Rowdy, reaching out to take his hand. Someone tall, willowy.

Maddy. It was Maddy.

Maddy!

Gillian woke soaked in sweat, her heart a blood-hammer, every mad, frantic heartbeat banging the gong of her head. She stumbled to the bathroom, popped three aspirin, and drank a glass of water. She leaned on the sink, breathed, trembled. Drank more water. Dust swam in the low light of the frosted window, the motes turning loop-the-loops and figure eights.

In the kitchen, on the counter, there was a note from Maddy: *Pizza tonight with the charity-drive organizers. I'll be late. Maybe ten or eleven? Love you, M.*

She must have passed out before Maddy came home last night—thank God she'd had the sense to make it to her bedroom—and had missed her daughter this morning as well. She hadn't really seen her in days now. And what day was it? Gillian grabbed at Maddy's phone, forgotten atop the microwave, and clicked it to life: Friday, October 2, 11:17 a.m. A hot wave of shame rolled through her. She remembered swaying in the kitchen, the wine long gone, Maddy still not home, and reaching for the handle of vodka in the pantry, taking a pull straight from the plastic bottle. White stars exploding in her skull.

For a time she simply wandered the house in her flannels, feeling terrible. She thought to call in sick but it was too late for that. Kent might cover for her. She sat at her computer and the glare of the screen spiked through her eyes and sent shards of pain arcing through her skull. She breathed high and hard, but there was only pain, and more pain, and shame. She would simply have to face it.

She opened her eyes and typed in the names. She couldn't find anything on Rowdy Burns. The only stories that mentioned Wendell Newman were six and seven years old, all about high-school basketball—*Tiny Delphia Poised to Make a Deep Run at State*—though she couldn't find anything about Delphia actually making State, which pleased her at first, then saddened her. There were more than a hundred schools in Montana's Class C, the designation for the smallest high schools, most often rural and remote. Of those, not many were smaller than Delphia, which in most years had only twenty or twenty-five students in the entire high school. If they had made State, if tiny Delphia had won a game or two, Gillian could have reveled all the more in the ridiculous unfairness of such luck blessing Wendell Newman, reveled in her own sense of the moral imbalance of the world, the way she'd felt at once crushed but giddy by the absurdity of George W. Bush mentioning clean coal or claiming they were winning in Iraq. She stared at the current headline of the *Billings Gazette*. Some county commissioner was suing the Obama administration over environmental regulations.

Gillian heaved herself up. She needed a glass of water. She drank it down—the water cool and good going down her throat, cold in her belly—and filled the glass again. She saw out the window above the kitchen sink the neighbor's tiny dog sitting smack-dab in the middle of her backyard, staring right at her, shivering with small-dog fury. She hated that animal. She took a long drink of water and turned from the window, and the dog—Bitsy, that was its name—exploded in a series of choking barks, each high yap lancing Gillian's skull.

She sat at her computer again. He had been taken from her by meanness and ignorance and idiocy, and there was nothing that would ever change that. But still she felt she owed her allegiance to the better world, even if it meant she had to sorrow and rage over the actual one. She

searched again, this time just for *Newman* and *Montana*. A few militia sites
came up, all referencing the father, the murderer, Verl. Gillian scrolled past
these—she knew that story through and through—and clicked on something about a Lacy Newman, who had been sentenced a couple of weeks
ago, here in Billings, for drug possession and child neglect and endangerment. There was a picture alongside the story—a skinny woman in a
jumpsuit in the foreground, head hung, dirty blond hair covering half her
face, and to the back right, in the grainy, pixelated shadows of the court-
room, a clean-shaven, lean-looking man. He was staring at the girl, his gray
felt cowboy hat in his hands.

Wendell Newman.

She went for a run, forced herself to turn up the road that led to the
trails below the Rimrocks. Her breath came hard. Her heart juddered
and shook. Liquor and sour wine burned from her pores. Not even slowing, she leaped from the sidewalk onto the dusty trail, made it over the
first hill, then stopped, put her hands on her knees, and retched. Nothing but bile, water, and the chalk of aspirin, all of it dripping down the
blue-gray leaves and woody stems of a sagebrush. She felt better after
that and ran nearly four miles, all the way to Shiloh Road. Her headache
was gone, and her heart, despite the run, had somehow slowed. She'd be
ready for her Saturday run with Maddy, she thought, walking back, her
fingers laced behind her head. Ready for her run with her daughter.

At the house she ate a piece of wheat toast with peanut butter, then
drank another glass of water. She called Kent and got his voice mail. She
told him she was upset about how he'd handled the situation with Rowdy
but apologized for missing work. All of this had been really sudden, she
said, and had sent her to some places she hadn't been in a while. She
needed to get herself together, but she would be back on Monday.

She poured herself some orange juice and drank it down, then found
herself, giving in, making her way upstairs and stepping into her closet
and unlatching the small wooden door that led to the attic. Up the ladder

she went, and with a hand on the ceiling for support, she stepped down onto the joists as the warm, mousy air enveloped her. She moved a box or two, a blue plastic bin full of Maddy's old toys, and there they were—Kevin's rifles, wrapped in garbage sacks.

Downstairs, she laid them out on her bed and unwrapped them. He'd always taken good care of his things—a trait left over from his days on the ranch, where, he always said, you had to make do with what you had—and his guns were yet beautiful, the wood gleaming, the steel slick and blue-dark. She hefted the smallest, a .22, set it against her shoulder, as he'd taught her, and stared down the length of the barrel and out the window, tracking the path of a yellow maple leaf skittering down the street. She picked up the biggest rifle, the 30.06, an elk-hunting rifle. She'd fired this one before as well. He'd started her out hunting deer, but the winter Maddy was three, they had gone out together for elk in the Bulls, on Glen Hougen's land. They walked most of a day and saw nothing. Then late in the afternoon they came across four elk cows grazing in the long, sunset light. Kevin let her have the first shot—a good shot, just under a hundred yards, with the elk stepping slowly, grazing—and she nailed a big cow. As they stood above the animal, Kevin smiled and offered her a tug off his flask. The whiskey boiled down through her, and as the sky went seven shades of red, they knelt and gutted the elk. Afterward she waited there with her kill as Kevin hiked back for the truck. The elk's hollow belly steamed in the cold air, and wind rivered the dead grass. The sky blackened. She waited a long time, but at last there was the sound of the engine, and the headlights bobbed in the night, and she knew Kevin was coming for her.

Gillian drew a bead now on Bitsy, who sat in rigid concentration at the fence, just waiting for someone to walk by. She pulled the trigger. A sharp, dry click.

She showered and crawled into bed naked and napped and didn't dream or even shift in her sleep, the rifles dark and still beside her. She woke feeling truly rested for the first time in days. It was nearly five p.m. She could make a nice meal for herself and Maddy, who should be home anytime. She tossed a few of her last garden tomatoes, tart golden cherries, into a pan with olive oil and garlic and a few slivers of sage. She boiled linguine and stirred in the mixture, along with a little of the salty pasta water, then stir-fried it all in the cast-iron. It wasn't until she plated it, and made a salad of arugula and balsamic reduction to accompany it, that she remembered Maddy wouldn't be home for dinner.

After dumping one of the plates into a Tupperware and putting it in the fridge, she took her own and a glass of water—there wasn't any wine in the house, thankfully—to the back deck, where she sat in the evening shade. For company she turned on the outside speakers, *All Things Considered* on Yellowstone Public Radio. More on Obama's health-care plan, the continued violence in Iraq, even a mention of the wolf hunt, the first of its kind in the nation, coming up in Montana.

An iridescent-throated hummingbird darted and hovered at the feeder. She couldn't remember the last time she'd filled it, which meant that Maddy, despite how busy she was at school, must have gone to the trouble of boiling water and sugar and refilling the feeder. Maddy had always loved birds, long before the fabled science project at Two Moon. Even when she was little she would point and exclaim at magpies and red-winged blackbirds but go silent whenever falcons and eagles circled high above in the white sky. Gillian twirled pasta on her fork and thought about how diffident and scattered Maddy had been this past month— quiet and withdrawn, home late, always forgetting her phone. Maybe it was just a little senioritis or, as Kent had intimated, some late, deserved rebellion. Still, she needed to figure out some way to spend more time with her daughter. Maybe they could bike to Two Moon again or, better yet, get up into the Beartooths one of these weekends. Bring the binoculars and guidebooks. Do a little bird-watching.

The sun arced down, spangling the city, setting the mountains in the distance aflame, and minute by minute the air cooled. Gillian went in for a sweater. When she came back, the station had cut to local news. She finished her pasta and took a drink of water and something caught in her throat. She coughed. What had they just said?

Gillian coughed and coughed and spilled her water. What was this about a "developing situation" in Delphia, Montana? She stood, tried to scoot back her chair but knocked it over, and the hummingbird at the feeder buzzed into flight and zipped away.

VERL

23?

I wake in the dark and it is god-awful cold. I would get up and walk to warm myself but need sleep. I do not want to make mistakes. I say the sky is a bowl but that puts the bottom at the top. What is it like? The sky? The sickle moon a wolf's tooth. The cold stars not salt or sugar but torn holes. Wolf-torn holes.

WENDELL

THE PICKUPS IDLED FOR A TIME, THE CHUG-CHUG OF THE QUAD-CAB diesel and the high whine of the Chevy S-10, then the rumbling ceased, the doors to both swung open, and the men climbed out. The three in the S-10 held back, positioning themselves behind the wide-open doors. The other four set their hats and holsters and rifles to rights and came forward. Betts led the way. He wore black boots and camo pants, a green long-sleeved T-shirt, a brown vest, black sunglasses, and a camo ball cap. He didn't carry a rifle, though he had a black pistol holstered at his chest and a black-handled knife at his hip. As if leashed, Freddie Benson walked three short steps behind Betts, still wearing his work clothes, cow shit and dust at the knees and cuffs. Freddie carried a scarred, unpolished 30.30 with open sights, and Wendell, despite the circumstances, felt a kind of pity for him, a wish that he wouldn't stick out so. And he knew now why Freddie had skipped the beer this afternoon, why he hadn't even come over to shake Wendell's hand this morning. All those years ago, when they were rehearsing for *Macbeth*, Wendell had taken it upon himself to help Freddie remember his lines, and Freddie did remember once, but only in dress rehearsal, and only the once.

Daniel McCleary flanked Betts on one side. Town kid that he was, McCleary had likely never ridden a horse in his life, yet he was done up anyway in boots, jeans, and a snap shirt, with a black Stetson on his head and honest-to-God pearl-handled six-shooters on his hips. Toby Korenko, hatless and a head taller than any of them, stood back by the S-10, along with two men Wendell didn't recognize. Toby had finally lost the last few sections of his father's ranch, and just a year earlier he and Starla had moved into a trailer in Delphia, where he'd taken the janitor's job at the school, the same school he and Wendell had graduated from not so many years ago. Toby cradled an AR-15, and given his size—hands like plates, forearms as thick as pines—the gun resembled nothing so much as a child's toy.

It was such an out-of-place, ridiculous tableau that Wendell nearly laughed out loud. He was loose from the beer, happy for the light rushing down through the thin high clouds, happier yet that Maddy was here. And Betts, Freddie, Daniel, and Toby all struck him as downright silly—their seriousness, their staged movements and goofy getups.

But the laughter went to gravel in his mouth when he saw the fourth figure walking toward him, on Betts's other flank, unhurried, sure, serious as all the rest. It was Tricia Wilson's boy, the pudgy, round-shouldered one whose name Wendell couldn't remember. He held a black semiautomatic rifle with a pistol grip and threaded barrel.

Between Wendell and the men, still in the V of her open car door, Maddy had tangled her hands in the scarf at her throat. She turned from the men to Wendell. And back to the men. She'd likely never seen men like this. Likely never seen so many guns. Wendell thought to say something, to reassure her, but then caught himself. He scanned the near trees, the dry creek north of the house, the hills and draws to the south. Where was Rowdy? Where was his boy? He swallowed and touched his back pocket, looking again for the can of Copenhagen that wasn't there.

Betts stepped forward.

—How are you this evening, Wendell?

Wendell brought his hand away from his empty pocket. Looked at Maddy, then at Betts.

—I'm confused is what I am.

Betts smoothed his mustache, and the corners of his mouth turned up into a smirk.

—I hope I might clarify things, he said.

Wendell had been ready for Rowdy to rush down the hill, his arms loaded with wood. Ready to take Maddy's hand, to show her the long blue view from the ridge and the meadowlarks throwing their little heads back and singing up and down the dry creek, to lead her around to the firepit and touch a match to the slenderest sticks and step back, watch the flame and shadow play across her face, and Rowdy's, and to be warm and amazed. But now, beyond anything he had been ready for, anything he had ever wished or hoped or feared, this, whatever it was, had come to him. He cleared his throat, nodded to Betts.

—I'll stand here and listen but if by the time you finish, I'm still confused, what then?

—Then we leave.

—You leave?

—We've been wanting to talk with you, Wendell. That's all. Don't take us for something we're not. We're men who know right for right. I imagine by now you've heard of us. It was us that left the wolf medallion for you on your table when the door was open.

The wind turned in the trees. A fist of blackbirds lifted over the trailer and veered away.

—But I personally would be disappointed if you remained confused, Betts said. Your father meant a lot to me. I bet you didn't know that. I was in Oregon when I first heard about him. They were closing the mills left and right, and we were all of us out of work. Everyone I knew was in logging somehow or other. Either running a saw or driving a truck or working the mill.

Betts sniffed and crossed his arms over his chest.

—My father shot himself, he said. That's what my old man did after he was laid off, and then rehired, and then laid off again, and then had his truck repossessed, and really his whole goddamn life stolen out from under him. Stolen all for the sake of the spotted goddamn owl. But your old man didn't knuckle under. No, he refused to be a victim. He didn't shove the barrel up under his own chin. He shouldered and shot back, shot that goddamn game warden who should have known better. Your father's a hero, is what he is. We admire the hell out of him for what he did, and we hope Verl Newman's own son might also see his way to what's right. Might stand with us.

Like wind-driven rain the light slanted down, burnishing the rusted steel of pickups, the dirty shine of gravel, the ash-black barrels of rifles, and Wendell stood all the straighter against its wash, against the words he'd just heard. There was the man Betts spoke of: the fence cutter, the wolf killer, the murderer, the man who'd run with his rifle into the mountains a dozen years ago and disappeared forever. And there was the man who yet at times stepped from the shadowed edges of Wendell's memory: the joke teller, the belly-laugher, the mountain trapper who'd take a knee as if in prayer to pluck a spray of Indian paintbrush for Wendell's mother. Wendell had spent half his life fatherless now, and in his father's absence he'd never been forced to reconcile these two visions. In the broken landscapes of his heart he could cherish the father who had a sprig of flower tucked behind his ear and blame the other father for everything— for Lacy's taking off, for his own drunken fuckups, for his mother's slide into despair.

There had been the early hangers-on and cheerleaders, a few of them locals, a few of them jackbooted, wild-eyed out-of-towners, who showed up at the trailer to offer their services to his mother during the manhunt. And though over the years Wendell had continued to hear—toward last call at the Antlers an old farmer might spill a story, or at a potluck, someone might sidle up—about the cattlemen's associations, about red-faced politicians, about militia types who wanted to make a martyr of his father, wanted somehow to call what he had done heroic, Wendell had long ago shut himself away from all that. He could still remember a man whose yellow eyes were loose in his skull going on and on about what a hero his father was, how right and brave. Snow was coming down, and he and his mother knew by then that his father was truly gone, one way or another. Wendell, twelve years old, stood there in the screen door with his mother for a time. Then he went and got his .22, slammed a shell into the chamber, and sent the yellow-eyed man on his way.

The wind, the light, the trucks and guns. Wendell tried to speak, to unravel this sudden knot, but Maddy, at Betts's words, had jerked, a string in her gone taut, and made a sound that was strangled and low. She shook her head at Wendell, her face simply falling apart, and stumbled back into her car. She revved the engine and tried to back out, rocks kicking from beneath her tires. Betts, Freddie, and Daniel stepped aside, but the Wilson boy stayed right where he was. He wasn't even looking. He was pointing the other way, down the road.

—Brian, he said. Someone's coming.

Dust rose in long plumes from the road, and the light glinted on the windshield of a sedan, then on the silent but unmistakable reds-and-blues of a sheriff's SUV behind it.

Betts turned to Wendell, his mouth slack. He looked nothing so much as hurt, as if everyone should have known this wasn't the way it was supposed to go. Maddy cranked the wheel to get around the Wilson boy and tried again to back out, but Betts snapped his mouth shut so hard his teeth clicked and strode over and slammed the flat of his hand on the hood.

—Stop the fucking car! he yelled.

He unholstered his pistol, told his men to take positions, and they did, falling to their knees, leaning over truck beds, shouldering their rifles.

Wendell leaped down the cinder-block stairs of the stoop, ran to Maddy's car, and pulled open her door. She stared at him, something shattered and shattering in her eyes, something beyond any of this. He held out his hand. She didn't take it but got out of the car and dashed for the trailer with him.

They were nearly to the steps when Betts cocked his pistol behind them.

—Nope, Betts said. No fucking way. Come on back. That's right. Stay close.

Betts turned them around, made them sit in the dirt up against Maddy's car, and told them to stay hidden, down.

The light was in their eyes. Soon the rising edge of the trailer's shadow would swallow them, but for now they blinked and shied. Wendell could feel the hard bite of rubber at his back, the cooler, somehow softer press of steel. He reached for Maddy's hand. This time, she let him take it. She was shaking. So was he. He scanned the trees, then looked at Maddy, mouthed, *Rowdy,* and shook his head. Maddy caught her breath and her eyes cleared. She turned her face to the trailer, the trees.

The crunch of gravel, the squeak of dusty brakes, the slowing of engines, and the rustlings of Betts's men. Now a scratchy, amplified voice:

—This is Deputy Sheriff Ryan Bouchard out of Roundup. Please lower your weapons and identify yourselves.

A beat of silence. Not even crickets or magpies. The shadow from the trailer had risen to Wendell's jaw.

—I repeat: This is Deputy Sheriff Ryan Bouchard out of Roundup. The vehicle with me belongs to Anna Prentiss of Child Protective Services, also out of Roundup. We are here to see Wendell Newman about Rowdy Burns. We understand Mr. Newman to be the child's caretaker and need to speak with him. That is all we are here to do.

Wendell tried to stand. Betts jammed his pistol into Wendell's clavicle and hissed at him.

—Sit. This is my show.

Then, with the nose of his pistol still pinning Wendell to the ground, Betts spoke up.

—Well, Mr. Bouchard, this is right interesting. I believe we have ourselves a bit of a disagreement about how to proceed. You see, how a man raises up his boy, well, that's a sacred thing, and it ain't up to you or me or anybody but him. So I'll kindly ask you and Miss Anna there to turn around, take your leave of us. Your authority ain't recognized here, which means you are trespassing, and as friends of Mr. Newman's, we are acting within our constitutional rights in defending private property. We aim to—

The first shot came from nowhere but the sky, as if it were riding the wide river of red light washing west over the mountains and pines. Though in the next moment, as the shadow of the trailer slid all the way over Wendell's eyes, he alone could see that the second—*pewwhg!*—tore from the corner of the living-room window. The bullet-ripped screen gusted and then settled gently back into the metal frame.

Betts, still standing, gargled another word, indecipherable, and a cup of blood sloshed from his mouth.

And the day deepened into itself. Became a thing that scratched and growled and drew breath. A great muscled beast rising on its hind legs, lifting up to its full and terrible height, pulling into its lungs the setting sun, the low wind, the evening songs of birds. It breathed them all in, every one of them, like so much dust, and breathed back out.

Betts dropped his pistol, swam his hands through the air, and toppled, the ripe weight of his head smacking the hood of Maddy's car.

Freddie screamed. Wendell pulled Maddy toward the trailer. The speaker atop the sheriff's SUV crackled once.

And Betts's men opened fire.

VERL

24?

It is like dreams no matter if my eyes are open or closed. I do not know where I am. Cannot even for the sun or stars figure it. I tried not to but circled some and am here in this country of broken ridges and box canyons. Do I know this country? Sometimes it seems I know it. Sometimes I don't. Sleep is what I need. I will lie down and sleep here in this country that I cannot even for the whole of my life in this country reckon.

Later

Fuck it. None of this makes any goddamn sense. I do not need sleep. I will even now get up and go deeper into the mountains this is the best time to go. I am greasy haired and lean. I am lunging. This moonlight road into the mountains. The spine of the mountains now.

GILLIAN

...Musselshell County authorities...shots fired...possible hostage situation...

Some static in the air, in her. Gillian coughed, wiped at her eyes. Bumped the table and knocked her water glass to the patio stones, where it shattered.

...multiple vehicles...Musselshell County plate...Yellowstone County plate...Oregon plate...

She nearly ran through the sliding screen door. They hadn't given plate numbers but said one was Yellowstone County. She'd heard that clearly. And where was Maddy? Where had her daughter been all these weeks? Something burned down through her. It had happened before— that was the feeling. This had happened before. Of all the many turnings of the universal tumblers, she hoped it wasn't happening again.

She found Maddy's phone on the microwave and punched in the security code, opened her recent calls, scrolled. Christ. There it was. A Musselshell County prefix and the name *Wendell*. Ah, God. And the voices on the radio so calm.

...property of Wendell Newman...shots fired...situation yet unclear...

Gillian did what she was supposed to do. She called the police, then sat there and cried and when they arrived told them what she knew, handed them Maddy's phone and a couple of pictures. She waited on the sidewalk out front until the red eyes of their taillights blinked out between the houses, then went back in and gathered what she thought she might need. She stopped once on the way out of town, at the Walmart in the Heights, and bought shells for the .22 and the 30.06. She didn't know what she planned to do. But the rifles felt important. And the need to close the distance between her and her daughter.

The sun had set and in the blackening night she drove north toward the Bull Mountains. Highway 87 fell down the slope of the divide, a thin gray line narrowing into shadow. Deer haunted the bar ditches. The shiver of dun haunches, the oval lanterns of their eyes. In her headlights she'd seen already three loose piles of bone, meat, and hide, rusty sprays of dried blood on the roadside. This was just the hour for it, the day having surrendered and the first stars dimpling the night's blue bowl.

She hesitated for a moment, then punched the radio to life. She wasn't much more than thirty miles north of Billings, twenty miles into the Bulls, but already YPR fuzzed and snapped as it came in and out:

...the developing story...tiny Delphia, Montana...shots fired... hostage situation...

The newscaster's voice chirruped, whined, and slid back and forth into the exhortations of some late-night preacher:

By the blood...a dozen years ago...I bind you...Verl Newman...that you may not ever...months-long manhunt...be unbound...

She cut the radio off. Checked her phone. Kent had called three times, Dave Coles once. She turned her phone off and tossed it in the glove box. Listened instead for the clink of the shell boxes in the backseat. She let herself consider her call to CPS yesterday and almost had to pull over for the roil of nausea and shame coursing through her. If she had something to do with this—but she could take the thought no further than that.

She slowed coming into Roundup and for the cool air rolled down the windows. Pickups and SUVs were parked out front of all the downtown bars, grimy windows lit with neon—the Sportsman, the Keg, the

Occidental, the Hitching Post, the Arcade. Roundup was one of only two towns in the entire county—Delphia the other—and had barely a thousand people, but there were so many bars, so many people out at them on a Friday night. Who was yet at home? Who was yet taking care? Though if they were here, she thought, at least they weren't out there, in the mountains. She remembered stopping at the Sportsman a time or two with Kevin. They used to have a cook there, an old Bulgarian, who made a spicy chopped-pork-and-cabbage dish with roasted potatoes and a salad of cucumber, tomato, sweet onion, and white cheese. Outside of their own kitchen, it was the only interesting meal they could get for ninety miles, with most everywhere else serving tasteless chicken strips, freezer-burned steaks, and whatever else came off the Sysco truck. Now the Sportsman's door hung open like a dark tongue, and pop-country music pulsed from somewhere inside.

She drove on. Turned east onto Highway 12, where the outskirts of Roundup—the feed and video store, the retirement home, the derelict sawmill—gave way in a matter of seconds, as if swallowed in the closing jaws of the night. Now there was only the pure dark of the highway, the black river, the abstruse pines, the intricate and tortured-looking sandrocks of the mountains rising like sentinels or slumped judges. She was close now, but she knew, too, she hadn't gone nearly far enough. Maddy was out there somewhere, in the mountains that had taken her husband.

She drove by the abandoned train yard at Nine Mile, the Antlers bar, and the burned edifice of the old hotel at Gauge, and as she turned through the S-curves, the Musselshell River below moved in mirroring oxbows and hairpins, scouring the north flank of the Bulls. She dropped down onto the flats, where some farmer was still running his center pivot, the *pock, pock, pock* of its end nozzle irrigating, for the most part, the weeds and deer bones in the bar ditch. Was this where it had begun? In bygone notions and blind myths? The idiocy of watering the bar ditch? The vanity of irrigating this dry land at all? The land where the failures of the nation, the failures of myth, met the failures of men. Where history went to die. Where rivers brimful in April slicked to gravel by August. Where the grass was tough and thick before the plow and ever after dust lifted from the sour, alkali hardpan left in the plow's wake. A land of ravaging pine beetles, of ever longer summers and shorter, dryer winters. The land itself animated sorrow and anger, birthed and cradled and raised up failure and fear, a raw and righteous violence. Gillian heard again the radio—*shots fired*—and imagined her daughter's terrified face. She mashed her foot to the floor and sped toward the heart of this dark place, her own dark parcel of violence in the seat beside her.

The lights of Delphia conspired in the distance. Still on this side of town, near the rodeo grounds, Gillian braked hard, the speedometer falling from eighty-five, and turned south onto the Delphia-Colter Road. The gravel was always a surprise, and the car fishtailed as she was forced to slow that much more. Her headlights hollowed the night before her— washboard road, fences studded with tumbleweeds, black snarl of cottonwoods along the river. She knew roughly where the Newman place was, fifteen miles or so south. She hadn't ever been out there but had seen the road plenty of times, when she and Kevin went hiking or hunting or just out on a Sunday drive. Kevin would have been able to trace on her palm every back road, every little ribbon of dirt, every two-track and ATV trail. She might get lucky, might take whichever road she could find north or south of the Newman place and eventually make her way there. Surprise them. But what then? The shells rocked and clinked. The empty rifles silent, waiting. She wasn't sure. She knew only what had happened last time. Out here the usual rules didn't apply. What was good and kind could be gunned down. What was violent and vile could disappear forever into the mountains. And there was no way, no fucking way, they were going to take Maddy from her too.

Her headlights caught the rusty trusses of the one-lane bridge over the Musselshell, and she saw to her right the turnoff to the old house by the river. It was just where it had always been, though she hadn't seen it in twelve years, and this night the sight of it snagged at her heart—the leaning, gray gatepost, its top still whitewashed, and the weedy cattle guard below, the dirt road beyond disappearing into the chokecherries and cottonwoods.

Some bit of blood memory turned the wheel for her. Before she understood what she'd done, the tires were rattling over the cattle guard and bouncing in the ruts. She hadn't meant to, and for the narrowness of the road she wouldn't be able to turn the car around now until she got to the house. She cursed her stupidity. It would take that much longer to find Maddy. But there was nothing for it. She drove on.

Tall grass scraped against the underside of the car. Frogs and owls screamed. She had to stop twice to move cottonwood branches that had fallen into the road. The second was even bigger than the first, heavy and not yet hollowed with rot, and as she tried to lift the thick limb, a chunk of bark slipped beneath her grip. The wind-torn end of the branch raked her forearm and ribs, and a stinging pain rolled in waves across her belly and chest, up her arm and into her shoulder. When she touched the spot, her fingers came away tacky.

She closed her eyes and squatted down and hefted the log again, managed to get it off the road, then got back in her car. In the dome light, the right side of her blouse was torn and dark with blood. Jesus. What was she doing?

She pulled up outside the old house, vacant now, she was sure, and probably had been ever since she'd left, as there was simply no one hereabouts to rent it. The only light fell from faraway stars, and she made her way along the path through the weeds and dry grass. The porch stank of mice and piss. Scattered here and there were silver cans and cigarette butts, likely from some teenagers who'd been out here drinking and fucking. The door, of course, was unlocked, and given the absolute dark inside she might as well have had her eyes closed as she moved through the front room, down the hallway, and into the kitchen, where with a screech and a pop she yanked open the door to the small closet beneath the stairs, reached in, fumbled about a moment, and got ahold of, yes, a candle and a box of matches.

Her fingers wet and sticky, she broke the first two matches. The third flared and evened into flame. She lit the candle, and the dark of the house rolled back to reveal dust-heavy spiderwebs and peeling yellow paint. She cringed at her ragged, blood-sheened shirt, then lifted the candle into the closet. Everything was right where they'd left it, though covered in a decade's dust—a half dozen or so candles and another box of wooden matches, a flashlight, a hunting knife, a wool blanket, a jug of water, two tins of sardines in mustard, a box of saltines, a silver flask, and a small leather valise that held a rudimentary first-aid kit.

She'd left the house here along the river less than a week after the memorial service. It wasn't what anybody had said. It was what they hadn't said. No one, not even Elner or either of Kevin's sisters, had spoken a word against Verl Newman, who at the time was still out there, still on the run. As the days went on, Gillian got angrier and angrier. The silence of her co-workers and neighbors and—worst of all—Kevin's family was so loud, it was like a roaring in her brain, and her need for the roaring to be silenced by their words was as raw as the need for breath or water. But they said nothing, and she packed what she could fit in her car and she and Maddy left for Billings. That was the very last time, until today, that she'd driven these roads, though Maddy had been with her all those years ago. Maddy, just six, sitting in the backseat, confused and wide-eyed and asking every few miles where they were going.

Maddy.

Gillian remembered herself. She had to move. She dribbled wax on the counter and stuck the candle in the mess of it, waited until the cooled wax held it firm, then lit another and did the same. Her forearm was scratched but fine. The cuts along her ribs, though, were deep and wouldn't stop bleeding. With materials from the first-aid kit she cleaned the wounds and tore open a package of gauze and held it hard against herself, hoping the pressure would help. Her ribs were slippery, and the gauze soaked through. She opened another sheet of gauze and made her way to the front room, lay down on her unhurt side on the old couch, in an attempt to elevate the wound—and like a small boat on a quick river, she drifted into sleep.

With a gasping breath she woke from dreams of drowning—water no matter which way she swam—and followed the flickering glow back into the kitchen, where the candles were merely wicks in pools of wax now. Christ. How long had she slept? She took a slug from the flask—bourbon. She took another. Pulled off her shirt and unclasped her bra, cleaned the wound again, covered it with fresh gauze, and wound the white tape tightly around herself. In an upstairs closet she found one of Kevin's park service shirts and pulled it on, his name as ever stitched on her heart. She walked back out to the car and hauled in the rifles and by candlelight loaded both at the kitchen table. Ought she to burn the house down? She decided against it. In the car she stowed the rifles, the bourbon, the crackers and sardines, the flashlight, and the first-aid kit, and after looking around the house to make sure she hadn't forgotten anything, she blew out the candles. A lake of blackness washed over her. By the blue-black at the windows she moved down the hallway. She stubbed a toe on something in the living room but righted herself and found the door.

God, the stars. The night had lifted and the sky was a shade of stone blue, lighter than the true dark of the house. The stars were softer now as well, no longer diamond points but a thousand-thousand small pools of white fire. She touched her breast, the embroidered thread of Kevin's name. He'd been wrong about some things, they both had, but he'd been right about the stars.

The night was still, the only sound the low patter of the river not more than a hundred yards away. She was nearly to the car when she heard it. For a time after, as she stood willow still, she couldn't be sure. But then in the great hush of the night, the voice came again, from the direction of the river. A voice she thought she knew.

VERL

I remember when me and Kevin were just little green-nutters and one day packed our wire snares and steel traps and made camp in the foothills above the river. We nicked our thumbs with our jackknives and held hands our blood on our hands and swore we'd never leave not for a million dollars. No we'd live on rabbit stew and dress in furs and live the good way the pioneers and mountain men and Indians and such lived. That night we ate tomato sandwiches his mother old Elner packed for us and fell asleep right there by the fire though of course we didn't stay. I don't remember how we got back home.

WENDELL

He took nothing but the .22, and then he and Maddy and Rowdy were out the back door of the trailer with their heads low as they ran through the dry weeds.

Behind them the roar of rifle fire gave way to a final, asynchronous volley of shots that cracked and zinged off into the trees. Rowdy tripped, fell. Wendell, not meaning to, dragged the boy a moment where he had him by his wrist and a scrape opened up below the boy's right eye. He lifted Rowdy into his arms, handed the .22 to Maddy, and they were off again along the lip of the junk coulee, their breath and steps hard and loud, no aim now but distance. Pine trees and a ridge were what he needed between them and Betts's men.

They ran the better part of a mile, and Wendell looked back only once or twice. Maddy was right there with him, the rifle at her chest. The hard earth was cold, dry, bone-rattling beneath their feet. The sun drowned itself behind the pines, and the night began to clamp down. Wendell cut into the mouth of a box canyon. At the steep back wall he finally slowed and picked his way along the crumbling sandrocks, a route he knew from time and time before. He scrambled up the final slope of the ridge, and only there, in the duff, among a tangle of pines and cedars, did he set Rowdy down. He held the boy's small shoulders a moment, their faces inches apart.

—You're okay, bud. You did good. You hang on, okay? We're gonna be fine.

Rowdy gave no response. The blood beneath his eye had blackened, smeared. His hands hung like dead fish at his sides. Wendell squeezed the boy's shoulders once more and took the rifle from Maddy. Leaning over a sandrock, he sighted down the barrel, studied as best he could, in the dark, the black grassy canyon and shadowed country they'd come through. Maddy leaned over the rock right beside him, her breath in his ear, the heaving of their lungs tuned to the same pitch and frequency. It would be easier if it was just him, Wendell thought. But he was glad of her beside him. And of Rowdy. Despite—no, *for*—the goddamn madness of what had just happened, he was glad he could reach out and touch the both of them.

—That Betts is dead, he said. That one doing the talking. I imagine the sheriff's deputy too. I don't think they'd shoot the woman. I don't think.

Wendell pulled the rifle back to his chest, thumbed the safety on.

—I expect they'll chase us. They might think I had something to do with the deputy showing up. They might think I shot Betts. I don't know. But it was either run or have them find Rowdy in the trailer and know what was what.

Maddy shivered beside Wendell, her shoulder just touching his. He wished he might put his hand there, on her shoulder, but rose and went over and checked on Rowdy instead. The boy stood there brushing at the dried blood on his cheek.

—I'm sorry you're mixed up in this, he said to Maddy. I don't even know what the hell this is myself, but I'm sorry.

The wind gusted, swirled along the ridgetop. Coyotes yipped off to the north, somewhere nearer the river. Maddy said nothing, just studied him, taking in every dark ridge and dry wash of his face.

Through the night they angled north and west. Given the shadows and the light of the stars, Wendell slipped now and again but managed each time to fall on his ass, keeping Rowdy safe in his arms. Maddy hadn't yet said a word, and he would have thought her in shock or too weak to talk save for the fact that she'd more than kept up, that she'd carried the rifle without complaint, and that she'd once reached out and steadied him as he fell, her thin arm sure around him.

They came to the crest of a hill, and on the other side a two-track road cut through the dark grass and greasewood of the plain below. Wendell paused, listened for what could be heard above the riptides of his breath and blood. Crickets, night birds, coyotes sparking the air with their cries. Then he led them down and across the plain.

The night wore on. And the miles. They stepped over cut fences, the slack wires coiled like shed skins in the grass. There were so many cut fences that Wendell figured Betts and the Wilson boy must have been at it for some time. They traveled on into the BLM land that mapped the heart of the Bulls, a land that had once belonged to the Crow, to the grizzly bears and buffalo. A land homesteaded less than a hundred years ago and abandoned not long after, a wilderness now of collapsed coal mines and yawing shacks, ghost towns not even old-timers could recall the names of, where the dry arteries of forsaken train lines bled into cactus and grass. A land leased and grazed and logged every so often but in large part empty, home to elk and antelope and mule deer, bobcat and cougar and coyote, and, for the past dozen years, a seldom-seen pack of wolves. A land beyond, traced at its edges by county roads but cut through its heart only by rutted, washed-out dirt tracks and faint horse trails.

They came slow and watchful. Wendell reckoned the way by memory, by story, by star. The night held them. The wind, the grass, the pines. He whispered to the boy of all the things they'd done, all the things they would yet do, of their lives together in the mountains. The coyotes were even now sniffing about their trapline, he told the boy. Somewhere a big bull elk bedded down in the tall grass was waiting, though he didn't know it, for them. He told the boy of the rich, grassy taste of elk, of the gray-orange softness of a coyote pelt. He told the boy about the planting season and the far-off harvest, about the calving season and the roundup, the known circle of the year in the mountains. Maybe they'd save up, the two of them, and buy a few head of cattle or sheep and raise them on grass, sell halves and quarters at the farmers' market there in Billings, like he'd heard was good business. They'd make enough to get ahead, to have new shoes and good winter coats and plenty of chicken noodle in the cupboards. He told the boy, too, about school and friends and reading and science experiments and all the good things to come. He told the boy what he knew of the world beyond, which wasn't much but was more than the boy knew, and in this fashion he slipped from memory to story and on into dream, until the edges between them crumbled in the dark. Then he narrated for the boy the tales of other voyages, other travelers, and for a time they could have been trekking through Middle Earth or following the Missouri across the unknown continent—their journey, like all such journeys, long, dark, and dangerous, full of will and happenstance.

Searching for a story to map the last black quarter of a mile, Wendell told, finally, the story of his own father, Verl Newman, the boy's great-uncle, who had taken off into the Bulls a dozen years ago and was never found, who for all anyone knew might yet be holed up fat and happy, living on deer steak and chokecherries, whose trail they might even now be following.

Deep in the night, atop a butte, in the lee of a half bowl of rock, Wendell swept up a bed of duff and dirt and laid the boy down and told him to sleep. He sat there and held the boy's hand for a time but eventually let go and stood and in the dark navigated the perimeter of the butte. There was nothing in the black distance, no movement anywhere that he could see or sense or in any way know.

He sat in the dirt, somewhat off from the boy so as not to wake him, and leaned up against a pine. Maddy, a shadow with a rifle, had stayed with Rowdy but came over to Wendell now.

—Do you believe anything you told him? she asked.

—I guess. I don't know. I was just talking.

—You're lying to him.

She sat on a low rock shelf a foot or two above him. From this vantage the stars were tangled in her hair.

—I don't know what you're getting at.

—Yes, you do.

He stood, though he didn't know where he was going and didn't take a step. Maddy stayed right where she was and went on.

—You're lying because whatever happens, it's not going to be the same and you know it. That man's dead. Even if they didn't see, like we did, someone could figure out who it was that killed him. It's not going to go back like it was. You and Rowdy living in the trailer. You and Rowdy together out here.

He sat back down, worked at his tired eyes with his finger and thumb. She was right. Maybe. But at least he could save Rowdy. He could bend the story the other way and say he was the one who'd shot Betts.

—That doesn't mean it's a lie, he told her. It was more like wishes, I guess. Like a dream.

Maddy leaned forward, starlight etching the curves and lines of her face.

—You might wish your father was out here in the mountains, she said. You might wish he weren't a murderer and tell the story that way, but then you're no better than those others. Those ones we're running from. Because that's what he was. He was a fucking murderer.

For a moment Wendell couldn't figure the glass in her voice or the way her face fell apart as she dropped it into her hands. But then, as if he'd been going sixty on a bad road and hit a rut that sent the steel frame bouncing and the pickup fishtailing, the full force of who Maddy was, who she had to be, came upon him, and his blood lifted, fell, slammed home.

—Oh Christ, he said. Jesus Christ. I never thought. I never thought at all.

He sputtered on for a time, waves of shame rolling through his gut. But then shocks of anger arced back up through him. He wasn't his father. This wasn't on him. He was just living out here, trying to make it. She was the one who'd called him, the one who'd driven all the way out here with her charity. Was it his fault she'd come into the mountains, even knowing what she might find?

—Why'd you come out here, then? If you knew?

She breathed and pulled her face from her hands, shivered as she leaned back into shadow.

—I didn't, really. Till tonight. I guess it never seemed real. I mean, my mom is always telling me stories about my dad, but those stories are about the two of them together, when they were young and traveling. She's trying to convince me of something, make me see him a certain way. She's told me about his death only once or twice, and just the facts. I can barely remember that time, and he's been dead so long it just seems like that's the way it's always been. Not like it could have been different. Not like, Jesus, someone *shot* him. Not like I could've ever had a dad.

Her voice broke, and she covered her face once more, and Wendell didn't know what to do. He didn't do anything. After a time, Maddy went on.

—My mom only talks about this place to say how he would come home from work and play with me and throw me in the air and how much he loved me. She never tells me what it was really like here. And he grew up here. I've got relatives here, a grandmother even. When I found out Jackie was from Delphia, I just sort of latched onto her. It felt like it was maybe a chance for me to finally know the place for myself. But then, well—then you were there at the bar that night. And then it was something else.

She paused, leaned forward again, looked right at him.

—I know it's the clothes, she said, the jeans and snap shirts, but even without them, if I didn't know you and you walked into Starbucks wearing whatever, I'd still know you weren't from Billings or just passing through on your way down the interstate. I'd know you were from here and nowhere else. It's the way you walk, like you're leaning up against a wind or something. How you hesitated when you stepped into the Antlers that night. You slowed and looked around, like you had to make sure of things. I was little, but I still remember how my dad used to do that. My mom would tease him, say he was casing the joint. It made me feel so bad when you got mad at me. Like my own dad was mad at me. Like I couldn't handle knowing something important about him and this place. That's why I called you. Why I came out. Maybe I'm like you. Maybe I was wishing too.

—And you never got my last name? You never thought to ask Jackie? You could've saved yourself a load of trouble.

—I didn't want anyone telling me anything anymore. I wanted to know for myself. And Wendell, I'm glad. I don't know any other way to say it. I wish we weren't here right now—fuck—but I'm glad I know you. And Rowdy.

He swallowed, tried to look at her. The stars were in her hair again.

—I knew your dad, Maddy. He and my dad—well, they went hunting now and again. I don't know that they were good friends or anything, but they were friendly. And I liked him. Your dad, I mean. He had a uniform and a green government pickup. He was a good talker, smart. He was someone I paid attention to as a kid. He was different. I liked him. Jesus, I'm sorry.

A scrim of cloud darkened the stars, though as the clouds thinned and disappeared, the Milky Way shone all the brighter, a river of white light.

Maddy stood and came over and sat down beside him, their shoulders touching, their hips.

—Thank you for that, Wendell.

Deep in the Bull Mountains, their hearts drifted and knocked about, and Wendell couldn't understand how they'd ever ended up out here, the two of them—no, the three of them. Not a father among them. Not a world unbroken. Each knowing the bone-deep emptiness.

Wendell stood and walked over to where Rowdy lay awake in his bed of pine needles and dry grass and picked the boy up and sat back down beside Maddy, who wiped her eyes with her shirtsleeve and reached for Rowdy as well. Together they held him, the three of them close enough that they cast a single shadow against the stars.

An hour later the night deepened, and Wendell woke to that stillness and sat up, his heart charging off in the dark. Maddy slept on. She was yet curled around the boy, as Wendell had been curled on the other side, the two commas of their bodies warming him. Rowdy shifted in his sleep for the new trickle of cold down one length of him. The silence was too much—Wendell rose to a crouch.

At the butte's edge he bellied himself down and studied the country to the east. A grassy, flat-bottomed plain flowing between more buttes and hills, the hills themselves cut with washes and the dark mouths of draws and canyons. There was nothing else to see. After a time he closed his eyes and simply listened.

When he finally heard it—the far-off slam of a pickup door, that metallic *whummpf* carrying through the windless air—he held himself still. He knew what he had to do. They were men moving angry and fast, men with guns. He couldn't carry the boy and outrun them. He couldn't. They'd have to split up. He made his way back. He gave himself only a moment, memorized them in his mind, the girl with her long dark hair and the boy with his hands knotted beneath the little stone of his chin, and he let himself dream a life of this—of honesty and forgiveness, of rest and touch—then knelt and woke them both.

With Rowdy wrapped in his arms, he told Maddy he'd lead Betts's men west and south, that she and Rowdy had to go north. Maddy took him in and closed her eyes and opened them, and he didn't know how it had ever happened that she was who she was, but he was thankful. She nodded and asked where, and he pointed north along the ridge, had her sight along his arm. He made sure she knew what was west, what was east, and to keep herself north, ever north. If she stayed true, he said, and kept the North Star in front of her, they'd likely be just west of the

Delphia-Colter Road when they came to the river, and then they'd be able to cross at a shallow rapids near an old abandoned farmhouse. That was Glen Hougen's property, and town would be only a few miles north and a dogleg east down the highway. He thought it might take four or five hours, all told. Less if Rowdy could walk some. There was a phone at the café. He told her to call who she needed to call, her mother or whoever, and then he would be grateful if she would call Glen. And she should ask at the café for the number to call her people. The Kincheloes. He knew them. They'd come. They'd keep her and Rowdy safe until her mother showed.

Wendell paused and hitched the boy up higher on his hip, wrapped his arms around him all the tighter. He told Maddy to tell them he had shot Betts—she couldn't waver on that, not even a little—and he told her not to let go of Rowdy for anything, not until she was sure. And talk to the boy, he said. Let him know they were safe, let him know what was happening.

Then Wendell held Rowdy in front of him, looked on his boy that way for a long time. The boy had slept, Wendell could tell, and perhaps he would be able to imagine the day past as a worrisome dream he could wake from. Maybe he could.

—All right, bud. I got a few things to do, but Maddy's going to take good care of you. You keep up. You know your way around these mountains now. You be a help to her.

He pressed the boy to his chest. How sleep-warm he was. How thin.

—Can I call you Rowdy Newman this once? Okay. All right. Good.

And he ran a hand through the boy's tangled hair, let his hand slide along the boy's cheek.

—I love you, Rowdy Newman. I do.

VERL

It is a season of wonders. I come to this high rock wall by moonlight and now by moonlight see two men carved into the stone. One has killed what looks to be a bear. He is the smaller of the two and the other is a long ways off but bigger. Behind them both there are the triangles of mountain peaks and between them nothing but a far space of rock. They were put on the stone together. Why so far apart? Why this stone? Was this where they killed the bear? This where they slept on their way home with packs of fatty meat? This where the bear killed one of them? Where the other came cowarding afterward with the screams in his ears? It is mystery and a wonder and it puts me in mind of how daddy my daddy used to steal things just little things a neighbor's shovel or a tank of gas when old Jake was asleep at the station. I would catch him at it now and again but never said a thing. One time your mother brought it up and that is the only time I put a hand to her popped her across the mouth and could feel her jaw-bone beneath the flat of my hand. ~~I need to tell you boy I feel it still. If I were to pick up a rock or stone out here and call it mine it would only fall back down when I die~~

GILLIAN

Branches slapped against her, scraped her arms and face. She took an awkward step and fell. Sticks and dirt and cheatgrass ground her palms, and the wound along her ribs ripped open once again beneath the gauze. She paid no attention to the smear of blood down her belly as she scrambled up and ran toward the river. Toward that voice. If the voice was but some conjuring, if the voice was but some crack in her furious, tired mind...

She broke through the willows, and beyond a gravel bar strewn with driftwood stood two figures, the one tall and lean, the other so small and slight as to be not so much a shadow as the intimation of a shadow. Shoes about their necks, pants rolled, the two held hands, the rippling water at their ankles and shins. They stared at her. The tall figure spoke, and it was the voice again—that voice that had carried itself to her through the silences of the night.

—Mom?

—Maddy! Maddy!

Gillian charged into the river, and in a moment had her daughter in her arms. She held her hard, kept asking again and again if she was okay, if she was all right. Maddy finally pushed her away and bent and picked up the boy, Rowdy Burns, and balanced him just so on her hip, as if he were her own, as if in the course of a night her

207

daughter had aged into a mother herself, into someone entirely away from Gillian.

—Why are you here, Mom? Where are we?

Beneath Gillian's feet the river gravel shifted. She wanted to tell the simple truth, to say, *I came for you,* to say, *We're here, where this all began.* But Gillian had no idea how any of this had happened, how the world would ever up and deliver such a thing. She'd never been farther from her daughter.

The boy's face was crusted on one side with dirt and dried blood. Maddy herself was as pale as river shells, her breath high and quick, a flame raging in her eyes.

—We're at the old house, Gillian said. Let's go. Let's get Rowdy cleaned up.

Maddy faltered, and Gillian reached out and took her elbow. Her daughter leaned into her, told her thank you, that she was so tired. Told her, with the fire in her eyes flaming once again, that they had to hurry.

—Wendell's still out there, she said. They're after him.

With no cell reception at the house, Gillian drove south down the county road—too fast, then too slow, then too fast again, as relief and terror washed over her in alternating waves. She bumped over the old iron bridge and up onto the first high pass into the Bulls, where she thought she might catch the cell towers across the mountains, and, yes, she had a single bar. She pulled the car over. But whom to call? What to say? How to make sense of her daughter, along with a mute boy, finding her way through the heart of the Bull Mountains in the night? Her daughter hiking ridges, fording rivers, some iron in the blood pulling her to her childhood home with the kin of her own father's killer in tow?

She glanced to her right to make sure, and it was no dream. There they were, Maddy and the boy, huddled up together in the passenger seat. Maddy had pulled the blanket up tight around him and opened a pack of saltines and by the green dashboard lights was trying to get Rowdy, who now had clean gauze taped to his just-washed face, to drink a little water.

Gillian dialed 911 first, but the call didn't go well. The dispatcher couldn't understand, and it was too hard to explain. She hung up and called Dave Coles.

When he answered, groggy, sniffing, she launched into it without preamble: Wendell Newman was on the run from a militia group out in the Bulls. Maddy and Rowdy Burns had been with Wendell after the three of them had escaped from his trailer, but he'd sent them off to safety and gotten Betts's men to follow him.

There was a pause.

—Oh, boy, Dave said. Oh, gosh. What else? Tell me everything.

All she could say was that Maddy had told her there were at least six of them at Wendell's property, that they had all kinds of guns, and that they'd shot the sheriff's deputy to pieces. There'd been a woman from CPS, and Maddy wasn't sure what had happened to her after she and Wendell and the boy ran. Wendell had shot Betts. He'd had to—it was self-defense, Maddy said. And that's why Betts's men were after him.

Dave promised to do whatever he could to help. He'd call every cop he knew.

—But where will you be? he asked. You've got to get somewhere safe.

From the pass Gillian could see for miles. The valley of the Musselshell turned and snaked off to the north; the badlands and plains unraveled in the east; the mountains rose and fell and rose to the south and west, where the lights of Billings were but a rumor.

—I'm going to Colter. We'll be at Kent Leslie's place. The three of us.

The county road unwound between the hills, dropped and then lifted through coulees and washes. The world was blue-black at its heights, full blue at the pine-studded horizon. One last time, Gillian thought, for this dusty gravel dance from Delphia to Colter. This last time. Maddy held the boy on her lap as he slept, his head against her chest, his breath halting as he jerked and shivered through dreams. The two of them even smelled cold, like rocks and knives. When they passed the dirt road that led to the Newman place, silent swirls of red and blue branded the far-off ridges and trees. Gillian reached over and touched her daughter's knee. Maddy startled, but stared straight ahead as she spoke.

—I didn't know, Mom. I didn't know about Wendell. Who he was. Who his father was.

The road fell into a tight, dry creek, then rose abruptly and leveled across an alkali-stained stretch of flats. Despite the loose gravel, Gillian had the speedometer almost at sixty. Maddy knew now, Gillian thought, and what would she do with this knowledge? What had she done already?

—But he's good, Mom. I'm not in love with him or anything, if that's what you're thinking, but he's a good person. He is.

Gillian gripped the wheel hard, held at bay the questions, the anger. There would be a time for all that.

—Okay, honey. I hear you. I believe you.

The dawn came on at last. The Prius's headlights pale and weak, everything at this liminal hour shading to nickel and bone, yet even from some distance Gillian spotted the dark hulk in the bar ditch. A car, she thought. An upended car, tires in the air, nose tangled in the broken four-strand barbed-wire fence. They were maybe fifteen minutes from Colter. Maddy and Rowdy were both half asleep beside her. Gillian didn't want to slow but skidded to a stop anyway just past the wreck. Likely there was no one in there, but she should check. Maddy blinked and swallowed. Gillian touched her on the arm, told her to wait.

If anything, the air had chilled a notch further. No birds, no wind, nothing but the crunch of gravel beneath her feet. Twenty yards from the overturned car she came on the undone body of a deer, nothing more than a blood shawl along the ditch now. She walked on.

The car was an Impala, an older make. The trunk had come unlatched, and pink boxes of Mary Kay were strewn across the road. The car's nose was accordioned, the headlights, she saw as she circumnavigated the wreck, spattered with hair, blood, and viscera. The windshield had held in place but was pure snowy-white shatter. Gillian bent down. She hoped no one was in here, that it was an untowed days-old wreck. But when she peered in the broken driver-side window, a shadow shifted, repositioned. Oh no—oh Jesus.

—Can you hear me? she shouted. Are you okay?

She swept away glass and gravel, got down on her belly. From inside the wreck came the scrabbling of breath. She turned and yelled back toward her own car for Maddy to bring the flashlight from the backseat.

A car door opening and closing then, followed by the crunch of gravel, and Maddy was beside her, handing her the cool barrel of the flashlight. Gillian clicked it on.

The woman was wedged beneath the collapsed dash, thin lines of blood ribboning her face. The blue-black hair, the deep, wide eyes—it took Gillian a moment, but then it came to her. It was Tricia Wilson, Tricia lifting a hand crusted with dirt and blood to block the glare of the flashlight.

—Oh God, Tricia, don't move. Don't move.

Gillian handed the flashlight to Maddy and scooted forward. Her own belly flared with pain, but she managed to reach Tricia's hand. She squeezed. Tricia wept, wailed.

—Fuck, she called out. Fuck, fuck. He took Tavin. Him and all those fuckers. I told him not to. I told him . . .

Her voice gave way to scattering heaves and sobs and Gillian tried to quiet her. She twisted her head around to her daughter, standing there shivering in the blue dawn. She wanted to let go of this woman's hand, crawl back out, and drive away. Didn't she have an obligation to her own before this other? Tricia coughed and shook. Gillian held the woman's hand.

—The keys are in the car, Maddy. You should get cell service in another ten minutes or so. Call Dave Coles. His number is in the phone. Tell him we're maybe twelve miles north of Colter on the Delphia-Colter Road. Tell him Tricia Wilson hit a deer and is hurt bad. He'll know what to do. Then call Kent—his number's in there too—and go to his house. Wait for me there. Go.

Maddy left to do as she was told. Watching her jog down the cold wing of the gravel road, Gillian almost called her back. But she swallowed the words, swallowed all the old fears. She let her daughter go. Her daughter so tall as she disappeared down the road and drove away.

Gillian had read somewhere that it was good to keep talking to someone who had a head injury, so she asked question after question, but Tricia shifted by the minute in and out of consciousness. Gillian, too, began to drift. She woke once to the sage going rose, to hard swaths of light in the pines, and felt the gravel beneath her belly and the wet blood of her wound. She remembered and began to talk again to Tricia. She got no answer. She talked and drifted and talked, and the two of them, these women grieving men, chasing children, bled there together at the side of the road. Twice she heard what she thought might be a far-off engine but was only wind. At times it seemed to Gillian as though Tricia were her younger self and it was her own blood-slippery hand she held. Then there was a howl, long and drawn, rising from a nearby ridge. It was close enough that she felt the shape of it in her chest, sloping, bell-like, heavy. When it fell away she could feel it still. Though she'd never heard a wolf, she knew it was a wolf.

—They're really back, aren't they?

Tricia said nothing. Gillian squeezed her hand and told her to hang on. Hang on a little longer.

VERL

I look back at what I've written and don't remember when. When did I taste meat? Why this field of wind? What color are your mother's eyes? Was this the night I dreamed the wolf? The day after the night? I see a ridge or line of pines and hours later see the same again. I find a spring and am scared by my own boot tracks as I kneel to drink. I don't know I don't remember

WENDELL

TWICE IN THE EARLY HOURS HE HEARD HOWLS. ONCE, A RIFLE SHOT. HARD to tell how close. A ridge away? Three? He kept moving. From east to west the sky paled from iron to stone to the blue of certain lakes he'd seen as a boy, the few times they'd gone camping, the three of them, up in the Beartooth Mountains.

The three of them. He'd sent Maddy and Rowdy straight north, making sure Maddy knew to stick to the rocks, to the ridges, and he'd gone south, through a grassy valley and across an overgrown road, his trail as easy as could be to follow, boot prints right there in the dust and grass. Though after the howls and the gunshot, he, too, took to the rocks and turned to the west. They'd follow him. He would lead them away from Maddy and Rowdy, give them time to get to town, and then—then he wasn't sure. For now, there were the mountains. That was all.

It wasn't yet midday when he heard the helicopter. He fell flat on his belly, nearly knocked the wind out of himself. It came toward and over him, flattening the grass, snapping dead branches, lifting great clouds of dust, and continued north and east. As the sound receded, he lifted himself up and brushed at his shirt front and went on. It hadn't even slowed or circled. Maybe they didn't know he was out here. Maybe Betts's men had killed the deputy and the CPS woman. Or maybe they had the CPS woman hostage in the trailer. Likely they had split up before the sheriff

215

could find out how many of them there were, and a few were coming after him while a few held the CPS woman. That must be it, must be why the helicopter was headed fast in the direction of his property.

Walking, he thought for a time on the CPS woman. He wondered if it wasn't Carol Hougen who'd called, seeing as how he'd left Rowdy there and gotten so drunk that night. But that was two weeks ago. And it wasn't the way things were done around here. Could have been a teacher from Delphia, still having to do with Rowdy busting that boy's arm, or it could have been one from Colter, about something he didn't even know. He'd been sick about it, though—a heavy ache—ever since he'd heard *Child Protective Services* crackle from the deputy's speakers. He hadn't had a chance to explain to Maddy it was nothing. He told her now, in his mind, and hoped that maybe she knew already.

Wendell came down a steep, eroded coulee and passed a tangle of chokecherries as the hardpan gave way to grass. He slowed and stripped a handful of cherries the magpies hadn't yet gotten and as he walked on popped them one by one into his mouth. The small, almost black cherries were sweeter this late in the season but still mouth-puckering. He worked the thin layer of flesh off with his tongue and spit out the stone. Rowdy would like chokecherries, he thought. His mother used to make a chokecherry syrup you could drink straight from the jar. Had he ever cooked the boy pancakes? He didn't think so. Maybe Rowdy and Maddy would get some at the café, if they'd made town by now, which they should have. Maddy had likely been able to call 911, call her mother. They might still be waiting, though. He could picture them beneath the snapping white fluorescents, where the linoleum was always tracked with the dirt of men's passings, see them sitting at one of the sloped tables, Rowdy on Maddy's lap while he reached to arrange the little packets of sugar and powdered creamer, Maddy with her eyes on the door, waiting.

He hoped no one there would give her a hard time. There were some that might. More than a few. They'd whisper, cut their eyes, even ask her to leave if she wasn't about to order anything. But maybe Glen would drive in and buy the both of them pancakes and eggs and sit with them. Glen, he knew, wouldn't have wanted any part of what Betts had done out at his place. Likely Betts hadn't even told him or Glen would've tried to argue him out of it. Glen didn't have in him whatever those others did. Or maybe Maddy would call her father's mother, old Elner Kincheloe. She was sick these days, but she'd always gotten her way. Wendell knew no matter what she'd make sure Rowdy got plenty of syrup on his pancakes.

Wendell followed a game trail across a dry flat. Despite the cool of the day, the sun was hot and sharp on the back of his neck, the glare of it in his eyes. He found a snakeskin wound around a dead yucca. He plucked up the skin, which was nearly whole, still preserved even where it had lifted off the snake's eyes. Once, twice he touched the eye caps themselves, and the skin began to tear, fall to pieces in his hands. The dry rattle made a small sandy sound when he shook it.

He knew then what the difference was between him and the others— they thought they were owed something. Freddie, Toby, Daniel. Betts. His old man. Someone had told them they were owed something. He wasn't yet sure who, hadn't had time to think that through, but that's what they thought, that it wasn't fair. Wendell crushed the snakeskin in his fist. *We aren't owed a goddamn thing.* He'd known that all along, known it so deep in his bones that he hadn't ever thought it outright before, and now that he did, he understood that Maddy had been right. That story he'd been telling Rowdy was a lie, pure and simple. Verl Newman might be out here, but if he was, it wasn't as anything more than bird-picked bones. Betts, too, was dead. Wendell didn't know what was in store for himself, if his story of shooting Betts would be believed, but no matter how this turned out, Freddie, Daniel, and Toby would likely see prison time. And that Wilson boy—good God. What would become of a boy like that? It wasn't easy out here—that was sure enough true. It was always something, hail or drought or poor cattle prices. But it wasn't like it was all of a sudden hard. It wasn't the EPA or the BLM making it all of a sudden hard. It had always been hard. That's why the wolves were coming back. They were built for it. They didn't worry about what was owed to them. They lived how the land demanded. Wendell could see it now. The land itself had taken his father, had left him with this sad riddle of a story, one those others were reading the wrong way altogether.

He smelled the water first, that mineral sharpness in the air, and followed the thickening grass up a box canyon. The cool stone walls narrowed as he went, passing wild rose and chokecherry in the shadows, and beneath a slick face of sandrock he knelt before the spring.

He leaned the rifle up against the rock and put his lips to the muddy seep. The water was cool and gritty. He hadn't realized how thirsty he was. He drank and drank, and fell back. The muscles of his legs cramped as he sat in the grass and he rubbed at the bruise on his thigh, where the calf had kicked him. After a time he pooled water in his palm and rinsed his face. Scattered about in the soft earth were the tracks of elk and deer, the delicate, intricate markings of raccoon and skunk—and then the wide, long-clawed tracks of what he thought might well be a wolf.

He drank again and sat and rested. He studied the wolf track, looked up every now and again, up along the rims of the box canyon, half expecting to see yellow eyes staring down at him. For the howls this morning, for the damp press of this track, they must be close. Maybe he would finally see that wolf he and Lacy had hunted.

It was getting on in the afternoon, time to find a place to hole up for the night. He'd put some distance between him and Betts's men. Tomorrow he might make his way north, to the highway. Catch a ride into town, turn himself in, call Maddy to see about Rowdy. He drank one last time and stood, his knees cracking, his hamstring tight enough to tear. The little muscles beneath his eye twitched, went still, twitched again. He was tired way down to his bones. Just a little farther, he told himself. A little farther and he'd rest for the night. He took up the .22 and did his best to skirt the mud, to avoid leaving any tracks of his own. As he was leaping from rock to rock, the ball of his right foot touched a slick stone and he slipped. His weight got away from him and with a wet pop his ankle turned.

He fell hard, wild rose ripping at him as he rolled. The rifle banged against the ground, was wrenched from his grip, but his finger was yet hard against the trigger, and a bullet fired, its report ricocheting through the canyon.

He breathed dust, smoke, and sulfur. He was on his back, his right ankle a jailbreak of pain. He laced the fingers of both hands behind his knee and lifted the bad ankle into the air, where it pulsed in his boot, bright and hot. It was the same one he'd hurt in track, the one that had never healed right and had kept him off the all-state basketball team his senior year. Pain rivered up through him, circled his hips and ribs, pooled in his guts. He ground the back of his head into the hard earth and after the hurt rose and broke and washed again through him, he pushed himself up onto his elbows.

The .22 was a few feet away, lying there in the grass. Goddamn. If Betts's men were anywhere close, they'd have heard that shot. He grabbed at the rifle and army-crawled toward the canyon wall, where he leaned against the cool rocks, his ankle already drum-tight in his boot. He hauled himself up, one hand on the rocks, and hobbled to the mouth of the canyon.

It was not yet evening. Low, tin-colored clouds scudded by, darkening with shadows that had begun to pull and stretch west to east. A faint road cut the broad, grassy plain before him, and the badlands beyond were thick with pines and tortured, wind-warped rocks. The grass would hold a track, but there was nothing for it. He had to get to the rocks.

He tried to step with both feet, but each touch of his right foot on the ground sent hot tracers of pain arcing up through him. His heart banged away. Lines of cold sweat trickled down his back, his every trembling muscle. Halfway across, he doubled over and retched, the water he'd drunk coming up warm and sour. He was nearly certain the ankle was broken. He used the rifle then as a kind of crutch the rest of the way, despite the clear mark it made, and on the other side fell to his knees and scrambled up the rocky flank of the rising hill. No use hiding his tracks now. No use at all.

He made the top of the ridge only to find another, higher ridge, rocks heaped on rocks. The path ahead was labyrinthine, overlaid and confused by the lengthening shadows of cedars and jack pines. Crutching with the rifle, his free hand on the cold, gritty stone, he started up a crevasse. He bent himself through twisted paths and ducked overhanging bulges and leaned into impossible whorls of sandstone. After navigating a tight stand of cedars he came to a high saddle between the mountains, where he exhaled and took his bearings.

To the south the ridge fell away and the canyon wall was vertical for maybe forty feet before angling off in a field of scree and greasewood. To the north and west the badlands lifted and turned, a mess of jack pines and sandrock that resembled nothing so much as a heap of broken bowls and plates. Likely someone could come through it. No one would. Whoever was after him would come from the east, which meant all he could do now was put his back to a rock, lay the rifle across his lap, and wait. Hope the helicopter showed up before they did.

From pine to pine he limped on. He used the rifle to negotiate two downed trees, then made his way along a game trail that led around an outcropping of stone. There, where the trail turned west, he found what he was looking for—a small clearing and the low, dark yawn of a cave beneath the far rocks.

He crutched toward the cave. About its mouth lay a scatter of weather-pitted rib bones. Deer, he thought. Or elk. A winterkill, anyway, a thing long dead. His foot connected in the pine duff with something hard. He balanced on his good leg and worked at the thin soil with the barrel of the .22, his movements awkward, ungainly. When he struck it again, it clinked. He moved it through the dead needles, and its dimensions clarified.

It was a rifle.

The night came on. The clouds blackened and lifted and thinned to nothing. Then the nail holes of stars, the brittle, copper-smelling cold, the dark, hard wind.

Wendell had found his father's rifle. He had found his father's notebook. His father's bones.

Out in these mountains he'd come around a ridge and walked into another kind of life. One where the cacophonous hollers and shouts might fall into rhythm, where chaos and pain might signify and resolve, where things for once worked out. He wondered at the rotted wood of the rifle stock, the ashen barrel. He held his father's bones, as if to warm them. Like the snakeskin, the clinging scraps of cloth disintegrated with even the lightest touch, and the old, tough Carhartt dusted away. Lacking dirt enough to bury his father, he gathered the bones, piled them together in the back of the cave, then laid the rotting .270 across the top of them. With his ankle, with the coming night, it was as good as he could do. The off-white of the bones, the black barrel, the dark wood.

To see his own name there on the cover of the notebook, the first few pages of his own scratchings, penmanship exercises, a couple of sets of math problems, and then to turn a single sheet and behold his father's gone hand: the letters blocky, wide, definite. For the shock, the embarrassment of it, he nearly dropped the notebook. He gathered himself and turned the pages. The dry air and shelter of the cave had kept the notebook well—the paper yellow and brittle but the letters and words legible. He leaned up against the rocks, laid the .22 in the dirt beside him, and in the last light began to read. Page to page, day to day. Until he arrived at the final lines, his father's last words, which slanted off and faded as the night came on, as though rising in the dark to meet the stars.

They'd never talked, he and his father. He'd been only a boy, but still.

Later, his mother had maybe tried to talk with him a time or two, but he'd likely turned away. He'd learned too well the old rule that said it wasn't okay for a man to let himself be open like that. Which was of course what he'd gotten in all those books, what he'd been so hungry for—the chance to be completely open. Yet here, beyond death and the wildest wish, he was being given this moment with his father. These words had been meant for him all along, and he'd found them, and despite all the time and confusions and fears coursing beneath them, they were between him and his father now, a bridge of sorts, one end in the mountains, the other end in the mountains.

Now, in the dark, he said his boyhood lines from *Macbeth* once more, said them aloud and timed them just so, to both ask and answer, as if he could be at once father and son.

—How goes the night, boy? The moon is down; I have not heard the clock.

The light of the stars was insufficient to the task. Wendell set himself to it anyway. He pulled the old blue pen from the spiral whorls of the notebook. It had been there since his father stowed it there, he thought, stowed it there and lay down to die. He clicked it to life and put it to the paper on the page after his father's last entry. It only scratched at first, tearing at the yellowed leaf. Soon enough, though, the ink stained the page.

It is October of 2009, he wrote. Then:

I am Wendell Newman, the son of Verl Newman, and like my father I am in the mountains. I have found my father in the mountains.

Also, I have shot Brian Betts and killed him with this .22 I have with me now.

I have sent Maddy Kincheloe—her father the man my own father murdered—I have sent her north toward Delphia and hope by now she is safe. She has Rowdy Burns, who is my little nephew, who I have been taking care of, who is like my own.

I have hurt my ankle pretty bad and am no good for running. I'll be waiting here. I hope for one of those helicopters to show tomorrow. Hope for it before those others show. I feel angry at and bad for those others. They are turned around about it all. My father was turned around about it all. You read this and you'll know. By the end, he saw it just the same.

I can't see what it is I'm writing. I hope it makes any sense.

The night is cold about me. The stars too. I am thinking now if it comes to it everything that is mine I give to my boy Rowdy Burns. Glen Hougen is a man I trust. Ask him, and he'll see it done. Rowdy, if ever you get this I want you to know you're a good listener, and a hard worker, and a fine boy for the woods. I love you. Your mother is having a hard spell but she loves you too. I know her. I know she does.

Maddy Kincheloe I want to thank for helping me here in the mountains. Maddy, I am goddamn sorry for the trouble. But I am glad of all things Rowdy is with you. I would have liked to talk some more with you. Maybe yet I will talk some more with you.

Goddamn. It has been a hard season. For me and so many. It seems there were times that were better. I don't know. I love those long hot harvest days. I love how they come every year. Every year, I guess, until they don't.

I sit here in the dark and am not sure what to write.

There's a lot yet for me to say. I don't know that anyone asked, but I feel it now in me. Maddy would have listened. Rowdy too. And I tell you, I would have listened back. Whatever they had to say, I'd have heard it. Every word. I wish them everything and that. Someone listening. Yes, goddamn I do.

VERL

Is it a month now? Two? I found the furry shit of an owl. There were bones in it. I ate them. The first thing I have eaten in some days. My head cleared a few hours. I sat down just where I was here in this high clearing a cave off in the rocks. I remembered my name. Remembered your name. Remember your name boy here it is on the back cover of this notebook I am writing to you boy the sky wide and dark and cut by stars what claws tear the holes of stars

TAVIN

They left before sundown, Tavin, Freddie, and Norris, while Daniel, Toby, and Clay stayed behind, with the CPS woman. On a two-track road they drove west from the Newman place as far as their stronghold at the cave and gathered what they needed—ammunition, food, water, jackets, blankets, and a couple of shovels—and turned back, knowing Wendell couldn't have gotten that far on foot. They drove without lights, in the true dark, and after a time they left the road and bumped over the prairie, then parked in a stand of pines in a wide canyon.

Earlier they'd rolled the sheriff's vehicle back behind the barn, with the deputy dead in the front seat, then locked the CPS woman, who'd pissed all over herself and wasn't making a lick of sense, in the trailer's back bedroom. They'd had a hard time deciding what to do with Brian. There was Tricia to consider, but they didn't want to risk a phone call. One of the out-of-town men, Clay, had gone to the same high school as Brian and been part of the free-state movement with him down there in Oregon, and he said Brian had a younger brother in Portland, though he was one of those who'd gone off to college and forgotten where he came from. He said, too, that not six weeks after Brian's old man had eaten the end of his shotgun, Brian's mother up and married a Mexican and moved to California. There wasn't anyone back home, he said, and spit.

It was agreed, then, that it ought to be Tavin's decision, and they turned and looked at him.

All six of them were standing in a rough circle in the front room of the trailer. Brian was laid out on the carpet, his blood dark and thick as jam in the dime-size hole below his jaw. They'd all been telling Tavin what a soldier he was not to cry. Telling him how proud Brian would be. Sharp metal stars spun through Tavin's bloodstream. He was sad, yes, but it was the rage that felt best, that felt good and clean and sure. In fact, it even seemed that because of Brian's fall Tavin had somehow grown. He hated and loved the feeling. He fingered the medallion at his neck. Picked at the scab along his jaw. The mountains were the only thing that made sense for this. They'd bury Brian there, then find Wendell.

By flashlight now, beneath the pines, they dug. It was slow going, the ground hard and dry, shot through with roots. Tavin thought of Daniel, Toby, and Clay back at the trailer, just sitting there, rifles across their laps, waiting for the cops or the FBI or whoever. They'd all voted for three of them to stay at the trailer. A standoff there would leave the other three more time to find Wendell in the mountains, and time, too, for those at the trailer, with a hostage and all, to get their message out, to give copies of Brian's manifesto to reporters. Tavin was glad, though, that he was one of the ones in the mountains. He was glad, too, that Norris had come. Norris was from north Idaho and was nearly as wide as he was tall. He spoke mostly in grunts and nods, his long yellow beard mashed against his broad chest. A tracker, he had shown up ten days earlier and, to Tricia's dismay, pitched an army-surplus tent right by the trailer. Most mornings he wandered off to chart the comings and goings of the Bull Mountain wolf pack, to ready them all for the hunt. Tavin had argued it should be just him and Norris who went after Wendell, but Freddie, the only one to cry as they stood there around Brian, insisted he should come.

They took turns, two of them shoveling, one holding the flashlight. Three feet down, they began to scoop up plate-size disks of sandrock and knew they wouldn't get much farther. Freddie and Tavin slid the tarp they had Brian on from the bed of the S-10, held its crinkling corners like impromptu pallbearers, and hauled him over to the makeshift grave. Given the darkness and the loose dirt all about, they were careful. But even so, the tarp, which they'd pulled from the rafters in Wendell Newman's shed, was old, and one of the corners Freddie had ahold of began to tear with the sound of a dry breath. Brian's body fell and rolled into the hole, landing facedown, arms and legs all cockeyed.

Tavin caught Freddie in the flashlight beam.

—Jesus fucking Christ.

Freddie made to get down into the hole.

—Don't even think about it. You'll just fuck it up.

Tavin handed the flashlight to Norris and slid into the hole and turned Brian's body over. He folded the arms across the chest, like he'd seen them do in the movies, then lifted himself out.

Brian had known the Bible, or had at least quoted lots of things he said were from the Bible, and Tavin recited, as best he could, the ones he remembered. Norris held the light on the mouth of the grave. Freddie started crying again. Tavin bent to the shovel. He didn't want to hear Freddie's sniveling and didn't want to look at Brian dead there in the ground.

Tavin didn't sleep so much as slide through the cold and the dark and the many visions Brian had fired in his mind. All the while he scratched at the scab on his jaw. Tricia had been telling him to stop, to quit fucking picking at it or he'd give himself a scar. Now his scratching tore the old wound open all the wider, until blood welled and stained the greasy sweatshirt he was using as a pillow. They'd been out cutting fence, and he'd been all fired up, not paying attention like he should have. When he turned his four-wheeler up a steep saddle between two hills, it tipped back ass-over-teakettle and slammed him to the ground, then dragged him through the sagebrush and cheatgrass halfway down the hill. Brian made sure he was okay, handed him a handkerchief for the oozing wound on his jaw. Remember, he told him, the land has its peculiarities. You have to know it to master it. Make it your own. Back in Oregon, Brian said, he'd seen a couple of loggers go soft, not want to fuck up a creek, say, or clear-cut a whole slope. But the land wasn't some kind of thing you baby-talked. No, the land was what a man pulled his life and wealth from. That's what it was there for. Loggers who went soft were the ones who dropped pines across their backs. Brian took Tavin by the shoulder and said once they were done with this wolf hunt, they'd get a tractor or a dozer out here and take the top off that saddle, make a proper road.

The night lifted. The stars shaded from diamond to cream. Off nearer the grave Freddie jerked in his sleep, whimpered and mewled. Norris came wheezing through the trees and said he'd found the trail, two sets of tracks, Wendell and the girl, not a quarter mile away. They ought to leave the S-10 behind, he said, as Wendell was sticking to the rocks, and they'd have to be careful he didn't double back on them. They gathered from the cab everything they might need—binoculars, ammo, canteens— and Tavin slammed the door hard, the crack and *whummpf* sharp in the still night air. He didn't give a damn who heard it. It would give Wendell and whoever that bitch was a chance. They would fucking need it.

For the first half hour the trail was faint, and they had to move carefully to make sure they were on it. Then the track cut south, plain as day, and they hurried. A low howl spilled down the hills like the sound of a bell, then thinned into a high, sharp cry. Tavin had heard wolves before, when he and Brian were out in the mountains, but never so close as this. He slowed and swung his head about, as though a wolf might be in sighting distance.

They ran on, rifles at their chests. Any moment, Tavin thought, any moment they'd come around a ridge and see them—he was goddamn sure of it. Brian had told him many times that they were all blind, his schoolteachers and playmates, most everyone. That for their fear of the truth, their shame at sucking at the government teat, they wouldn't open their eyes and see. They were sheep is what they were, following the herd, never questioning, never realizing that they could make their own decisions, that they could just fucking stop living that way, that they could live a new way. It took only the strong shoulder of a free man to knock things off-kilter, to send the usual rules toppling like a load of badly stacked bricks. When you got right down to it, there was only your word and your will and your rifle. Everything else a lie. Do you hear me? Brian would ask. Yes, sir, Tavin would say, then quote Brian's favorite line of Scripture back at him: *Those who have eyes for seeing should see, those who have ears for hearing should hear.* Tavin ran, knowing in his bones that he'd see Wendell Newman before Wendell saw him.

After shortcutting across a series of rocky hills, hoping to find Wendell running south in the valley below, they came to a blind creek. At the bank, a coyote in a leg-hold trap leaped at them. The animal had been bellied down in the yellow grass, and as they ran on, it charged and snarled and clacked its jaws, and the trap, clamped on the left foreleg, reached its chain length and spun the animal around in midair. The coyote landed sprawled in the dirt and scrambled back up and stood there, its gray winter coat still shot through with streaks of red and orange from the summer. The animal bared its teeth and growled low in its throat.

Tavin, who'd slipped and fallen over when the coyote vaulted at them, stood and swore. Who in the hell was running a trapline out this way? He'd thought he and Brian were the only ones running traplines in the Bulls. Without caring who might hear and before Norris or Freddie could say a thing, he raised his rifle and shot the damn animal through the head.

Night found them at the spring. The sky stone-colored, dark clouds banking in the west. They'd nearly lost Wendell's trail late in the afternoon. Tavin and Freddie had sat and waited as Norris circled and circled, his nose to the rocks like some bloodhound. And that's when they'd heard the rifle shot. They simply ran in that direction and had picked up the trail again, as night fell, here at the spring.

Now they lay about and ate granola bars and beef jerky. They passed around Freddie's Copenhagen. They talked and laughed and made sport of that dumb bastard Wendell Newman, who, given the evidence around the spring, had barely made it a day before he'd fallen on his ass and hurt himself. Old Verl must be shaking his head up there in heaven or wherever he was. They'd find Wendell easy tomorrow. Tavin didn't even feel too bad that somewhere along the way they'd lost the girl's trail and that Wendell was alone now. They'd likely just have to trace back to find her. Freddie, though, kept talking about the boy, who had to be with them, he said, who was with Wendell at Hougen's roundup and was why the deputy and the CPS lady were there in the first place. He was all worked up about the boy, about the helicopter they'd seen, about what might be happening back at the trailer with the CPS lady and the dead deputy and Daniel, Toby, and Clay just sitting ducks. But Tavin didn't care about the boy or about Toby and Daniel or any of the rest of it. As long as they got Wendell, things would come out right. He was the one responsible for what had happened to Brian.

Some of them had thought it was the sheriff, that he must have realized how fucked he was and shot first. Others studied the plum-size hole in Brian's throat and said no, the shot had to have come from behind, so it must, somehow, have been Wendell—maybe the rifle had been in the girl's car or something. But whether Wendell had actually shot Brian or not didn't matter, Tavin said. It was still Wendell's fault. If he'd done what he was supposed to do, if he'd done what his old man would have had him do, it would have been easy. There would've been no mess at the trailer.

What no one challenged Tavin on, so as not to dishonor a dead man, was that a number of them hadn't even wanted to go out there. Brian had insisted. He said it was the symbolism of the thing. He said people were ignorant but that they could come to know. Part of what the Bull Mountain Resistance needed to do was educate people about the real issues, about the unjust ways the federal government was controlling their lives and land. In this respect, the wolves were more than the wolves, and if they had Verl Newman's own son beside them, people would understand they weren't just killing wolves—no, they were joining a long line of rebels and freedom fighters, from Verl Newman all the way back to George fucking Washington.

Tavin had listened and believed, but in his boy's heart he was jealous of Wendell Newman, of his unearned status as the son of a hero. Before Tavin was even born his father had fallen out of a pickup bed and broken his head wide open. He was at best a sorry case and at worst a drunken idiot. A boy at school, a town kid, had razzed Tavin about it all last year, after the class had written personal histories for their unit on Indians and pioneers in Montana history. What kind of an assignment was that anyway? He'd hated that teacher, Mr. Lloyd, with his sandals and shaggy hair, his long lists of books and class debates and the big papers they had to write. Why couldn't he just have them do worksheets like the other teachers did? Why couldn't he teach them the facts and be done with it? Why—when they all knew damn well where he was headed anyway—were Lloyd and Leslie and Houlton always on him about his future? And how in the hell did Wendell get so fucking lucky as to have Verl Newman for a father? It wasn't fair. Not by a long goddamn shot.

Freddie curled himself against the cold now, hugged his knees to his chest. Norris was on his back, already sound asleep, like it didn't even bother him. Tavin rubbed at the dried blood on his jaw, the tender, infected wound. It felt good, that easy pain. He lay down, put his hands beneath his other cheek, and studied his slice of sky: black clouds, the blacker shapes of mountains against the clouds. At least he'd been born to the Bulls. And when he'd been given the chance, he'd made the right choice—he had chosen Brian. They couldn't take that away from him.

A light, cold rain woke them, fat drops splatting in the dust, the first real rain in months. They cached their supplies at the spring. Carrying only rifles and sidearms, they jogged across the plain and up the rocks. Atop the ridge they stopped and took a breath. Norris fingered a bunch of grass, a stick, then cut up a twisting coulee. The rocks were tight about them, the cedars too. In the rain a runnel of water widened beneath their boots. Tavin couldn't hear much of anything save the whir of his own breath. Like bees in me, he thought. Wasps.

The rocks opened onto another, higher ridge, the view to the east, south, and west miles long beneath the tin sheet of the clouds. The mountain reared up to the north, which was the way they went, slipping through cedars and around bulbous sandrocks and as the rain came a notch harder stepping into a small clearing.

There sat Wendell Newman, maybe fifteen yards away, rifle at his shoulder.

A blackness filled Tavin. Black liquid waterfalling in his guts. Wendell had heard them first, seen them first. Wendell was ready for them. But Brian said, Brian said, Brian said! Brian said they were the ones who would *always* be ready. They weren't ready. Fuck, fuck, fuck!

The rain runs down Tavin's nose.

Norris sets his rifle on the ground, and Freddie does too, saying something unintelligible, working himself up to tears. The smell of rain and sage everywhere.

Tavin licks his lips. Lifts his rifle to his shoulder. As easy as that. He clicks the safety off, aims at Wendell's neck, that soft hollow low on the throat. For a moment the two of them stare at each other, down the barrels of their rifles through the rain.

Then Wendell sets his rifle on the ground. He hauls himself up, his hands on the rocks, and Tavin can almost feel, beneath his own palms, the grit of rain-wet sandrocks.

—Freddie, Wendell says, do you remember that play we did? I was just thinking about it. I think about it all the time.

And that's what does it. Or undoes it. Undoes everything Tavin knows. A man keeps his rifle at his shoulder. A man doesn't worry about what comes next. Why isn't Wendell staring straight down his rifle at him?

Tavin fires. Fires again.

Norris grunts. Freddie screams and wraps his arms around Tavin's shoulders.

But Tavin's making time. All he'll ever have. The world has taken everything from him and he's taking it right the fuck back. They'll wear each other down to nothing, this world and him, right down to sulfur, dust, and bone.

Tavin shrugs Freddie off and fires again and again, each bullet ringing out, thudding home.

VERL

I dream a loping she-wolf beside me can you imagine boy the barrel of a
wolf's body kneeling there I thought to take her in my arms she was as
perfect as anything I have known that time last summer we went down to
the river to swim after a long day of bucking bales and you stripped out
of your jeans and I looked up from the river where I was already shaking
my wet head and saw you were a man boy the arc of you as if the light
itself had some flesh and heft light is all that is left the wash of light or
the wash of night the night your mother turned fifteen we lay down in
a field of grass and the moon a fool I mean a full moon that night over
us and the hard earth beneath us we held one another and the land held
us as if the land cannot hold us anymore as if the line of earth and sky
has fouled we are falling through the wolfholes of stars boy we are falling
down

ROWDY

He sits in the backseat, sits up straight and tall and in the hard winter light counts the old wooden fence posts as they whip by his window—one, two, three, four, five, six, seven...Just this side of a hundred, a hawk dives and from the matted grass lifts squirming in its talons a prairie dog, and Rowdy loses count. He switches to pretending he's got a blade he can lever out the window and hold just so to trim all the weeds and cheatgrass in the bar ditch. Tapping his cheeks with his fingers, he looks up. The driving man—Mr. Leslie, Mr. Leslie, Mr. Leslie, he tells himself, trying to remember—eyes him in the rearview, then gives him a small grin, realizing he's been caught, and shifts his gaze back to the road. Maddy, whom he knows and doesn't have to make himself remember, sits across from him, staring out her own window, at the mountains. He squirms in his seat, the seat belt pressing at his neck, and reaches out to touch her elbow. She smiles at him, her face red and splotchy, eyes just about to break. She takes his hand. He likes it when she takes his hand.

They turn off the county road and onto a dirt road whose entrance is framed by thick timbers, with a horned cow skull nailed to the oiled log across the top. Mr. Leslie slows across the cattle guard and bumps through the ruts and on the dirt straightaway picks up speed. Rowdy knows this road. He sits up all the taller and leans to the middle to watch the land shift and unfold out the front window. His teacher—Ms.

Houlton, Ms. Houlton, Ms. Houlton—turns in her seat and smiles that same sad smile they've all been giving him.

Ms. Houlton tells him that Mr. Hougen had been a friend of his uncle's and asks if he remembers him.

Behind his eyes Rowdy sees a big red calf coming right at him, sees Wendell scoop him up and swing him out of the way, then the old bald man, Mr. Hougen, lean down to hand him a five-dollar bill.

Rowdy nods once, twice, three times. He knows he needs to respond. That's one of the things his new teachers keep teaching him. When he doesn't have the words, he can just nod or shake his head, give a thumb up or down. He needs to talk to them, even if with just his body, so they can take good care of him. Just like his uncle Wendell did.

Rowdy picks up his notebook, pulls his pencil from the whorls, and flips through—trees, mountains, traps, the dinner table set with two full bowls. He finds a blank page near the back and begins to draw the calf and the dust. The biggest person is his uncle Wendell—there's not even enough room on the page for his uncle Wendell.

Mr. Leslie noses the car in beside the row of work pickups outside the house. Everyone gets out, their breath billowing and disappearing, the tang of wood smoke in the cold, still air. Mr. and Mrs. Hougen are right there, waiting by the front door, smiling those same sad smiles, though Mr. Hougen's smile, when he sees Rowdy, cracks and shatters, like Maddy's eyes. Mrs. Hougen puts her arm around his middle. Ms. Houlton touches his shoulder. Mr. Leslie shuffles on his feet and looks the other way. Rowdy lets go of Maddy's hand and comes right up to Mr. Hougen, who pulls out a white handkerchief and loudly blows his nose, then leans down close, his breath warm and bitter on Rowdy's cold face.

—I'm short a hand, Rowdy Burns. And grieving it. Just as soon as you get your feet back under you, you come on out and put in a day's work for me, okay?

Rowdy reaches out to shake hands. There are laughs and tears, and Mr. Hougen takes Rowdy's hand and shakes it up and down, up and down. Doesn't let go until Mrs. Hougen tugs at him. He turns to Ms. Houlton, takes a long breath, and pulls off his cap, rubs at his bald head.

It's a goddamn mess, he says, and he's goddamn sorry about it all. He just didn't ever think for a second they'd go so far as this. Now there are three down on the ground and half a dozen in jail, the whole place torn this way and that. Mr. Hougen pauses to haul in a big ragged breath. The trouble, he says, is that a young fellow can't make a living out here any-more. Even if his daddy has land to hand him.

—It ain't a living, he says. It's a dying is what it is. I don't know. Maybe we pull up stakes and give it back to the wolves and buffalo. I just don't know—

He cuts himself off, presses at his eyes. Ms. Houlton touches him at the shoulder again.

I'm sorry, Glen. I am. You were always good to Kevin and me. I was grateful for that, in spite of everything.

She tells him that considering the circumstances, the state is letting Rowdy stay with her while her foster application is being approved. As for Mr. Hougen, she makes clear that what he's done is more than gen-erous, covering Wendell's debts and paying more for the Newman land than it would've fetched at sale. The state has set up a trust for Rowdy, she says, and two different therapists are visiting him each week. He's making good progress.

Mr. Hougen wipes at his eyes, blows his nose again.

—Hell, it's only what Wendell wrote down. That's what I'm doing. I wish I could do more.

The trailer is cleaned up, he tells them. Rowdy can go over when-ever he's ready and take whatever he wants or pick up anything Lacy wants.

Ms. Houlton thanks him. Then reaches out and takes Maddy's hand. She says she doesn't know that she did right last time, just leaving like she did, without a word to anyone, and she doesn't want to do that to Rowdy. She visited Rowdy's mother at the prison the other day, and she plans to see her again next week. The day before, meanwhile, she went to the hospital to see Tricia Wilson.

Ms. Houlton gets stuck on something there, swallows, stops. Maddy takes her mother by the elbow and speaks up for the both of them. They've been talking to Rowdy about what happened, she says—the therapists tell them that's important—and they've got a picture of Wendell up by Rowdy's bed.

This starts Mr. Hougen in to crying again, and Mrs. Hougen rubs his back.

—That's enough of this, at least with little ears around, she says. Rowdy, I've got a treat for you here.

She pulls a paper bag of something from her pocket and hands it over. Rowdy crinkles down the neck and peeks in. Gummy worms. Must be a pound of them.

Just then Tyler comes running around the back of the house wearing a fringed leather jacket and a coonskin cap, two toy six-guns stuck into his belt. He hands one of the guns to Rowdy, who fists a mess of gummy worms up for him in return.

Tyler grabs the worms and angles off across the yard, cuts around the henhouse and the machine shop, now up a deer trail. Rowdy's right behind him. At the tattered line of jack pines, Rowdy slows and turns, looks back at the low, sprawling house below, where curlicues of wood smoke lift from the chimney into the sky. His chest heaves, his lungs burning with each big, cold breath, and his sneakered feet tingle with an itch to run.

He's only making sure, is what he's doing, counting once again everyone who's in that house—Maddy, Ms. Houlton, Mr. Leslie, Mr. and Mrs. Hougen, one, two, three, four, five. And even though they're not there, his uncle Wendell makes six, his mother seven, and seven is a nice, good number. Seven is all the people he knows who love him very much. That's the word his uncle Wendell used when he left them in the mountains, *love*, and that's how Maddy says it now when she tucks him in at night. *He loved you very much, we love you very much.*

The hard snow glisters beneath the sun. A magpie veers overhead, settles on a killed pine, and makes its *hack-hack-hack*.

The Bulls shift with winter shadows, winter light, and Rowdy's thinking he likes living with Maddy and Ms. Houlton in the new big house in town. He's thinking, too, that he'd like to live again with his uncle Wendell, out here in the mountains. But his uncle Wendell's dead, that's the word they keep using, *dead,* which means he's nowhere anymore but in Rowdy's heart. That's what Ms. Houlton says. Rowdy looks down, his breath blooming and fading before him, and taps his chest.

That's where his uncle Wendell is.

He smiles and takes off running, carries his uncle Wendell with him up into the mountains.

ACKNOWLEDGMENTS

Jennifer Sahn shepherded portions of this manuscript into publication at *Orion;* her early support and critique were essential. Derek Sheffield suggested I keep following these characters; I'm thankful he did. Shann Ray, Jonathan Rovner, Lex Runciman, and Liz Wilkins read early drafts and offered wise guidance. Sally Wofford-Girand and Ben George—both simply extraordinary at what they do—believed in this story and worked to make it all the stronger; I am so, so grateful for their efforts. And a final thanks to the Sustainable Arts Foundation, the Margery Davis Boyden Wilderness Writing Residency, and Linfield College for the time and space necessary to write.

ABOUT THE AUTHOR

Joe Wilkins's memoir, *The Mountain and the Fathers,* won the GLCA New Writers Award for nonfiction, and his work has appeared in the *Georgia Review,* the *Harvard Review,* and *Slate,* among many other periodicals. He is a Pushcart Prize winner and a finalist for the National Magazine Award and the PEN/USA Award. Wilkins lives with his wife and two children in western Oregon, where he teaches writing at Linfield College.